RAINIER'S LEGACY

RAINIER'S LEGACY

CHAD CORRIE

DARK HORSE BOOKS

Published by
Dark Horse Books
A division of Dark Horse Comics LLC
10956 SE Main Street
Milwaukie, OR 97222

DarkHorse.com

Library of Congress Cataloging-in-Publication Data

Names: Corrie, Chad, author. | Burgess, Dan, artist.
Title: Rainier's legacy / writer, Chad Corrie ; cover art, Dan Burgess.
Description: Milwaukie, OR : Dark Horse Books, 2024.
Identifiers: LCCN 2023031702 (print) | LCCN 2023031703 (ebook) | ISBN
  9781506741048 (trade paperback) | ISBN 9781506741055 (ebook)
Subjects: LCGFT: Fantasy fiction. | Short stories.
Classification: LCC PS3603.O77235 R35 2024 (print) | LCC PS3603.O77235
  (ebook) | DDC 813/.6--dc23/eng/20230922
LC record available at https://lccn.loc.gov/2023031702
LC ebook record available at https://lccn.loc.gov/2023031703

First edition: September 2024
Ebook ISBN 978-1-50674-105-5
Trade Paperback ISBN 978-1-50674-104-8

1 3 5 7 9 10 8 6 4 2
Printed in the United States of America

ALSO BY CHAD CORRIE

THE WIZARD KING TRILOGY
Return of the Wizard King
Trial of the Wizard King
Triumph of the Wizard King

GRAPHIC NOVELS
Sons of Ashgard: Ill Met in Elmgard

STANDALONE NOVELS
The Shadow Regent

SOJOURNERS' SAGA
As the Sparrow Flies

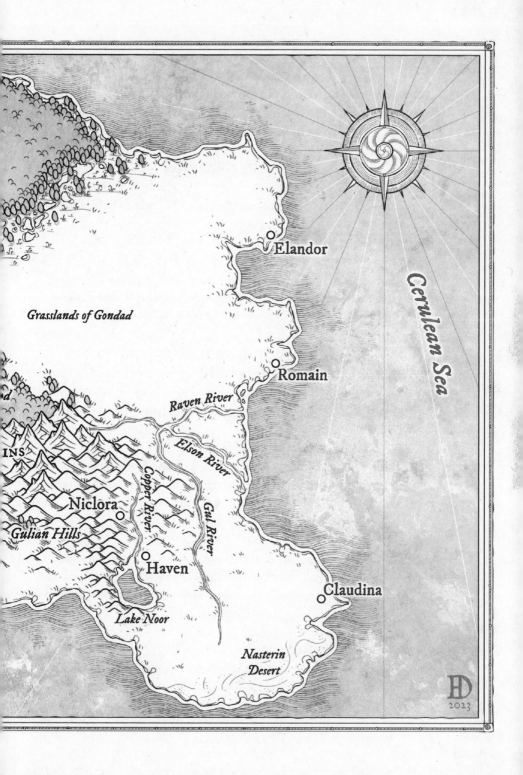

Elandor

Grasslands of Gondad

Cerulean Sea

Romain

Raven River

Elson River

INS

Copper River

Gal River

Niclora

Gulian Hills

Haven

Claudina

Lake Noor

Nasterin
Desert

HD
2023

TABLE OF CONTENTS

RAINIER'S LEGACY

1

The sun was sinking into a reddish-orange bank of clouds as the *Phoenix* made its way through the Yoan Ocean. The frigate had recently left the port kingdom of Elandor headed for the colder waters of the Northlands. Seasoned in waves far to the west, it flew the flag of Breanna from its mainmast. Few this far east had seen the white flag with a medium-sized powder-blue stripe across its center. And certainly no one in the Northlands knew the gnomish nation's standard.

The *Phoenix* had left Elandor in fine weather three days earlier. It was spring in the Midlands. The fresh winds were just gaining strength, aiding the vessel's voyage and cheering the crew. The captain and his men were mostly traders and adventurers who offered themselves as transport and guide for various clients, taking a share of the profits in addition to an initial fee.

The crew itself was a ragtag bunch, like most men of the sea. A majority were tall and tawny Telborians—with sharp green or blue eyes—whose leathery skin had been lashed by sun and cured in salty surf. Mixed among them were a varied host of dark-eyed, dusky-skinned Celetors; a few Patrious with pale gray skin and black or silver hair; and even a handful of Napowese, whose black hair accented their olive complexions.

All were loyal to their captain, a powerfully built Celetor named Hirim Koofehi. A skilled and accomplished sailor, he'd decided to embark on this recent venture after learning of its potential gain. Just what this venture involved, though, Hirim hadn't revealed to his men. Only his lieutenants had any inkling but kept it to themselves. For now, the crew contented themselves with scrubbing the deck, maintaining the order of the ship, and dreaming of the rich reward awaiting them.

While they worked, Hirim and his guests rested in his cabin at the vessel's stern. The cabin actually comprised more than one room. Hirim wanted a larger area than was commonly found on such vessels and had the space custom fitted for his needs. None saw the spacious personal quarters but himself. The other room off his private area, however, served as a common room. Though smaller, it wasn't as cramped as one might expect, allowing comfortable seating for five people around an old circular oak table nailed to the floor in the room's center. Currently, one of those seats remained vacant.

"I see you're courting Saredhel now, eh?" Hirim's strong jaw clenched a thick cigar. The pungent smoke curled above his shaved head, adding to the hazy halo encircling the other men. Angular eyebrows outlined his dark brown eyes, which flirted with mirth. Dressed like many Celetors of the West, he was the most colorfully garbed at the table. Billowing red breeches, leather boots, and a large khaki shirt opened just low enough to outline the dark valley between the twin mounds of muscle on his large, hairless chest.

"One does the best one can." The gnome, Josiah Brookshire, fanned his playing cards wide before him. His deep blue eyes complemented a rather congenial face. He, like the others gathered here, spoke Telboros.

He wore a white shirt under a modest coat that was the same brown as his pants. His most distinguished piece of attire was a leather vest whose breast pocket housed an elegant ivory pipe. Josiah was slender but tall for his people, rising above a human's belt by a head. His height granted him just enough clearance at the table to function as his taller companions did.

"Well, read them and weep, losers," said a scruffy-looking halfling named Charles de Frassel. His wide grin highlighted pointed ears. "A full court."

He thrust the cards onto the table. They revealed colorful portrayals of a Telborian king, queen, prince, princess, and priest. Their suits weren't matching, however, revealing all five in the deck: clashing silver swords, a yellow circular shield, a green oak leaf, a bright red heart, and a soft blue four-pointed star.

"Looks like I win." Charles' bloodshot eyes lusted after the small pile of copper coins in the table's center. His combed-over wisps of auburn hair failed to hide the pale moon rising behind them. Dark stubble peppered his cheeks and neck, muddying his otherwise clear features.

He wore a rather simple outfit. Simple, that is, for a halfling: blue silken breeches with white stockings and black shoes. His white shirt was left slightly undone, showing off his hairy chest before stretching over a protruding belly. A wide black belt kept both it and his pants in place.

"Not so fast, Charles," said Corwyn Danther, a Telborian bard. Though tall for a halfling, Charles didn't rise above four feet, making Corwyn a giant in comparison.

"Got something on me then, do you?"

Corwyn was young and clean faced with reddish-brown hair and blue-green eyes, which added to his natural good looks. Unlike Charles, he wore more subdued attire: a common pair of pants and a cream linen shirt, a coin purse dangling from his side.

"This ought to be good," said Hirim, stroking his long mustache. "What you got, Corwyn?"

"The court of leaves," he replied, laying his cards on the table.

"Let me see that!" Charles hopped on his chair and leaned forward. All five cards bore the green leaf: a king, queen, prince, priest, and jester.

"Hmph." The halfling slumped back into his seat. "Jester's wild. Why does it have to be jester's wild?" Charles hadn't won a hand since they'd started playing after lunch. This wasn't that uncommon. During the infrequent games they'd adopted shortly after leaving Breanna, he rarely broke even and usually lost.

"So now I'm out of coin." Charles flung his cards into the center of the table. The others did the same. He tried not to look too longingly at

Corwyn moving the copper mound into his own modest pile. Even with this newest addition it remained about even with Hirim's and Josiah's.

"I'm surprised you've kept what you had so long, playing as poorly as you have since coming onboard," said Hirim.

"Just a run of sour luck is all. I'll be back on top and you'll be my debtor soon enough. I just need one hand to win it all back . . . and something valuable to get me that one more hand . . ." Charles' eyes darted back and forth between the players.

"You still got that map, de Frassel." Hirim poked at another of the halfling's sore points.

"And it's *staying* in my possession, thank you very much." Charles removed a slender cigarette from a rectangular silver carrying case in his shirt's side pocket. He tapped the end of the cigarette on the table and put it between his lips. Gaining a spark from the dying embers of his previous cigarette, still smoldering in an ash-and-butt-filled tin beside him, he took a lengthy drag.

"Ah." He exhaled a thin jet of creamy smoke. "Halfling-cut tobacco, the best there is."

"One would disagree," Josiah submitted between pipe-clenching teeth. The distinct fruit-and-nut aroma of his own smoke wafted past Corwyn, who, for his part, sought to avoid the mingling clouds. He was thankful at least one of the windows in Hirim's quarters was open. Yet even with this small boon, bluish-white smoke hung above their heads, strangling the copper oil lamp swaying over the center of the table before snaking out the open glass portal at the room's rear.

"So *now* what are we supposed to do for entertainment?" Charles took another slow drag. "If I can't play cards, how am I supposed to endure this godsforsaken boredom?"

"A troubling thought when you consider we have quite a long trip ahead of us, if your map is to be believed," said Josiah.

"You certainly believed it enough to take on this venture." Charles chased down his words with a swig of wine from an open bottle beside his chair. Finding the bottle empty after his assuagement, he returned it to the floor, crestfallen.

"Hey now! Try to ration yourself," Hirim scolded while shuffling the cards for another game. "I don't have enough booze to keep you going, if that's what you're seeking. We already had to stock up in Elandor after you almost drank us dry."

"Then you should have bought more."

"I want to make a profit on this voyage." Hirim kept his gaze leveled against Charles. "Having you drinking all of it isn't going to sit well with me or the rest of the crew."

"Indeed, Mr. de Frassel, it would seem your indulgence has been quite excessive since we left Breanna." Josiah adjusted some locks of his white hair; the longer strands, though thinning, had fallen down his crown as the boat rocked back and forth. They were touching the neatly trimmed but still thick and bushy sideburns descending from his jawline.

"Well, I have to do something around here to keep myself entertained if I can't gamble anymore."

"Why not help the crew?" Hirim asked sardonically.

"Pah," Charles snorted. "Work like a dog with common men? You have got to be *joking*. Now, if your superstitious sailors allowed me to take aboard *all* my cargo, I might not be so apt to complain."

"Mr. de Frassel," Josiah began in a paternal tone, "you know full well Coggsbury, Elliott, Chesterfield, and Company is a moral enterprise, and your entourage of fallen persons of the weaker sex is not something with which Coggsbury, Elliott, Chesterfield, and Company wishes to be associated."

"Blah, blah, blah," Charles said, using his free hand like a mocking puppet, opening and closing its mouth in time with the halfling's words. This only raised Josiah's dander.

"Mr. de Frassel, I trust you are aware I am the representative of the company whose bountiful investment in your offer has made this whole venture possible in the first place. I will not be mocked. You were aware of the terms and conditions laid out in your contract, which, I might add, you signed quite readily. So I would ask that you conduct yourself with a modest amount of tact and decorum whilst we are on this journey."

"Or what?" Charles smirked.

"Or I can find some creative places for you to spend the next few weeks." Hirim's reply brought some sobriety into the halfling's face.

"Fine." Charles extinguished his cigarette on the small tin dish. "Can anyone lend me some coin for another game?"

Hirim's eyebrow rose. "You don't know when to quit, do you? Why should anyone lend you anything?"

"Well, I would have won more if we had that bookworm in here."

"So you think." Hirim cut the cards one last time.

"Hey." Charles jabbed a stubby finger at the Celetor. "It took him forever to get over being seasick. Shows he has a weak constitution."

"And that would make him a bad card player? Seems to me you said similar things about Corwyn here before he came onboard, and now he's mopping the deck with you."

"Just a run of good luck," Charles said dryly. "Which can and will change if I can get another chance here. So is anyone going to loan me some coin or not?"

"Fine," said Hirim. "I'll loan you some coppers if it'll shut you up for a while." He started dealing out the cards.

"Thank you." Charles gave a slight nod, though there was little gratitude in the words.

"I'll win it back soon enough anyway," Hirim added with a smirk. "Oh, and jester's wild."

Sometime later Corwyn sought fresher air while checking in with a certain Patrician scholar whose quarters were in the ship's lower deck. Mathias had been on board since the ship's departure from Rexatoius, the first place they'd stopped after leaving Breanna. He'd been hired by the gnomes for his insight into old languages and grasp of ancient history. Because of this, he'd been given the task of deciphering Charles' map. And that map, Corwyn learned, had something of a history.

Charles had approached some gnomes on Breanna about a year ago with a moneymaking idea. The halfling was convinced the old document led to some kind of treasure and tried enticing the gnomes with the promise of great wealth. The gnomes, though, were a practical bunch, and therefore hired a skilled translator and an expert document crafter—Mathias—to guarantee the map's authenticity. It *was* coming from a halfling, after all.

Once the map had been authenticated, Mathias made a discovery that piqued the gnomes' interest. A few lines of text near the image of an island in the Northlands, which none knew existed before, were translated to read: "The secret of eternal life here." Naturally, the gnomes were more than willing to fund and assemble an exploratory venture with such documentation as motivation. After all, if they could corner the market on a product granting eternal youth and life, or at the very least keep people from getting any older, they'd be rich indeed. So Coggsbury, Elliott, Chesterfield, and Company was formed—named after the three largest contributors. Following that, the *Phoenix* made its way from its port in Rexatoius to Talatheal—and Corwyn.

"Mathias?" Corwyn knocked on the door to the elf's room.

"Come in, Corwyn." Mathias Onuis watched Corwyn enter. "I thought you were with the others, playing cards." The elf sat amid a clutter of chests, scrolls, and stacks of books. He wore a rather common gray robe. It was darker than his pale gray skin but complemented his high-strapped black leather sandals, pale sapphire eyes, and short black hair quite nicely.

"I got tired of winning, and Charles' whining wasn't helping any." It took a moment for his eyes to adjust to the dark interior. There were no windows below deck, and the only light came from the dirty glow of an oil lamp hanging from a beam and the candle resting on Mathias' desk.

"Halflings . . ." Mathias mused dryly.

"I needed some fresh air, too. Between those three chimneys, I think I know what a smoked pig feels like," he continued, moving closer to the scholar, stepping over the precarious literary panorama in the process.

Corwyn had been approached by Waylan Coggsbury, one of his supporters, promoters, and organizers, to chronicle this venture. Though the company hired Josiah Brookshire to represent their interests, Coggsbury didn't see any harm in safeguarding the safeguard, obviously appreciating a story or song as well to further capitalize on the expedition. That, and he didn't think Waylan liked leaving Charles alone with the map.

The halfling's bold demand to share in the profits by being made a junior partner was bad enough—hence the "and Company" appended to Coggsbury, Elliott, and Chesterfield—but his insistence on being the lone keeper of the map and remaining the sole owner was an annoying thorn in the gnomes' side. Corwyn didn't mind. The whole thing sounded interesting enough without any outside prodding. So far it hadn't been too bad, though he'd have some time to change his mind before they arrived in the Northlands.

"So, have you made any progress?" He came up alongside the elf, glancing over his shoulder at what he was reading. "I wish I could be more help, but what I know about the Northlands would make a pretty short scroll."

"You more than make up for it by keeping an eye on things, I'm sure."

"I'm just helping him out, not spying for him, Mathias," Corwyn explained. "Waylan Coggsbury can certainly take care of himself."

"No need to convince me of that. He was the one who signed my agreement for payment. I don't think he'll be out on the street begging anytime soon."

Of all those he'd gotten to know since coming aboard, Mathias was still unfamiliar to him. The elf didn't often leave his quarters and fraternize with the others. His days were filled with reading and transcribing, recording what he'd read, and then trying to pull out meaning from it.

This, of course, was all while keeping his stomach under control. He'd only recently been able to overcome seemingly unending bouts of seasickness. A scholar and scribe by trade, he didn't have much of a grasp of social skills, nor did he often put himself into places where such talents were needed. Even so, Corwyn liked their visits. He figured they did them both good, and he enjoyed learning more in the process.

"If you're looking for any fresh insight, I don't know much more than I did when last we spoke." Mathias took fresh interest in his book. "I've been able to find a few faint leads here and there, but nothing has panned out yet."

In their previous conversations, Corwyn discovered just how much progress Mathias had made since leaving Rexatoius. During the journey, he'd translated more of the ancient text on the map as well as having compiled an interesting background on the island itself. Though it was cobbled from myths and legends, the emerging tale remained intriguing and insightful.

Apparently, Nordicans had avoided the island for centuries. Only in the last three hundred years had a pair of adventuresome souls made their way to the shores of Troll Island, another locale not commonly frequented. This is where they had found Charles' map.

It had been buried in the skeleton of an ancient vessel long since beached, picked clean, and half-submerged in the soupy sand like the remains of some decayed whale. These same explorers had lost the map later in a game of cards with some fellow seamen, who then took it south from there. And so it traveled about for some three hundred years. That is, if what Charles said was entirely true. Though Charles declared he'd won it in a game of cards, the gnomes hadn't been able to verify how he came to possess it or even its supposed origins.

But however it came into Charles' possession, the map proved authentic enough. Mathias had been convinced of that much at least. The worn vellum displayed an island farther north than Troll Island, making this unknown landmass the northernmost of all the Northlands. Near this unnamed isle was the text which so excited the gnomes. The only problem was that at first, the island hadn't seemed to exist.

Mathias had been able to track down some Nordic legends supporting the claim of an icy isle off the shores of Troll Island. He'd informed Corwyn that he'd come by this information through a handful of sources, many located in the Great Library of Rexatoius. Through some of these sources he'd also found the name of their destination: Sigmundson's Isle—or, in some renderings, Rainier's Island.

The last time he spoke with Corwyn, he'd confirmed the island was small and almost totally covered with ice. None of his books and scrolls spoke of any Nordic sailors going on or near it. Once they sighted it, it seemed they'd always sail around, for some reason steering well clear of its frosty shores.

"The island is still real, though, right?" he asked.

"Oh yes. The island is certainly real."

"Good." Corwyn carefully took a few steps back from Mathias' squat desk. Elsewhere in the room was a bed Mathias uncovered each night where he could rest his eyes and dream about finding additional answers. "I'd hate to be on some wild-goose chase or lost somewhere in the middle of the Northlands."

"That remains to be seen," said Mathias, turning another page. "The island may be real, but I can't vouch for any of the other things we're seeking. It still seems more fantasy than reality."

"I thought followers of Dradin believed anything they recorded?" He hadn't yet met any Dradinite or scholar who believed what he read or recorded was entirely false. Even myths were seen by sages and priests of Dradin as holding some kernel of truth or as being true events that had become misunderstood over time.

"Most do, but I have a hard time finding any truth in what we're searching for," Mathias confessed. "Even if there is an island and people lived there at one time, I doubt we'll discover what your investor friends are seeking."

"Why not?"

The question pulled Mathias away from his reading. "Because I believe we romanticize history too much and that over the years people have made a history of their own liking. Now, to be fair"—his tone became very respectful—"Dradin and his priests have done a very good job at sifting through false history and true tales. The Great Library of Rexatoius has been very helpful, too, with keeping an accurate record, but what we're dealing with here are fragmented tales and dusty myths and legends."

"Legends with enough conviction behind them to pull together the investors for this venture and get you hired," Corwyn countered. "And you just said you believed our destination was real enough."

"Yes, the destination, but not necessarily the object we're hoping to find. Think about it logically for a moment. We're talking about the secret for eternal youth being hidden on some frozen island. Don't you think it sounds a bit far fetched?"

"It might seem odd and perhaps unreal," he conceded, "but what could it *really* be? *That's* what a true follower of Dradin would ask."

"Would they now?"

"What if it really *is* something that helps restore youth?"

"Then why has no one gone after it before us?"

"Because *they* didn't know where to look, and *we* do."

"You have the makings of a good story." The elf returned to his work. "But I'll believe it when I see it. *If* I see it."

"Well, I don't want to give up hope just yet," said Corwyn, surveying the mass of materials covering most of the floor. "I think you have enough to head us in the right direction. I just hope we're able to get there without getting lost."

"We won't as long as Hirim can keep to the course the map conveys."

"Great." Corwyn backed up, meandering through the vellum valleys and hardbound mountains with graceful strides. "Say, it's bound to be dinnertime soon. You want to get out and have some food on deck?"

"Thank you, but no, I have to keep at this." Mathias kept his focus on his book. "The firmer the factual footing I can create, the better it will be for all of us."

Corwyn managed to get back to the door without disturbing the contents of the room. He turned around once the door itself was in hand, using it to steady himself as the vessel shuddered. He'd almost gotten his sea legs, but every so often found himself needing a sudden refresher. "You've been in here since I've been on board. Stay any longer, and you'll start sprouting roots."

"I'm fine, *really*." Mathias didn't look up from his book. "I was hired to do a job, and I intend to see it through to the end."

"Are you sure you don't need any help? I can come back later and try narrowing the search. Maybe I could clear up some things with what I *do* know."

"That's okay. It's easier having just one person in here at a time," he replied, motioning around the cramped chambers for emphasis. "Besides, I work better alone."

"Okay, let me know if you change your mind." Corwyn closed the door behind him.

The next night Hirim's guests were invited to a meal celebrating the commencement of the second part of their voyage. It was a simple affair, with fresher food than they'd be eating for the rest of the trip, and a welcome respite before the monotony of life at sea returned. The celebration took place in the room off the captain's private residence, which allowed comfortable seating for all Hirim's guests.

The spread was plain but favorable, with wooden bowls of steaming-hot stew set before the four diners and a fifth seat still awaiting its occupant. Some loaves of bread were also in the center of the table—the freshest among the batch they'd acquired from Elandor.

"I say we start without him." Charles stared at his bowl with eager eyes, careful to keep any stray ashes from his cigarette away from it.

"Give him just a little more time," Corwyn advised. "I'm sure he'll show." He again found himself contending with the incessant smoking of his dinner companions. But he was confident he could manage for a short while, given tonight both windows in the room were open.

There was enough of a breeze to allow some fresh breaths now and again within the growing haze. All of them were seated around the table save Mathias. The food had been served almost a quarter hour before, and the courtesy of waiting for their missing guest was wearing thin.

"I do not think we should wait forever, though, Mr. Danther." Josiah did his best to look relaxed and unaffected, but Corwyn knew he was as hungry as the rest of them. With provisions rationed on journeys like this, the mind often invested more time meditating upon food and its consumption or the lack thereof. Josiah consoled himself with his pipe, slowly puffing away.

"I'm sure he's just—"

Mathias' entrance interrupted the conversation.

"*Finally.*" Charles watched the scribe make his way to the open high-backed chair beside Corwyn. "You forget the way up here?"

"I just had a few last-moment things to attend to." Mathias took his seat.

"Now that we're all here," said Hirim, picking up a clay jug resting beside him, "I think it's time we had a toast to set this evening off right and invite the continued good graces of Perlosa on the rest of our journey." He gently placed the jug down on the table, pulled the cork, and grinned. "A fine vintage of port I picked up when I first bought this ship." He poured a small amount into his wooden mug. "I've kept it with me to savor now and then. I thought it fitting we share some tonight, since this is the farthest the *Phoenix* has ever sailed."

Charles' eyes lit up. "Now you're talking."

"To *savor*." Hirim hammered the point home. "Not to drink bone dry." He rose and poured a small portion into each diner's mug. When he'd finished, he recorked the jug, placed it back down beside him, and took his seat.

"A toast then." Hirim raised his mug. "To fair seas and prosperous ventures."

"Fair seas and prosperous ventures!" Corwyn and the others raised their mugs.

"Fine stuff, eh?" asked the Celetor.

"A most well-rounded flavor," Josiah agreed, taking a final pleasing puff from his pipe before placing it beside his meal.

"I've had better," Charles replied flatly, though no one seemed to hear.

"Just how long have you had this ship?" Corwyn asked.

"Close to twenty years." Hirim extinguished his cigar by pinching it between his thumb and index finger. "Some days it seems longer, others like I only got it yesterday." He rested the cigar beside his wooden spoon.

"Can we *eat* now?" Charles' tone became an almost caustic whine.

"This would be one of those long days." As soon as Hirim picked up his spoon, Charles dug into the stew with reckless abandon. He would have swallowed his half-spent cigarette too if he hadn't remembered to take it out of his mouth and crush it out on the table.

"So how long have you been a bard?" Hirim asked Corwyn between bites.

"I've been back in the Midlands for a little over two years but I've been a bard—getting trained and practicing my skills—for the better part of ten years."

"You have to be *trained* to tell stories?" asked Charles, wiping his mouth with the back of his hand. "I thought you just made up stuff. How hard can that be?"

"If you want to be good at it, you'll seek training. Not just that but musical training and voice lessons and basic knowledge of myths and legends."

"Pah." The halfling dismissively waved the notion away. "Waste of money if you ask me. So, that all we get to drink tonight, Hirim?"

The captain bent down and retrieved another ceramic jug from beside him. The halfling's eyes lit up once again. It looked newer and slimmer than the previous jug, but its obvious heft in Hirim's hand told all it was full. "There." He placed it on the table near the bread with a heavy thud. Charles made an effort to grab it, but it was out of reach.

"Here." Mathias brought the jug closer to the other's searching hands.

"Aha." He pulled out the cork with his childlike fingers.

"Just remember it's for *all* of us tonight," Hirim warned.

"I know, I know." He lifted the jug and, after some skillful maneuvering, filled his mug to the brim.

"Is there anything of note you have discovered in your studies, Mr. Onu—"

"Hey," Charles shouted in disgust. "What kind of game you playing, Hirim? This is *water*!"

"What did you think it would be? *Wine?*"

"Yeah."

"Not tonight." Hirim reached for a hunk of bread and tore off a piece. "You can be sober for one night." The halfling's face contorted into a scowl but he said nothing else, merely contenting himself with finishing his stew.

"As I was saying," Josiah continued, "have you found anything of note in your studies thus far, Mr. Onuis?"

"Not anything more than I've already told you." Mathias took a piece of bread for himself.

"I, for one, am most intrigued by the notion of this venture," said Josiah, sitting back in his chair. "Think about what could be at stake and your mind does indeed travel far in the field of speculation. Immortality," he continued, taking the jug and filling his mug. "What wonders one could work and see and even accomplish, I daresay, if one could indeed not have to worry about his best years slipping away from him."

"Do you want to know what *I'd* do with immortality?" Charles inquired.

"No," Hirim returned curtly, receiving the jug from Josiah.

"And why not?"

"Because I'm trying to enjoy my meal."

"I sense a real fear of imagination here." Charles managed to secure his own loaf and angrily ripped it apart. "I bet you couldn't think of *half* as many things to do with immortality as me."

"Let's just take your word for it." Hirim passed the jug Corwyn's way.

"So did you learn any good tales in your training?"

"A decent amount, I guess," he replied.

"Then why not share some with us tonight? Maybe you have something that might fit with our current venture."

It actually sounded like a good idea. "I think I have a few tales that might fit . . ."

2

Within weeks, Charles had grown stir crazy. And the crew was growing crazy from Charles. Occasionally Corwyn would pull out his lute and strum a few songs, distracting the halfling for a spell before he'd lose interest and declare his boredom to all present. And he made sure to let every crewman know of his increasing boredom every day. After all, they had a responsibility to keep him—the junior partner of this expedition—entertained. On top of that, Charles was running low on wine. He easily drank his daily rations before late morning. Worse still, there were only a few fat handfuls of cigarettes remaining to his name, forcing some painful self-discipline.

One crewman, a Napowese sailor well known by all the crew for his calm, controlled nature, nearly got into a fight with the halfling as the whining continued. His redemption came through a strong-bodied Napowese named Chal, one of the lieutenants, who kept any daggers from puncturing Charles' gut. Even Hirim had reached the point of threatening to send the halfling off in one of the rowboats to fend for himself, but he was held back by Josiah, who rebuked him for such pleasant fancies, citing contractual obligations.

During all this, Mathias had been able to update them on what he'd discovered on the map, along with its possible origins and the nature of the island itself. Once every few days he'd brief the group on his findings. Some days were more fruitful than others. Today only offered slim insights. Mathias was getting low on notes and tomes despite constantly feeling the pressure to provide answers to those gathered around the table in the room off the captain's quarters.

"That's it?" Charles inquired with more than a little disappointment.

"That's all I've been able to discover in the last few days, yes," answered Mathias.

"Well, I better get some big payoff for being put through this dreadfully awful trip."

"You have already been compensated." Josiah bristled beneath his calm and dignified demeanor. "And I would like to stress you are indeed looking at healthy compensation for your investment in any shared profits Coggsbury, Elliott, Chesterfield, and Company experience."

"It's not that bad." Corwyn voiced some optimism, pulling the map across the table and turning it so everyone could see it better. He'd been learning a new part of the puzzle from Mathias' frequent updates and their snippets of conversation over the past weeks.

"Now, we already know the place is off Troll Island. We also know the Nordicans supposedly avoided it for unknown reasons, which, if true, would mean it's probably not been disturbed since this map was created. That means whatever is there probably hasn't been touched in centuries." He peered back at the stubble-faced Charles. "So your profits, and those of all involved, are more than secure."

"I still need some bearings to go on," Hirim explained, jabbing a finger at the drawing of Troll Island. "I can't trust this map to be accurate, and I don't want to end up getting lost in the Northlands or going over the Crown of the World."

"I believe, Mr. Koofehi, we all share such a sentiment."

"Right." Corwyn considered the map once again. "I'm more interested in figuring out what this island is supposed to have on it. Mathias has almost exhausted his books and scrolls and has yet to come across anything but vague rumors."

"We can just as easily find out what's on the island when we get there," offered Charles.

"I don't think that would be wise, really," said Corwyn. "What if there's something there we should be aware of? I mean, this map says it holds the key to eternal life or some such thing. If that's true, won't such a thing be guarded or protected in some way? *I'd* guard something like that, if it were me."

"So what are you proposing, Mr. Danther?" Josiah was studying him, as were the rest in the room.

"I think we should visit one of the Northlands and try to gather more information before we get to the island. Maybe we could get better bearings from the locals."

Hirim stroked his mustache in thought. "That does make sense. How about it, Josiah? You think the company would be willing to take a detour?"

"Speaking as its representative, I can say that while the merits of the idea might be sound enough, we would open ourselves up to the possibility of losing our unique claim on the find. That and we could possibly invite Nordic hostilities into our endeavor. Having read accounts of their savage nature, in which they have been known to attack their own kin for basic supplies, I think it wise to avoid contact with them altogether."

"I hear the Nordicans have lovely maidens—*giants* of women." Charles chuckled to himself. "I'd be more than happy to climb *those* mountains. Maybe we all could do with a little shore leave, just for some recreation. We wouldn't even have to tell them what we're after."

"The matter has been decided, Mr. de Frassel," Josiah replied firmly.

"You've been pretty quiet, Mathias. This all seem okay with you?" Corwyn's question shifted all eyes toward the scribe. "I could help you gather information from what you still have to look over, I suppose. I'm not as skilled with Nordican as you, but it's still better than nothing if we aren't going to be allowed access to seek new information."

"I suppose." Mathias' voice was dry and low. "Maybe an extra pair of eyes could be helpful. I guess I could have missed something."

"How much longer till we reach Troll Island?" Corwyn asked Hirim.

"We're probably about three more weeks out if the weather and winds hold."

"Three weeks?" Charles whined. "I'm going to be stuck here for *three more weeks*?"

"Believe me," Hirim muttered, "we feel the same way."

"Hey, you all haven't been the best of shipmates either," Charles snapped back.

"That's the longest it could take, Charles." Corwyn tried his best to calm the situation. "It might be much faster."

"If we had a priest of Endarien or Perlosa on board it would be," said Hirim. "We don't, though, so we'll just have to rely upon both gods' favor. So far they've been more than gracious since we left Rexatoius."

"I think I can speak for all, Mr. Koofehi, when I say I look forward to a safe and rapid arrival at our destination. Mr. Onuis, I expect both you and Mr. Danther to come up with a bit more from what you have on hand. Any small fraction of insight could be of great benefit if it provides a better picture of what this island is all about. I am sure, with the added help, your efforts will be even more fruitful. I have faith and confidence in both of you and your abilities."

"Don't you want anything from me?" Charles smiled sarcastically.

"To be honest, Mr. de Frassel, if you could find something to safely entertain yourself and hold your interest, I would be very supportive of such an endeavor."

"I see." Charles studied Josiah's dry expression with an amused eye.

"I am told reading is quite the most powerful of pastimes one can undertake."

"*Reading?*" Charles' head slouched forward.

"Yes, reading." Josiah was as congenial as he could be. "Of course, someone of your . . . immense appetites might find themselves better suited to writing."

"Writing what?"

"Perhaps a log of the journey thus far."

"I thought the bard was doing that," he said, nodding at Corwyn.

"He is, but maybe yours can be from another point of view, or you could even write a story."

"Write a story, eh?" Charles' face entertained a rather unsavory lopsided grin. "That would be something, wouldn't it?"

"It certainly could be. I myself know of no modern-day halfling writers. Perhaps you might be the first one to gain the world's attention." Josiah joined Mathias and Hirim in rising from the table.

"Well, you just don't get out much, Josiah." Charles leapt from his chair and followed the gnome from the room.

"That may be. But I am sure with your mind and some modest degree of dedication to the task, you can come up with something that would make the days just fly by."

"Yeah." Charles nodded. "Why not write? I mean, it's about time *true* culture and proper tales were put into the public square, right? And who better to do so than the most cultured race in the world?" He followed Josiah out of the room. "I even have a title: 'Charles the Great and the Ship of Fools.'"

"Oh my . . . that is . . . certainly *boldly* original."

"Now I just need a plot . . ."

A week later, Corwyn was back in Mathias' quarters, studying the map by means of the swaying oil lamp above. He was focused on a small section of the old vellum which had held his eyes for the past quarter hour. "What are these things?"

"What things?" Mathias looked over from where he sat with books and scrolls piled about his feet and a few volumes on the desk.

"These black spots?" He turned the map to face the elf. "Here." His fingers pointed out a small section at the top right of the vellum.

"I just assumed they were ink spots or stains."

"Just a thought," he said, turning the map back to face himself. He paused. "I hope this isn't too inconvenient for you. I didn't want to impose, even if Hirim said—"

Mathias cut him off. "No, it was needed. I'm not going to get all the answers before we need them; that's apparent now."

He didn't like the defeated tone in Mathias' voice and felt partially to blame for it. In a way he was muscling in on the scribe's domain and probably making him feel even less useful, since Corwyn made him more or less second-guess everything. Not to mention that Mathias had to tutor him in the Nordic language along the way, which further slowed his progress.

"Have you changed your mind yet?"

Mathias was caught off guard. "About what?"

"About the truth of what we're looking for. When I first came onboard you said you didn't think it existed."

"And, to be honest, I still don't believe it to be something real." Mathias resumed his studying. "It's a nice allegory or story perhaps, but little else."

"But it has to be based on something, some kernel of truth."

"Ever the romantic." Mathias turned another page.

"I'd like to think I'm more of an optimist. So why are you on this ship if you don't think what we're seeking is real?"

Mathias shared a soft smile. "I need the money. Though it isn't that great an amount, it's still some coin."

"So you're more *mercenary* than *scribe*," Corwyn teased.

"Perhaps, but then that would put me in good company, since all here are doing this for the money."

"I'm actually just curious to see what might await us on that island."

"Which is probably nothing."

"You *really* think nothing's there?"

"I think something might very well be there, but it won't be the secret to eternal youth or life or anything like that. That sort of thing is impossible."

"But we live in a world with wizards and priests. And the stories of dranors and the titans before them talk about some pretty amazing things—some of which people have even found. How can you think nothing will be there?"

"Spoken like a bard." Mathias shared another grin. "I just don't see the world like you do, Corwyn. You live in a place of pleasant fiction and fantasies. I do believe in the gods and know about priests and wizards and the power they command, but that doesn't mean everything that's been spoken or written down over the years is true.

"If you can show me something—something *tangible*—then I'll believe it. But if you ask me to take too great a leap of faith, then I just can't do it. I know the gods are real because I see the power of their priests. I know the wizards have power; I've seen that too. But there's no real documented proof or evidence for what we seek. We only have some old tales, legends, and myths. That's all. No trustworthy eyewitness accounts. No documented evidence. Nothing."

Corwyn let Mathias' words sink in. He could see the scribe's position, and while sorry for the difference of opinion, he wasn't going to let it come between them in their work. He also knew carrying the conversation further would risk offense or argument, which wouldn't be productive for either of them.

"Then I guess I'll just have to be the optimist for both of us," he said, making his way over to another book on top of the pile beside the elf. "So what else can I help you with?"

3

The *Phoenix* slowly skirted the cold, empty coast of Troll Island. In these northern waters the pale, lifeless waves were tipped with frost. While it was nearing spring in the Northlands, the chill of the past winter hadn't yet relented its grip. The temperature had greatly changed in just the past few days as they crossed into the Sea of Glass, taking on a colder snap. It would only decrease as they neared their destination.

Hirim didn't want to sail too close to the island. He thought it wise to heed the old Nordic sailors who steered clear of the Troll-infested land. The frigate remained just close enough to be seen from land in the partially hidden sun but not within striking distance of anything keeping a lair on the shore or in the shallow waters near the pine-forested coast.

The pace was slow going, the winds weak and conflicting the further north they went—small flurries of snow dusted the crew and deck in fluffy frenzies of flakes. Soon small chunks of ice appeared bobbing in the water beside them. They were nearing the fabled Crown of the World—the division between the known and unknown.

The frosty air and water made the *Phoenix* creak and groan. It seemed the colder it grew, the louder were even the weakest of sounds. Whispers carried farther, and every movement—from the flapping of the sails to the creaking of timber and the motion of the rigging—could be heard distinctly.

Everyone had donned winter garb: fur-lined coats, boots, thick woolen tunics, mittens, and padded leather pants. All had also done what they could to keep out of the wind. This proved difficult, since it came at them from a new angle every few moments. In these chaotic battling gusts, it didn't take long for red noses and cheeks to bloom among the crewmen and passengers. Facial hair was soon matted with hoarfrost, and mucus trickled from frigid noses, dripping onto chapped nostrils and lips.

Hirim pondered the waves from the upper forecastle with his spyglass, orange woolen scarf flapping in the breeze. Josiah, Corwyn, Mathias, and Charles stood nearby, eager for his report, nestling together like chicks for warmth.

"I don't see anything." Hirim's voice was grim.

"My calculations have to be correct." Mathias stood beside him, fur-lined hood drawn tight about his face. He held the map in his mitten-covered hand, making triple sure of his work. "Corwyn and I went over this map with a fine-toothed comb."

"Well, I don't see anything," Hirim repeated while passing over the rocky outline of Troll Island with his spyglass.

"It should be just two leagues north of Troll Island," Mathias continued.

"Well, we've gone *seven*." Hirim collapsed the spyglass with a snap. "Let me see that again." He claimed the map with a rough tug.

"Hey, be careful with that now," Charles whined between shivers. He'd shoved both mittened hands under his armpits, focusing all his energy on staying warm. In so doing he'd given the crew a small respite from his typically disruptive behavior. But the crew had no time to enjoy it. They were constantly cleaning the snow off the deck and keeping the rigging free from ice. Continually working their fingers kept their digits fluid enough to keep up their efforts. None spoke, saving their energy for staying warm.

"Are you sure you calculated correctly?" Josiah huffed on his pipe.

"Positive," said Mathias. "I've done the work ten times now . . . it's all come up the same. Corwyn can verify my efforts."

"He's right," added Corwyn. "It should be here."

"Well, *this* is exciting," Charles huffed.

"You're just lucky we haven't tossed you overboard yet," Hirim growled.

"Well, it's about as useful as an empty cask of wine," Charles grumbled. "We don't even know where we're going."

"Could I see the map again?" Corwyn asked. "I don't see how, but we must have missed something."

"Why not?" Hirim surrendered it to him. "Not much good it's doing us now."

Corwyn considered the map with a feverish intensity. Though he'd studied it already for many an hour with Mathias, he tried looking with fresh eyes. He saw the old inked outlines of the Northlands: Baltan, Troll Island, Frigia, and Valkoria; the waves around them and the island off the coast of Troll Island . . . off the coast, near some other specks on top of the map . . . And then something hit him right between the eyes. He was amazed he'd never actually thought of it before.

"Look here," said Corwyn, pointing to the mysterious island. "The map has it no more than two leagues from Troll Island, right?"

"Correct."

"But what if the island was there when the map was made but has since drifted off?"

"Drifted off?" Mathias shook his head. "Now you're just wasting time."

"No, I'm not. Think about it a moment." He lowered the map to his side.

"I've never heard of an island floating away on its own," said Hirim.

"It could be magical," Josiah added. "For all we know the whole *thing* could be a magical island. If it holds eternal life on it, then it probably would have some type of magic to it."

"*Magic?*" The doubt in Mathias' voice was impossible to miss. "Now don't go telling some bard's tale, too."

"Not magic," said Corwyn, "but a large piece of ice and debris."

Charles frowned. "You haven't been drinking, have you?"

"Listen, I read a few old sagas from Mathias' books that claimed large blocks of ice float around the Crown of the World before disappearing into the other side of Tralodren. A similar tale was even mentioned in Argos when I was being trained. It was one of the few from the Northlands the college verified as truthful."

"So?" Charles sniffed back some snot.

"If the island isn't here, then it must be something like those ice chunks and has floated away."

"Either that or he read the map wrong." Charles glared at Mathias.

"Or there may never have been an island in the first place," Josiah countered. "We have to acknowledge that possibility as well, gentlemen, should we understand the full nature of this venture. There might never have been an island at all, and this whole expedition might have been in vain."

"It may not be *here*"—Corwyn fixed his eyes on the gnome—"but what's the harm in looking a little farther? Let's just go a little farther, till we get to those ice floes, and then see if there's anything there. If we don't find anything, we can turn around. Why not be thorough for your employers?"

Josiah puffed on his pipe, thinking. "Why not indeed, Mr. Danther."

"I'm not going over to the other side of the world chasing after floating ice chunks."

"Not at all, Captain." Josiah eased Hirim's displeasure. "Simply in that direction, no farther. I have no desire to see such a spectacle as the other side of the world. I may have an entrepreneurial soul, but I am not a fool." Hirim huffed and made his way for the deck, shouting orders to his crew. As he did, Josiah studied Corwyn with a pragmatic eye. "It still might not exist." He took another puff from his pipe.

"I guess we'll all find out soon enough."

"Interesting theory." Mathias sidled up next to Corwyn, while the rest cast their gazes back onto the frigid waves.

"I got the idea from those ink spots on the map. After I saw the floating ice in the water, they reminded me of islands."

"Smaller masses of ice I can see, but one as large as an island floating around out here is something else."

"It's hard for me to imagine too, but wouldn't it be the perfect place to hide something important—on an island that kept moving?"

"Assuming you knew how to find it in the end." Mathias took another view of the expanse of waves. "They really told you Nordic stories in college?"

"A few. They helped give a greater breadth to our lessons."

"What was the story about?"

"A giant slayer named Erik the Tall. It's a saga about how he travels to the far north to seek out his archenemy, the Jotun named Latham Life-taker. It's not that popular anymore and wasn't widely sung by the skalds, I guess, either." Mathias nodded absent-mindedly before joining the contemplative silence they all shared while considering their surroundings.

A few hours later, the *Phoenix* plowed along the slushy waters surrounding the last known bastion of reality before everything turned and shifted to the other side of Tralodren. The Northlands were no longer in sight. Only small blocks of ice and half-frozen waves greeted them. Colder than any thought possible, the temperature plummeted below frigid—beyond freezing—a marrow-cracking numbness hanging low and thick over everything. Even the previously soft breezes had become honed razors dashing exposed skin with their cruel touch.

Charles had gone to bed to hide from the cold, taking his map with him. Mathias remained with Corwyn on the stern. Both were tightly wrapped in their coats, studying the horizon, searching for anything useful. Josiah paced nearby, his pipe ever smoldering. So far neither they nor the crew had found anything. There had been a few larger collections of ice, but nothing matching the size of Rainier's Island. The farther they sailed, though, the greater the chunks of ice became, some even resembling small hills. In the distance others resembled mountains.

The crew had slowed considerably, their bundled frames trying to keep up with the needs of the ship while fighting the numbness slowly soaking into their bones. Hirim wasn't pleased and often cursed while pacing the upper deck. His black mustache had become frosted with ice and specks of snot. He'd taken a spot on the upper forecastle again, placing the cold lens of his spyglass to his eye. His manner was tense and his crew ever alert; they'd discovered that oftentimes a greater portion of the larger chunks of ice dwelled below the waves than above. This meant they had to constantly maintain a safe distance or risk running into one or gouging the hull.

"I think I see something," he shouted to the others, making his way down to the lower deck. "Take us hard to port and then steady on until I tell you otherwise." The crew scattered and the wheelman huffed out steamy blasts as he fought for mastery of the wheel, steering the ship in its new direction.

The sun was already slouching in the slate-gray sky when the *Phoenix* approached the large floating isle of ice. All on board remained silent as the white island drifted closer, like a giant buoy. Around it bobbed a few smaller fragments of frozen water topped with crusty snow. Another light dusting of thin flakes in the crisp air forced them deeper inside their warm coverings.

The water had thickened over the last hour. The previous soupy slush had become more like clay. When the crew found an acceptable spot, they laid anchor. It hit a piece of ice beneath the waves with an echoing thud.

The island was pure snow and ice. Jagged peaks sprung out of and around it like faux mountains around an empty beach sliding further inland. The island's frozen mass appeared larger than they'd expected, perhaps over a mile in both directions. Beyond the powdery beach, a large structure jutted out of the landscape alongside an icy, snow-swathed mountain. All eyes were drawn to the structure, nestled behind curtains of low-riding hills and jagged, frozen mountains of ice. White, half-covered by snow, and caked with ice in spots, it certainly possessed the look of something made by mortals.

"I think we may have found our destination, gentlemen." Josiah smiled. "Can you make anything out of it, Captain?"

Hirim accompanied them atop the forecastle once more, spyglass in hand, observing the landmass. "It looks like it's a citadel or tower of some kind. It's covered in snow and ice here and there, but still standing. The building is about halfway into the island itself—"

"But through ice and snow the whole way," grumbled Charles. He'd reluctantly rejoined the others when news of a possible discovery reached his hammock.

"No one said you had to come along," said Hirim.

"And miss out on the *prize*?" Charles cast a disparaging glance Hirim's way. "Hah!"

"Well," said Josiah, rubbing his cold-reddened chin. "We have some gear that should allow for safe snow travel, but nothing allowing us to get near that structure in good time. And I fear though we might be able to traverse the snow, climbing those hills and sharp peaks will be quite hazardous indeed."

"Not to mention what might happen if we get caught on that ice heap when the sun goes down," Mathias added. "I'm not too wild about spending the night on an island of snow and ice. The ship's cold enough already."

"Maybe we can convert the landing boats into some kind of sled," offered Corwyn. "It might gain us some time."

"Interesting idea," said Hirim. "It might be possible."

"You probably should get what books and scrolls you will need too, Mr. Onuis," said Josiah. "I trust we will still have some quandaries of mental obscurity and challenge which only your muscular mind will help solve." The gnome inhaled deeply from his pipe, flushing out smoke through his nostrils. Charles observed the action with a fair amount of jealousy.

Mathias nodded. "I'll get a working collection together. With my notes and what I've read so far, I think we should be prepared for anything we might encounter."

Josiah blew out another thick cloud of scented smoke as Mathias departed for his cabin. "I would imagine the rest of us should make ready as best we can, too. We do not know what we shall encounter."

"I was born ready," said Charles. "Just get me on that island and near that secret of eternal life!"

"Now, Mr. de Frassel, you know we have to follow protocol. We must be cautious and not rush into something that might indeed prove perilous, not just for the individual, but for all involved. I would much prefer if you deferred to the captain, Mr. Danther, or Mr. Onuis before lurching ahead like some wild animal, half-crazed with thirst upon catching sight of water."

"You talk a lot, you know that?"

An hour or so later, the crew and guests finished their final preparations. The two smaller boats which they used for making landfall—as they were about to do now—had been converted into rough sleds in a way that kept their structural integrity and seaworthiness. The adaptation was simple yet sturdy enough to protect them from the rough terrain ahead.

Each also grabbed a weapon of some kind: cutlasses for the crewmen, a mace for Josiah, and daggers for Mathias and Charles. Not that the last three were skilled in the use of such weapons, but when it came to self-defense, each felt safer having something at hand should the worst befall them.

"You're not carrying any weapon?" Mathias asked Corwyn as he made his way on deck. The elf had bundled what he could into the small chest he carried.

"No." Corwyn briefly glanced at the dagger sheath girded about the scribe's waist.

"Aren't you afraid of being unprepared in case something happens?" Mathias climbed the stairs with him. Though it was small, the elf struggled with the chest, huffing white gusts of breath with every other step.

"Not really."

"Oh," said Mathias, reaching the deck first. Both made their way to the others, who were dividing up the crew. "I guess I believe in being more cautious than that." His breathing was returning to normal. "I'm not as free in my ways as you bards have a reputation for being."

"And that's fine. The world would be a pretty boring place if everyone was like me."

As the *Phoenix*'s crew completed their preparations, a set of eyes held them fast. This stare came from inside the rougher section of the island, where the beach was overshadowed by large, jagged pieces of ice mimicking cresting waves frozen solid in midascent. Near a patch of smooth ice, now bashed open and allowing access to the frigid waters beneath, a white bear took in the shape of the ship and the men on board. Its blood-covered muzzle wrinkled while sniffing the air. Under its gore-splattered chest and stomach lay the carcass of a seal, whose contents had been eviscerated and strewn across the colorless ice by bloody paws.

The bear licked at its muzzle, clearing off some of the congealing blood, then abandoned the seal in favor of keeping a tighter focus on the ship. The activity of the crew sparked its interest, making it aware of thoughts and understandings it hadn't experienced for quite some time. Rising, it began cautiously lumbering toward a dune of ice and hardened snow that helped conceal its shape. The longer it spied on the ship, the brighter the glimmer in its eyes became.

4

Disembarking from the *Phoenix* was a fairly routine and simple affair. Even with the modifications to the smaller landing boats, it took just a short row to get to shore. But once they'd made landfall and dragged the boats onto the powdery beach, all routines ceased.

"Are you sure this will work?" Charles cautiously stepped into the back of one of the modified rowboats.

"Shut up and get in!" Hirim snapped.

A crew of twenty men, led by Hirim's two lieutenants, accompanied the five adventurers clambering into the modified rowboats. In one of these boats sat Josiah, now joined by a muttering Charles. The two were too short to make good progress in the deeper snow on foot, and there was concern they might get swallowed whole through a simple misstep, tumbling into a deep snowdrift or hidden chasm. Mathias stood beside the other modified boat, shivering.

"Get those shoes on," said one of the lieutenants, a middle-aged Celetor. Upon the order, all the men donned their snowshoes.

"Just sit down and relax," Corwyn told Charles while fixing his snowshoes to his fur-lined boots. "If this works, we'll be there in no time, and both you and Josiah will stay dry and safe."

"And if it doesn't, we'll be stuck on this chunk of ice to freeze to death," Charles grumbled.

"And the world wouldn't be too troubled over the loss of one halfling," came Hirim's retort. Charles' face soured. "If you're not careful, your face might freeze that way." Hirim snickered, adding, "It might actually be an improvement."

"Shut up and get this thing moving," Charles snarled. "I'm already colder than Perlosa's tits."

Upon Hirim's orders, five crewmen took charge of each vessel, pulling them along the snowy landscape. A handful went ahead, using fifteen-foot poles to judge the ice and snow, prodding and tamping down any drifts that might block their path. They managed to make good time until they encountered the hilly region surrounding the citadel. As they neared it, they could see it rested at the center of a crater-like valley, alongside the long, stalagmite-like ice mountain at its center.

All kept their words to a minimum. This only added to the unsettling quiet around the place. It seemed as if the very ice and snow soaked up every sound, creating an odd sensation of stillness and peace. And while the daylight helped tremendously, its continuous reflection off the endless stretch of white cast a bright shimmer all around. This forced everyone to squint for glimpses beyond the brilliant glare.

The battle getting up the hill proved harder than they'd expected, especially for the ones pulling the boats. These strained their legs and backs while staying atop the ice-coated, hard-packed snow, which creaked and cracked beneath their tread like tired hinges. Even so, this was by far the easiest path to their destination; other parts of the island were jagged and impassable.

Despite the sluggish ascent, they still had daylight with them. Their location near the Crown of the World would assure a few more hours of it, but it wouldn't hold back the night forever. They managed to reach the top of a hill and take a short rest. The sun sank lower, bleeding orange light across the horizon. Whatever mercy they'd gained from Rheminas was fading.

The firn in which they stood swelled into a white foundation from which the company of men peered into the alien landscape. Below them rested the low valley, stained a tarnished gold and silver by the sun's fading fire. From their new vantage point, the expedition could see the entire circular depression. Around them small drifts of snow gave rise to pregnant hills and then jagged cliffs of ice encircling the low-lying tract of land in a sort of hedge. Indeed, it seemed like the whole circle around the citadel was planned. Such thoughts, though, went unspoken. All focused their eyes on the ice mountain in the center of the valley and the citadel attached to it.

Sharp spears of ice shot heavenward amid the white marble spikes boldly stabbing the sky. Angled slabs of silver joined them and buttressed the white marble walls. Together they made a towering fortress anchored to the rising mound of ice beneath, itself like some archaic set of worn fangs. The citadel was of solid stone, allowing for no windows or openings. Thick icicles the size of men hung from the overhangs of the sloped roof, a snowcapped peak some two hundred or more feet above the empty, snow-smothered ground.

"That's *it*?" Charles scowled from under his hood. "The secret to eternal life lies in *there*?"

"It looks deserted," said a crewman.

"And riddled with snow and ice." Hirim nodded. "Can anything of value still be in there?"

"Only one way to find out," said Corwyn, climbing into one of the boats.

"I must concur with Mr. Danther," said Josiah. "We have not traveled this far only to squelch the potential benefits of this venture. If what we seek is indeed inside, then we have almost completed our mission and shall be quite handsomely rewarded."

"Get in, Mathias," Corwyn told the shivering scribe beside the boat.

"I'm not so sure this is such a good idea." The elf's complexion was noticeably paler. "After all, I mean, it's already dangerous now. Why not just trek down to the valley on foot? Why add to the peril with this makeshift sled?"

"You know why." Corwyn tied a rope snugly about his waist and bound it to a small iron loop which he and a few crewmen had affixed to the inside base of the boat. "If we climb down, it will take far longer and be far more dangerous and we'd lose what daylight we have left." Mathias remained shivering, watching Hirim and the rest of the crew get into their respective seats.

"Come on already," Charles shouted. "I'm so cold I could piss ice."

"Just hop in and close your eyes." Corwyn motioned the hesitant scribe forward. Mathias slowly climbed over the lip of the boat and stepped inside one leg at a time, testing its stability. Once assured it was safe, he took a seat beside a Napowese sailor, who handed him a rope.

"If I die, I'm going to blame you," Mathias informed Corwyn. He tied the rope about his waist, then bent over so he could run it around a metal loop, accompanying the other ropes already anchored to it.

"Everyone set and tied in?" Hirim asked from the other boat. When confident all were, he continued. "All right then, heave off, lads," he told the two stalwart Telborians connected to their boats with rope belts. Each bent low and began shoving the boats off the frozen hill.

Within moments, each boat moved up to and over the edge. The Telborians pushing the boats quickly leapt into the spots allowed them at the rear. The vessels slid over the lip of the hill and into the valley below.

At first the boats were slow, but they quickly picked up speed, sliding down the slope at an ever-increasing rate. The two Telborians used oars as makeshift rudders, steering the vessels as best they could, keeping them headed in a straight line while avoiding ice spurs and troublesome areas. Everyone else did their best to attach their white-knuckled grips to anything solid, praying all the way.

At the top of the same hill where the others began their sled ride, the lone white bear lumbered over and studied the fresh tracks, sniffing about the trampled snow. Satisfied with its investigation, it sauntered over to the lip of the hill and peered down at the rapidly descending boats. It tilted its head, then pushed some snow over the crest of the hill with its red-splattered paw. It stood there a moment longer—silent as the landscape—as if pondering something profound, then turned around and slowly backed down the hill with its large rump until it too slid toward the citadel.

The makeshift sleds continued speeding down the hill, the two crewmen ferrying their course. Icy rocks bumped them to and fro in their rapid descent. The wind sliced into everyone's skin like cold knives, tearing tears from their eyes before they could fall or freeze. All held their breath. Struggling with their stomachs in their throats, they jostled around the smaller bumps and lumps of the hill with the icy citadel rapidly rising ahead.

"So how do we stop these things?" Hirim asked Corwyn over the rush of wind.

Corwyn had seated himself beside him, allowing a full view ahead. It was a good question, and he did have a good answer, just not one the captain might want to hear.

"Snow." His voice barely rose over the noise of the ride.

"Snow?" Hirim's cold-chapped face wrinkled in confusion. "I don't—"

He stopped short when the boat hit a particularly sharp bump. The ice mountain and the small snow mounds around it were getting closer—too close.

"Somebody stop these damned things before we crash," Charles shouted.

"Slow us down! Slow us down!" Hirim shouted at the two helmsmen.

Each strained on their oars but could only create so much drag against the brittle snow and stubborn, clumpy ice. The surface of the hill was rapidly leveling as they neared the center of the crater. While this did some good in decelerating them, it wasn't enough.

"I'm too young to die!" Mathias clenched his eyes shut and clamped a white-knuckled hand on the rope about his waist.

"I do not believe any of us shall die, Mr. Onuis," Josiah remarked, though his voice betrayed his own agitation.

"Shut up, you overstuffed bureaucrat!" Charles barked. "If anyone shouldn't die here, it's me."

"Snow!" Corwyn spoke louder this time, motioning to a pile of white powder near the citadel's base. "Steer for the snow!"

The two crewmen wasted no time. Grunting curses beneath their breath, they managed to veer the boats toward the snowbanks.

"This better work," he heard Mathias say.

The two boats slid closer to the banks and then into them. First one boat, then the other sheathed itself in the cold diamond dust. For a moment no one said anything. The first few feet of the boats, along with the crewmen seated there, had slammed into the white mound. They emerged looking like living snowmen, spitting, sputtering, and shaking the snow from their faces and frames.

"Great," said Charles, shaking snow out of his hood. His face was covered with it, his eyes peering out between white cheeks and frosted eyebrows. "As if I wasn't cold enough." Those seated farther back weren't as coated but were still dusted with more snow than they would have liked. All wiped their faces and cleaned their garments in quick fashion.

"Are we dead?" Mathias dared open one of his eyes. His mittened hands still clung tightly to the rope about his waist.

"No." Josiah retrieved a grooming brush from an inside pocket and cleaned himself off more thoroughly than the others. "We seem to be all right and whole, Mr. Onuis . . . at least as far as I can tell."

"Everyone okay?" Hirim climbed out of his seat. Like ants emerging from a disrupted hill, the crew instantly went into action, clearing the boats and themselves from the snow mound. This time they allowed themselves a few muttered curses and complaints while undertaking their tasks.

"How do we stand, Chal?" Hirim asked his Napowese lieutenant, pulling out some of the annoying icicles clinging to his mustache.

"They're solid enough, Captain," Chal replied.

"That went better than I thought." Corwyn worked the snow off the back of his neck, letting the small clumps slide down his back and out his coat.

"Yeah." Charles stepped out of the boat with a scowl. "Real fun."

"I wish you would have told us about this first." Mathias fiddled with his rope belt.

"Ah, it wasn't that bad," said Corwyn.

"Speak for yourself." The elf finally untied the knot.

"We made it here in one piece." Hirim's tone was gruff and businesslike. "Now we need to get inside this thing before it gets dark."

"Yes." Josiah joined them in a rough circle as the crewmen finished cleaning out the snow from the boats.

"And that would be Mathias' territory." Charles peered at the scribe.

Mathias took in the white marble building with a silent, contemplative gaze. He, like the rest of them, stood viewing the most bizarre thing he'd ever seen: an edifice of ancient architecture in the middle of nowhere.

The outer walls were smooth and clean. Silver accents could be seen through the frost, ice, and snow, which appeared to outline the spear-tipped roof on each of its four corners. The blocks still appeared fresh and unaltered by the passage of years.

"Mathias?" Charles clapped his mitten-clad hands.

"Wha—" The elf returned to his senses.

"How do we get inside?" asked Hirim. Shifting restlessly from foot to foot in a small dance for warmth, the others watched Mathias approach the walls. The front of the citadel was partially covered with a snowdrift; the rest merged with the ice of the towering mountain.

"Something's here," he said, gently tracing what he saw with his hand. Corwyn joined him in clearing away the crusted snow, scooping it with hands and kicking at it with feet. After some digging, they revealed a white stone door. A single line of runic text was carved deep into its surface about one third of the way down from its rounded top.

"Looks like Nordican." Corwyn stepped back, mirroring Mathias, who was already engrossed in the discovery.

"Seems to be an older dialect," Mathias added.

"Can you read it?" Josiah moved beside the two men.

"I think so." Mathias stared at the text in heavy concentration. The rest of the crew had finished tending the boats and joined the semicircle of bodies around the newly discovered doorway.

" 'Eternal life . . .' " Mathias trailed off.

"A promising start," Josiah mused under his breath, stuffing his pipe with tobacco.

" 'Eternal life, for all who dwell inside these gelid, mundane walls,' " Mathias continued his translation.

"Are you sure?" Josiah worked his sparker above the pipe's bowl, keeping the stem clenched between his teeth. The device reminded Corwyn of the large pins sometimes still used in holding cloaks or other items of clothing together. "I do not mean to doubt your talents, Mr. Onuis, but I want to be sure we have the right information before we proceed any further." Good to its name, the sparker dropped a handful of sparks into the bowl, allowing the gnome some fresh puffs of flavored smoke. "Safety is of the utmost concern."

"Yeah, he's got it right, I think." Corwyn could see some sense in the runic text the longer he went over it. "From what I've learned so far, that's what it says."

"So we get eternal life only if we live inside this place?" Charles reasoned aloud.

"I do not think that is the case, Mr. de Frassel. It is more poetic, I believe, referring to the potential of there being the secret for eternal life residing therein. If I understand the basic idea."

"So then how do we get inside?" Hirim's frustration was increasing.

"I don't know," said Mathias. "I don't see any lock or even a handle."

"Well, I can fix that." Hirim stepped forward, drawing his sword. Josiah's hand reached up and wrapped itself around the Celetor's meaty wrist.

"I doubt its creators would have envisioned such a method of entry. There is a proper and safe way to get inside, and we must be diligent in discovering it."

"So, in the meantime, we all freeze out here in the dark?"

"Hardly," Josiah continued. "I have the utmost faith in the combined talents of Mr. Onuis and Mr. Danther to procure our answer."

"Then hurry it up." Hirim sheathed his sword with a huff.

"No pressure," Corwyn muttered Mathias' way.

"No. None at all," the elf replied.

5

The remaining embers of daylight had nearly expired and still Corwyn and Mathias hadn't found a way inside. The crew had long since finished their tasks, and the whole collection of men stood idly in a semicircle, hands shoved deeply under their armpits, shifting their weight from one foot to the other amid white clouds of breath.

All eyes were trained on Mathias and Corwyn. Both were pressing their faces close to the runic designs, their fur-wrapped digits brushing away fine particles of snow, when Mathias touched one of the runes. Though he'd touched the runes before, this instance birthed a faint silver illumination and a soft humming sound.

"What did you do?" asked Corwyn.

"Nothing, I just touched a rune and then—"

"*What* rune?"

"*This* one." Mathias held his hand above the runic letter for *r* inside the word *eternal*. Corwyn pulled off his mitten and pushed the rune himself. The faint hum returned, and the rune glowed a soft, icy silver before going quiet.

"Found something?" Hirim stepped closer.

"I think so." Corwyn put on his mitten. His fingers felt like chunks of ice from the brief exposure.

"You don't think you can hurry this discovery up some, do you?" asked Charles.

"I might have one idea," Corwyn replied. "What was the island's name again?" Mathias merely stared at him in wonder. "You said it had two names, right? What were they?"

"Rainier and Sigmundson."

"Okay, give me a moment." He returned to the door, eyes feverishly playing about the runic text.

"Mr. Danther, I would encourage whatever discovery you may have found be completed in a most expedient manner."

"Don't worry, Josiah. If I'm right we won't have to be outside much longer. You might want to stand back, though. I don't know what will happen."

All gathered gave him some space.

"Okay." He removed his mitten again. The cold instantly bit into his naked fingers, turning knuckles and muscles into stiff chunks of stone. He'd have to move fast. "Here goes."

"R." He spoke aloud while pressing the rune in *eternal* again. The light and noise returned. "A." He pressed the runic *a* in the same word. The silver light on the runes grew brighter and the humming more pronounced. "I-N-I-E-R." He pressed additional runes as they lined up in the text, increasing the glow and the hum, which had grown to a volume equal to a casual conversation in a crowded dining hall.

"S-I-G-M-U-N-D-S-O-N." He punched out the last name and donned his mitten. The light from the selected runes blazed a brilliant, icy silver. The humming had become both louder and higher pitched. "That did it," Corwyn shouted over the din.

Mathias cautiously rejoined Corwyn's side with wide, wondering eyes. "What did you do?"

"It was just a hunch, but I thought it might work to spell out his name . . . the letters all matched up, so . . ."

"But what now?" Hirim's voice boomed over the hum.

"I don't know." Corwyn retreated a few steps. "I suppose we just wait and see." His reply did little to inspire the others. A moment later the ground shuddered, and the door ascended like a portcullis, light spilling into the dark interior.

"Get some torches ready." Hirim's command jerked the crew back to their senses.

"I'll need my chest." Mathias headed for the sled.

"Well done, Mr. Danther." Josiah gave Corwyn a pat on the back. "Well done, indeed."

"That's just getting inside," said Corwyn. "Let's hope things are a little easier on the other side of the doorway."

Josiah, Hirim, Charles, Mathias, Chal, and ten other crewmen entered through the dark doorway. Five stood in front and five behind, weapons drawn. Their nervous eyes took in everything. The other fifteen from their party were told to stay beside the door and watch the boats and entrance in case something should happen. None knew for certain how long the door would remain open.

Marcus, Hirim's Celetoric lieutenant, oversaw these remaining men. Needless to say, none were happy with the prospect of staying out in the cold but did as ordered. Each took turns standing in the doorway, staving off the chill as best they could. Inside, Corwyn held his torch high; the three other torches were carried by the crewmen scattered among the group.

"I still think it's madness you wear no armor." Hirim's head turned in the darkness. "If you aren't going to carry any weapons, you should at least be protected."

"Slows me down." He politely dismissed the matter. "Besides, you haven't seen me wield a weapon." He lifted the torch higher, seeking the ceiling. He could only see for a short distance before the darkness obscured everything. "I'd be more help to any would-be attacker."

"So you *are* an Olthoan." Charles curled his upper lip. He couldn't see much from his vantage point, since he'd moved into the midst of the others' taller bodies. "I'd my suspicions before, but—"

"I'm not an Olthoan," said Corwyn. "Though I do like what some of her followers are about." He couldn't find anything amid the dense blackness. "We're going to need more light."

"Get five more men with torches," Hirim instructed a nearby crewman.

"Yes, Captain," the other responded before getting swallowed by the darkening sky.

"So, what now?" Charles whined. "I mean, we're inside, so where is it? There isn't anything here but an empty room."

"Patience, Mr. de Frassel." Josiah also stood in the middle of the others, cocooned by the taller bodies. "When one is in the field of endeavor, one does not heedlessly rush headlong into such matters."

"I'm going to need more light to read my texts," said Mathias. A crewman toting his chest stayed close at hand. "Who builds such a large place without any windows anyway?" He brought a scroll closer to his face.

"Maybe they wanted to stay warm," Corwyn offered.

It was warmer inside than out, even with the cold creeping in from the open door. He studied the stone wall at his right. The torch light revealed solid white marble. Craning his head, he got the impression the walls ascended for many feet—probably twenty or twenty-five, if he had to guess.

"Well, you know what I'm going to do with eternal life once we find the secret?" Charles' face displayed a more puckish nature than usual as he made his way out from among the others. Josiah followed his lead.

"Still don't want to know." Hirim swung his torch around as he scanned the room. "It's scary enough imagining you living longer than you already have."

Charles sneered as five more crewmen entered, each bearing a torch. By aid of the extra light, they could see the room acted as an entrance chamber. A cold, empty, and featureless entrance chamber, whose blue-veined white marble walls climbed for twenty feet until meeting a marble ceiling. The hall itself ran for about thirty feet before fading into dim, flickering shadow. No friezes. No candelabras or censers, nor any other source of light.

"This is odd," Corwyn muttered.

"You're telling me," said Hirim.

"Why have no light source at all?" Josiah searched the walls and ceilings for an answer. Unconsciously, all of them nestled closer together than before. The proximity of the torches gave the illusion of a miniature sun in the frozen darkness.

"Who was this Rainier anyway?" Corwyn moved further along the wall, cautious of his steps. "I didn't find anything on him when I searched some of your books."

"I wasn't able to figure that out," said Mathias, moving parallel with Corwyn. "I only gleaned he was a Nordic warrior of some repute back in the early days of the Shadow Years—even before the Imperial Wars. He was in some sort of dispute. They don't say much in the text, but some skald scrolls speak of a curse or him being cursed."

"We're in a *cursed* man's house?" Charles couldn't keep the dread from flowing out of his throat. "You didn't say anything of this before. That can't bode well."

"I just found it out a short while ago and didn't have time to share it until now," Mathias calmly replied while reading his document. "I brought the rest of the volume in the chest should we need it."

"Anything that has curses in it, I'm not about to be involved in." Hirim's gruff sentiment murmured down the darker sections of the chamber in a faint echo. "What's going on here, Josiah?"

"Peace, Captain. We are in no danger, I assure you. Coggsbury, Elliott, Chesterfield, and Company does not subscribe to ventures of excessive risk with little reward, and neither does it give credence to the notion of curses."

Hirim stopped. "I don't care what your company thinks or believes. I have enough sense to stay clear of any curses on any man, possessions, or abode. I'll not risk my crew or myself being exposed to a curse in the name of profit."

"A lot of old texts say that sort of thing," Mathias explained, peering up from his reading with a disbelieving smile. Corwyn thought it the type of expression worn when humoring someone who still believes in childish things they should have outgrown years ago. "It was their way of saying, 'He didn't have good luck' or 'Don't touch my things after I'm gone.' Most of the writers took a lot of artistic liberty in crafting such tales anyway. It takes a lot of reference sources and some common sense to peel back the layers of legend and myth and get to the truth behind most tales."

"So is this curse real or fake?" Charles' voice asked from near Mathias' waist.

"I think it's safe to assume the information we have isn't from any source tied to Rainier. That's to say, he didn't have any people to tell the tale to in his own words. We only have the story as told by those who opposed him.

"Now as to the curse, the Nordicans did and still do raid one another from time to time. Wars, feuds, and other such matters aren't uncommon.

It's probably just a general sort of thing, like, 'Curse that thief.' No one really believes you're actually cursing that person in any way . . . unless you're a wizard or perhaps a priest . . ."

"So you're saying he's a wizard?" asked Charles.

"He wasn't a wizard," Mathias firmly assured him. "Wizards didn't appear until several thousands of years *after* the time Rainier reportedly lived."

"Well, can we move one way or the other?" Charles' biting tone grated on all who heard it. "I'm freezing just standing here—even in this forest of crotches and legs."

"Fine," Hirim grunted, "let's keep moving. We'll survive the night better in here, I suppose. Make sure the others rotate inside until we get back," he told Chal.

The sailor nodded and made his way back to the entrance. Corwyn watched his torch light bounce in the spacious gloom along the way like a firefly in the night. Once the crewman was out of sight, the rest moved on.

Outside the citadel the sun had finally disappeared behind the white, craggy peaks of ice. A cold gray sky dominated much of the formerly blue canopy, dimming into a deep, smoky sapphire. Under this twilight sky, the ten crewmen left at the doorway huddled against the citadel's walls, keeping watch over the boats and peering into the black opening every few breaths.

To fight off the creeping sensation of chilled numbness pulsating deeper into their marrow with every heartbeat, they huddled together a few feet from the open doorway. It would get colder yet, but no one had brought firewood. They had thought they wouldn't need it. Foolish indeed and the worst planning they'd done while in service on the *Phoenix*. They'd all thought they'd be back well before nightfall.

But instead of resting back on the ship, they hobbled around each other, observing the bleak scenery and hoping they'd leave as soon as possible. Everyone was too absorbed in staying warm to take notice of the large white bear, who'd waited for this moment, edging closer. None of them heard the soft crunch of snow beneath its heavy tread or knew a set of red-rimmed black eyes watched their every move, waiting for the most opportune moment.

When it saw Chal run out the door into the cold, it knew its time had come. While the other sailors turned their backs on the unknown threat, the bear leapt forward, charging with a deep bellow. Upon hearing the noise, the sailors turned, but it was too late.

Beefy, fur-covered paws slashed two crewmen's abdomens before they could react. Both fell to their knees even as the bear's jaws found the throat of the third crewman, puncturing the very scream in his throat while it shoved him down to the red snow and sated its fiendish hunger. Those who remained drew their cutlasses along with Chal and Marcus. Roaring as they engaged, each swung their blade, half-mad with grief over what had just befallen their comrades.

Their attacks were useless.

"Strike harder!" Marcus shouted. "Bring it down!"

It didn't matter where the blade connected; the blows all met with rock-like resistance or slid off before even splitting a hair. But the cold, and now senseless fury, had crept in and they could do nothing but continue vainly hacking at the beast. The bear lapped up the warm blood of its victim, even going so far as to shake the man's neck back and forth between its jaws like a rag doll, squeezing out every scarlet drop.

When it finished gorging, it reared on its hind legs and thundered forward toward the remaining crewmen. The beast stood eight feet tall, adding a new dimension to the fight. The crewmen backed against the wall. Relentless and stubborn to the last, they jabbed and sliced, swung and hacked with their cold, useless steel.

Four strong swipes and a bone-crunching bite laid low over half the crewmen. The three who remained—Marcus among the trio—ran about the bear, ringing it with their cutlasses. The crewmen let out one final yell, but three more swipes swept all into silence.

Left on its own, the bear continued its ravenous feasting. When finished, it turned its bloody muzzle toward the open doorway, sniffing the area. Leaving the chilling corpses, it shuffled for the open portal and into the citadel itself. Once the bear was inside, the door closed with a slow, grinding descent.

"I think we might be here a little while longer than I first thought," Corwyn announced.

They'd found another hallway beyond the entranceway. This one was smaller but more polished and full of potential clues. He held his torch close to the wall beside him. A deep relief covered the white marble surface, rising from floor to ceiling. The chiseled forms told a tale with runic script and a linear progression of images he found both confusing and compelling.

The ceiling was about half the previous room's height and more rectangular. Carved of white marble, the same as the larger room from whence they'd come, the room was lined with a solid stone relief stretching around all the walls to the far end of the hall. Here another stone door frame, this one blocked with a wooden door, faced them. He guessed the hall stretched another forty feet. As they entered, the others fanned out, the extra torches revealing various parts of the hall with a dirty yellow light.

"This could be very important," he continued, staring at the runic text and images in greater concentration. "Do you have anything to help make sense of this, Mathias?"

"What's it say?" Hirim too had found a section of wall that caught his eye. It showed what appeared to be some Nordicans killing another by running their spears through him.

"I'm not sure yet." Mathias examined his own section of wall, torch in one hand, the mitten on his other hand tracing the outline of the runes. His wooden chest rested open at his feet. The image he studied revealed a large number of bears savagely attacking a group of Nordic-looking humans.

The brutal nature of the attack was rather gruesome. The stone relief detailed flailing limbs, severed appendages, and internal organs spilling out from the many victims. It appeared there was a person directing them in their attacks. "It's the old Nordic tongue, of course," said Mathias, "but these phrases are very archaic, almost cryptic."

"Anything about the mention of eternal life?" Josiah halfheartedly considered a series of images beside him with a mild disgust. He'd taken up his pipe again as a way to soothe his growing unease.

"Yeah, where is it?" Charles droned. Like Josiah, he'd only a faint interest in the images, his limited view probably adding to the disinterest.

Mathias kept his attention on the frieze. "Nothing yet, but—"

There came a heavy thud from behind them. The echoing clap stilled all present.

"What was that?" Charles finally dared speak.

"It sounded like the stone door at the entrance," said Corwyn, watching the black opening they'd just walked through.

"We're trapped!" the halfling nearly shouted. "By all the gods, we're trapped and now we're going to die in this accursed place!"

"Shut up!" Hirim growled. "Get a hold of yourself." He motioned to a nearby Patrician crewman holding a torch. "Take three men with you and check it out. It could just be Chal getting back in. He might have tripped the door." Two rough-faced Telborians joined the Patrious. "Just take a look, no heroics."

"Aye, sir." The Patrious nodded, and all three merged into the inky doorway back into the entrance hall.

"Brave man sending his crewmen to fight for him," Charles mocked.

"Feel free to join them," Hirim sneered.

"Please, gentlemen, let us strive to keep a civil tongue. This is hardly the time nor the place where strife and dissension should be entertained." Josiah's words soothed some of the tension. "I recommend while waiting, we make better sense of this work of art before us." Neither Hirim nor Charles responded to the gnome's plea, instead staring blankly at the relief. The other crewmen silently peered back into the dark portal through which their friends had disappeared.

"I might have something," Mathias said after a short silence.

"What is it, Mr. Onuis?" Josiah made his way for the elf, puffing as he went.

"It's a line from what looks like a ballad." He directed the gnome to the line of text. "Seems to be talking about this place. It reads: 'Pale is his flesh yet paler still his keep.'"

"Okay." Charles resumed his shifting from foot to foot. "That almost makes sense."

"Captain." A younger, torch-bearing Celetor on the opposite end of the room drew all eyes his way. "I think I've found something, too."

Everyone moved around the crewman, eager to lay eyes on his discovery: the image of a Nordic man, taller and more regal than the others, who were bowing around him in a circle. The central Nordican was young, lacking even the beard or mustache of the other men. He wore a common tunic and pants while holding up a skull. He had the expression of a haunted figure; his eyes, even in the relief, looked forlorn yet sinister at the same time. Under the image was more runic text, this longer and larger than the other runes around it.

"What does it say?" Josiah leaned closer.

"'Rainier Sigmundson.'" Corwyn pointed at the fat line of text. "I got that much out of it."

"'To him has been given the secret of eternal life.'" Mathias translated the smaller runes under it.

"*Finally*." Charles slapped his mittens together with an eager grin. "Now we're getting somewhere."

The three crewmen walked with careful steps through the darkness. Their torches allowed some light but couldn't pierce the gloom stalking their every step. Without the failing sunlight from the entrance, they were unable to navigate the room by sight, having to rely on memory and guesswork. It was more like a blind, drunken stumble than a confident progression, but they persisted.

It was, after all, probably just as Hirim had said: Chal and the others had stepped inside from the cold and hit a wrong rune or leaned on a wall or something and triggered the door to close. It was certainly feasible, given they were all numb with the cold and unable to feel anything they happened to brush up against. Hopefully, they'd be able to figure out how to undo it . . . though none of the sailors knew how to read the Nordic runes.

"Chal?" one of the Telborians asked of the darkness.

"Chal?" he tried again.

Nothing.

All three felt the hair on the back of their necks bristle and brought their cutlasses higher. Slowly and seemingly eternally, they trod on until catching sight of the stone door in the outskirts of the torch light. When closed, it nearly blended in with the rest of the wall. They would never have known it was there if they hadn't known what to look for in the first place. And, unlike the outside of the door, the interior side was bare. No runes or markings marred its surface.

"What was that?" One of the Telborians turned his head.

"What?" the other asked.

"I could have sworn I saw something."

"Chal?" the elf called out. "Gregory?" He moved his torch about, circling himself and the others. "Anyone?" The increased light showed nothing but empty space and more darkness.

"Think they're stuck outside?" The elf dared a cautious look at the closed door.

One of the Telborians reached out and touched it. Feeling braver, he put his ear to it, not bothering to remove his hood. "If they are, then we can't get to them."

"They have to be if they aren't in here," the elf replied.

"So what do we do?" asked the other sailor gloomily. "We could wait until they opened the door again, I suppose."

"Do you think they know how?" The Patrious sullenly considered the Telborian. "Do any of them even know *how* to spell?"

"Marcus would." The other Telborian shifted his feet and peered about the shadows. "So would Chal. Where is he anyway?"

The elf interrupted any further thought with a brisk turn on his heel. "We need to get back to the captain and tell him what we found."

"But what about Chal?"

"He's probably working on the door right now—at least if Perlosa's feeling kind tonight." The elf started back the way he'd come, the first Telborian falling in beside him. "There's not much we can do here anyway." The lagging Telborian nodded solemnly, then followed.

Above them, the bulky white bear stared down in silence. Its whole frame sat on the ceiling as if it were the floor and gravity simply reversed. Red glowing eyes beamed out from the murky air cloaking it from sight. It watched the three crewmen wander under it to the door, and then return the way they'd come. When confident they were gone, it waddled toward the adjoining wall and climbed down the smooth surface with an eerie, graceful silence. It reached the floor a moment later, moving in the direction the crewmen had followed—its gait slow, measured, and quiet as the grave.

6

"So the secret is here, but where?" Josiah took a deep draft of his pipe. "Or it could have *been* here, but isn't around now for anyone to benefit," said Corwyn, scrutinizing more of the friezes. These depictions were simple and crude compared with the others: men and women adorned in animal hides and bone jewelry.

They appeared huddled around a fire amid a cold and snowy landscape. Text was sparse in this section of the relief, but he could discern the word *Perlosa* amid the runes for what seemed to be *curse*. The words were close together but also far enough apart they could be unrelated too. He'd learned archaic Nordic runes were hard to fully understand, and on this section of the wall with the various scenes all tied together, it was even harder to make sense of things.

"This might not be anything, but I read 'Perlosa' and 'curse' from this image."

"A figurative curse, though, right?" voiced a hopeful Charles.

"It only says the word 'curse,' not what kind."

Mathias joined Corwyn at the next section of the relief. "The ancient Nordicans were very into curses and luck. Remember what I told you all earlier. It's probably just as simple as that."

"Probably," Corwyn echoed, though not with the same confidence.

"It looks like no one's been here for a long time. So if this secret hasn't been disturbed, it must be here somewhere." Charles ventured toward the closed doorway opposite the one they'd entered. "And if it isn't in here, then it must be through that door."

"Mr. de Frassel, I would think embracing such a reckless attitude toward this venture would be very detrimental to say the least. Let us progress toward this discovery together." Josiah took a step in the halfling's direction. "After all, we are not entirely sure what we are looking for. It could be a scroll or a relief on a wall or something else altogether. I do not think—"

"Captain." The returning elf, flanked by his Telborian crewmates, interrupted the gnome.

"Where's Chal?" Corwyn watched Hirim's face grow grave.

"Nobody's there. They must be outside. The door's closed and we couldn't see how to open it from our end."

"Wonderful," Charles grumbled.

"Why would it close if no one else triggered it?" another crewman, this one a young Napowese near Corwyn, asked with obvious concern.

"We don't know they didn't," said Mathias.

"And we don't know they did," countered Corwyn. "Maybe it was only to remain open for so long, keeping out the cold or something."

"Or keeping others in." Taking up his scroll once more, Mathias stopped short of continuing the thought.

"Friends," started Josiah, "let us not dwell upon such a negative prospect, but rather search out and lay hold of the positive." The gnome sounded more like a statesman than a company representative. "If we explore more of this citadel, then we shall increase our odds not only of getting out of it but of finding what we seek."

"Then let's get moving before we suffocate or freeze or something worse," said Charles, continuing his march toward the closed wooden door. "Course, the best thing is I'll outlive you all if we *do* die from lack of air. You're all such gangly giants, and my perfect size has reduced my chance of suffocating by at least half."

"Thank the gods for small favors," Hirim told himself.

Everyone moved for the closed door, eager for progress. Frozen solid, it was made of ice cleverly carved to resemble wood. Corwyn pushed it inward with a small grunt. It didn't have a handle or lock of any kind, but its archaic silver hinges unleashed a high-pitched squeal.

All held their breath, shining a few torches inside the dark doorway. Behind the fleeing shadows appeared a large room full of dangling chains, some of which had metal cuffs attached.

"This can't be good." Charles stuck his head through a narrow gap between a pair of legs and the doorjamb.

Corwyn inched his way inside, raising his torch higher. The chains descended from another high ceiling, some fifteen feet overhead.

"How is *this* part of eternal life?" Hirim inspected a chilled chain with the blade of his sword as if it were some sort of dangling vine. The more torches entered, the more the room revealed its secrets—ghastly ones at that. While the room had a tall ceiling, it was smaller than the last, about twelve feet in width and fifteen or sixteen feet in length.

The fieldstones of the floor tightened and packed together around circular depressions holding a tarnished silver basin underneath each collection of chains. All in all, the room held five such basins. Corwyn drew closer to one of them, squatting for a closer look. His torch showed its lip was encircled in runes. The rest of it remained murky, the inside bottom of the container stained darker than the rest of the basin.

"There's some writing here. Mathias, can you help me decipher it?" Corwyn peered back at the scribe, who was studying the collection of chains dangling over another basin a few feet away with great dismay. Curious, Mathias joined him, bending low beside the basin, careful not to touch it. "These runes seem older than those on the door and relief wall."

"So what does *that* mean?" Hirim watched Mathias closely.

"It means they were either written using an older script or were made in a time before the runes on the door were carved." He squinted as he continued his study.

"I understand we have not been able to date the map specifically, only claiming a pocket of years in which to hedge it." Josiah leaned over Corwyn and Mathias while they worked. His smaller stature kept him from getting much more than a glimpse of the tarnished silver between them. "So what does this discovery add to the chronological placement of this place and prize?"

"It means," answered Corwyn, "that these basins are probably older than the text on the walls we just passed. And *that* was already older than most of the runic script Mathias has on record."

"Brilliant," Charles snorted. "I always found exploration and scholarship to be such *invigorating* subjects."

"We don't know what we are looking for here, Charles, and that's slowing us down." Corwyn stood, bumping into Josiah in the process. "I can't make any sense of them. They're too old for me, so it looks like Mathias has to struggle with them. If you want to make yourself useful, feel free to explore this room. See if there are any more doors or help figure out what these basins were for."

"That's easy enough." Charles' smile bordered on haughty. "They're there to collect blood." All eyes swung to the basin over which Mathias stood. He stopped his work, wide eyed at the halfling's words.

"*What?*" Hirim watched Charles carefully.

"It looks like when you gut a deer. You string it up and clean out the guts and let it bleed clean."

"So, then, you are saying this place is for, what? Killing deer?" Josiah did his best to keep his upper lip as stiff as possible.

"Could be. Course, where are they going to find deer here, huh?" The halfling's yellow-toothed grin didn't encourage anyone.

"Captain—"

The crewmen were hushed by Hirim's hand. "Hold your ground. We'll be out of here soon."

"Well, it wasn't deer, that's for sure." Mathias moved his torch around the basin, stepping around it like some squatting ape. "At least part of what I can read here says they were to 'collect the tribute befitting their king.'"

"Gold?" Hirim wondered.

Corwyn gestured to the shackles. "More likely a torture chamber for people who didn't agree with him. I assume it mentions Rainier?"

"Yes, but it only calls him the 'son of Sigmund,'" said Mathias.

"Who would torture people way out here?" Josiah pondered. "For that matter, who would build a place so bizarre to inhabit a floating piece of ice? This is a very odd thing indeed."

"Captain, there's a strange marking here on this wall." The same crewman who'd spoken before drew the others' attention.

"Let me see." Corwyn hurried to the spot near the far end of the room.

"Anything else, Mr. Onuis?" Josiah began pacing around the area.

"Just something else here I can't quite get figured out. It says, 'The Eternal King's empire shall never be extinguished.'" Mathias stood. "That's about all I can make sense of without having more time to study it."

"Eternal King, eh?" Charles mused devilishly. "I like the sound of that."

"But nothing about eternal life?" Josiah's face was troubled.

"Nothing."

Josiah sighed. "This is indeed a difficult mystery. I had thought once we arrived, the object of our quest would become clearly evident, but it seems that shall not be the case."

"This might prove interesting." Corwyn's voice brought the others' attention to a wall with a large crescent moon carved into it. The raised relief was close to four feet wide and covered with silver. On the moon itself was a small series of scratches that the others couldn't see but were plainly visible from his present distance.

"What is *that*?" Mathias drew closer.

"A last will and testament." Corwyn ran his mitten over the text. "The runes are in the same manner as those on the basins, but the first part of the text is more modern, and from what I can understand, they claim the runes that follow are the final will and testament of 'the Great Rainier, the Eternal King.' What do you make of it?"

Once close enough, Mathias studied the tight block of runes arranged in a square-foot area on the plain white marble portion of the moon. The runes were smaller and carved deeper into the stone, but still readable in most places.

"Seems to be a bestowing of blessings and curses upon various people . . ." Mathias translated.

"Curses again." Charles frowned.

"Standard Nordic practice, as I've said before."

"Still not comforting," the halfling muttered.

"'He curses those that would defile his stronghold and who come to seek his harm'..." Mathias explained, "and..."blesses those whom he highly favors with life eternal.'"

"That's more like it." Charles' demeanor instantly brightened.

"I don't understand," said Hirim. "So this king—this Rainier—has eternal life in his possession and gives it to people he likes?"

"Sounds that way," said Mathias.

"But what is it, I wonder?" Corwyn tried gleaning more from the text, but just met with frustration and confusion. "Does it say anything about how he did this or whom he favored? We don't know if it's an elixir, a spell, or something else—like a poetic metaphor."

"It better *not* be a poetic metaphor after all I've had to suffer through." Charles wiped fresh snot from his nose with an already-mucus-smeared mitten.

"I'm still looking," Mathias continued, concentrating on the text. "It just follows up with a litany of how he wants his empire to be divided should he meet with death—"

"Wait a moment," Josiah butted in, having joined the others by the crescent moon relief. "How can the 'Eternal King' die? I thought you said he was immortal."

"That's just one interpretation," Mathias explained. "Runes can be read in many different ways, the same symbol being understood as something else with the same expressive thought...like a synonym of sorts. The rune they have for 'eternal' here, if I'm reading it right, could be read as 'eternal,' 'everlasting,' even 'undying,' as well as 'immortal.'"

"Don't those mean the same thing?" Hirim took in Mathias' pale gray face.

"For the most part. But one could interpret them to mean slightly different things."

"All those words don't sound that different to me," said Charles.

"Well, in this case I think we can all agree that they mean what we seek is here and Rainier's somehow tied to it."

"Then if Rainier's still alive, where is he?" Hirim scoured the room once more. "We haven't seen anything but this torture chamber and that image-covered hall."

"True, but this is a big place and there's got to be more rooms... somewhere," said Corwyn.

"Well, you better find them soon," said Charles, reaching for the silver moon. "I don't want to spend my last hours of life here with you. If you're going to die, you should go to Mortis in bed with a smile on your lips and four very tired women beside you."

"More halfling wisdom?" He raised an eyebrow.

"Common sense."

Corwyn was about to say more when he heard a soft click where Charles' hand had been. The halfling heard it too, his face mirroring the same surprised wonder as Corwyn's. Cautiously, he touched the same spot Charles had on the silver moon. Again, he heard the faint click.

"I think we've found something."

"*I've* found something," Charles corrected, trying to stick out his chest but only succeeding in making his gut swell into even greater proportions.

Corwyn pushed slightly harder and felt the silver crescent release from its ties to the wall. It wobbled a little to the right. He carefully moved it in that direction and found some writing on the stone underneath. He pushed more until it stopped at one hundred eighty degrees from where it'd been before. Another faint click locked it in place. All could see a small chunk of runic text in the same archaic style of the exposed block on the left side of the relief.

"What does it say, Mr. Onuis?" Josiah was near breathless with wonder.

Mathias feverishly pored over the symbols, tracing the lines with his finger. "It seems to be a poem. It's a bit rustic and my translation isn't totally clear with all of it, but what I can read right now says:

"'He who seeks eternity is brave indeed'... ah... 'The sun is not his ally, for it burns the days away. To he who breaks the'... no, that should be 'through.' 'To he who breaks through the barrier, a new world shall be given. For Rainier, son of Sigmund, favors the brave, and those who seek to cast off their former life in favor of the undying must seek him out'... umm, 'the King of Eternity' . . ." Mathias stopped. "It goes on like this for a little longer . . . More titles and exalting the greatness of Rainier . . . but nothing else about eternal life."

"Only that Rainier's the one who has to be sought to gain it." Corwyn continued peering at the rustic scratchings.

"But why hide this?" Hirim wondered. "What's there to protect in a poem?"

"A secret?" Josiah mused.

"This Rainier is a Nordican, right?" asked Charles.

"Yes, from what we can tell," said Mathias.

"Don't they worship Perlosa?"

"Most pay her some form of respect as the goddess of both the icy wastes and sea," Corwyn replied. "But this type of moon isn't her symbol— at least as it appears today. It could be a sign of their devotion, however."

"Why would one place a token sign of adoration and worship of Perlosa within a torture chamber?" Josiah rubbed his chapped chin. "The two, to me, do not mix well at all."

"This whole place doesn't mix well," Hirim agreed. "And I'll be happy to be rid of it when I can see daylight shining through some chink or crack in a door leading out of here."

"That is another thing," said Josiah, seeking a better view of the solemn crewmen and unnerving room. "Where is the light source in this structure? There are no windows anywhere, which I could argue might have been excluded to keep out the cold, but it would stand to reason they would have set up some sort of conveyance of illumination."

"Yeah, I wondered about that myself." Corwyn traced some of the formerly hidden text with his mitten. "There's got to be another doorway here somewhere—some passage or something to get us deeper inside and help us find a way out. This place is too large to have only the few rooms we've seen."

"So where are they?" asked Charles.

"Somewhere here. Just start looking," replied Corwyn. "Maybe it's a wall, or something we missed. Let's just start searching everything and anything . . . but carefully. This place could still have some deadly surprises, even after all these years."

Everyone broke into groups and began combing the walls, the floor, and even the chains and basins. Corwyn and Mathias stayed at the moon carving, trying to tease out more lost secrets. Together they shared some texts from Mathias' chest.

None in the room noticed a pair of eyes watching them from the top of the wooden door frame at the room's entrance. The blood-splattered bear leered at them, hanging as would a bat behind the door. Only its head peeked inside the doorway. The bear's eyes were devious and reflected a keen mind and less-than-kind plans for those present.

While the others searched and thought, Corwyn made a discovery of his own. He'd taken a tome from Mathias' chest and was turning to the back portion of it when he stopped as a stray page came loose.

He gingerly pulled the parchment from the other pages. It had been folded and seemingly stashed between the pages for some time. Closing the book and placing it back with the others in the chest beside him, he carefully opened the heavily creased page. It was an epic poem—a saga—of Rainier Sigmundson, also oddly written in a more modern styling of the Nordican tongue, which aided him greatly in making the translation.

"'Hail to the slayer of Jotun, the savior of his kind,'" he whispered. "'He who was cursed for the sake of saving many. The White Prince, the Crimson Lord, blessed with a curse and cursed to be a blessing.'" He stopped. Poetic or not, they were certainly odd comments to ponder. Seeing the others were fruitlessly examining the room for clues, he continued with the folded parchment. "'Son of Sigmund, great chief now gone. Son of the tribe now faded away. Hail to Rainier, who stared down the goddess and yet lived. Hail to Rainier, who forged his own tribe from the ashes of the old.'"

"What are you reading?" Mathias' question jarred him from his thoughts.

"Something I found in one of your books. It's a saga of some kind—about Rainier."

"Really?" Mathias' eyebrows lifted in surprise. "That's a little fortuitous."

"That's what I thought, but it was stuck fairly well in the book. The cold must have loosened the pages and freed it."

"Anything useful?"

"Nothing yet."

"You can read it?"

"It's written in a more modern style, so I recognize most of it. Not that I can make much sense of it, but I've learned a fair amount on our voyage. Have you found anything?"

Mathias shook his head. "I'm beginning to think we've reached a dead end. I don't know where to go next and what I brought along isn't proving too helpful. We should be trying to find a way out of here, if you ask me." The elf sighed. "There won't be any point in looking around for this secret of eternal life if we don't have a way out of this tomb."

"We'll find a way. Don't lose hope just yet."

Mathias only nodded and returned to his tome.

The white bear slid down from its vantage point with incredible grace and preternatural skill. Keeping clear of the door frame so none would see its descent, it treaded down the wall onto the floor in utter silence. After a few moments it made its way to a section of carved reliefs lined with people getting beheaded and run through with swords.

The bear stopped and sniffed. Once satisfied, a soft nudge with its blood-caked nose pushed in one of the severed heads resting on the ground next to its owner's dying body. Doing so birthed a faint click. This was followed by a thud behind the carving and then a grinding, scraping sound as marble rubbed against marble. The whole process unveiled a secret door in the chaotic stone mural.

Waiting for the doorway to completely open, the bear tilted its head, let out a snort, then shuffled into the darkness.

"Nothing," Charles grumbled. "This whole gods-cursed room is a waste of my time."

"Let's just calm down." Corwyn shifted his attention from the silver half-moon he'd been examining. He'd finished reading the saga and returned the refolded page to approximately where he'd found it. It hadn't been much help after all. For a few more stanzas it declared the wonder of the great White Prince and the empire of ice he spread over the southern lands. It also referred to him as the Crimson Lord of Night who reigned supreme from his citadel, killing all who opposed him. Then it just stopped. Again, not much help at all. "There has got to be an answer here—"

"To the Abyss with your patience." Charles stomped toward the hanging chains and tarnished silver bowls. "We're all going to die here unless we start making some progress."

"A modest degree of self-control would indeed be most advisable in such a situation as this—"

"Shut up!" he spat back.

Before anyone could say anything else, there came a noise similar to the low grinding sound they'd heard earlier when the door had closed.

"What was that?" Hirim rapidly inspected the doorway.

"Something from the other room," said Mathias, joining the captain's stare.

"You don't think the door opened back up again, do you?" Charles' face took on some cheer. "Maybe they got it open."

"Hope springs eternal." Josiah spoke in tepid tones.

"You think it could be the others?" an unsettled crewman asked Hirim.

"I don't know." Hirim didn't hide his anxiety.

"Well then, someone should make an inquiry." Josiah directed his gaze Hirim's way, his demeanor the subtle pressure of diplomatic urging.

"You volunteering?" Hirim reflected the gnome's stare.

"I would be able to do so, yes, but only with a handful of others to help safeguard the representative interests of Coggsbury, Elliott, Chesterfield, and Company."

"Maybe we could all go." Corwyn started for the door. He noticed the other crewmen's relief at the suggestion.

"All right." Hirim's thinned lips disappeared into his mustache. "Come on then," he added, motioning his crew forward with his sword. "We'll make sense of this yet."

Everyone made their way back into the hallway. Careful steps and cautious eyes found the area as they'd left it. Nothing had really changed.

Almost nothing . . .

"Where did *this* come from?" Charles traced the seamless outline of the secret doorway with his mitten.

Josiah slapped the halfling's hand away. "We do not know what this is about, and I would strongly advise keeping your hands away from *anything*— only touching what we must."

"How this got here, though, is still a good question." Corwyn pushed his torch inside the opening. The darkness was too thick to see much of anything save the beginnings of a white marble hallway.

"More importantly, where does it lead?" Charles took a step toward the blackness, intent on moving inside, but Hirim's strong hand grasped his shoulder and held him fast.

"No you don't," said Hirim, reeling him back. "You're staying right here until we know it's safe."

"I never knew you cared so." Charles smiled with the sweetest sarcasm he could muster.

Hirim huffed a gossamer cloud of breath.

"What if it's like the entrance door and closes?" Mathias kept his distance. "Should some of us stay outside to get it open again?"

"How did it open in the first place?" Corwyn countered.

"Is that really the question here, my friends, or is it rather, why are we not pursuing this fortuitous occurrence?"

"If that's how you feel, then you can lead us." Hirim bowed, extending his hand in an inviting gesture for the gnome to do just that.

"Very well." Josiah sighed. "If that is what needs doing to keep things moving along, then I will do so."

"Whoa." Hirim stopped Josiah from moving forward. "I didn't think you were actually serious."

"We are running out of options, Captain. And quite possibly air. As far as I see it, this is our best course of action."

"All right, but we do it wisely," said Hirim, releasing his grip.

"I would not do it any other way." Josiah shoved his torch forward and took a step into the darkness, revealing a white marble staircase further inside the hall. "It seems we have a set of stairs to climb, gentlemen."

"Then let's start climbing," said Charles. "The sooner we find what we're after, the sooner we can leave and get rich. And then the sooner I can warm up in a bed full of well-endowed, nubile young maidens." Charles chuckled to himself while Josiah shook his head in silent disdain.

7

At the top of the stairs, the bear shoved aside a large oak door with its beefy shoulder. Beyond the door was a splendid room drenched in darkness. With the bear's low growl, a ring of sconces lining the walls of the circular chamber came alight. The sconces possessed no flames, bringing forth only a cold, silvery-white glare in the otherwise windowless chamber.

Silently, the bear entered.

Spacious and lovely, the chamber resembled more a royal mausoleum than a simple room. The perfectly circular chamber's walls rose to a domed ceiling. The distance from top to bottom and side to side was equal, creating a strange span of nearly spherical dimensions. At the chamber's center rested a plain white marble altar. It stood atop a marble dais that rose some six feet off the floor. A silver chalice stood alone in the middle of the milky rectangle of stone.

Around the dais were eight granite slabs hewn to resemble beds with pillows of stone accompanied by immobile sheets. All these beds rose some three feet from the floor. And all but one of the slabs were empty. On the one opposite the doorway rested the shape of a woman carved entirely of ice: hands folded over her breasts, long hair pooling under her head and down the stone pillow. Though the shape had a feminine aspect, the rest of the body did a disservice to the other physical graces common to women.

Under the white dress covering much of the sculpture's crystalline frame, her features were sharp and cold—almost feral in nature. Her cheekbones rose to near spear points, closed eyes deep in their sockets belying a bestial origin. Her crossed arms showcased bone-like hands—as if they might be some type of talon or claw rather than slender, appealing digits. The body itself, though lean and muscular, possessed curves and two mounds of flesh atop her chest. But all this supposed feminine beauty was literally only skin deep.

The bear sniffed about the icy woman's face and hands, then reared up on its hind legs and vomited all the blood lapped up from its recent victims. Teetering from one foot to the other, it walked the whole length of the sculpture, making sure to cover all of it with the steaming red gel. When finished, the bear plopped itself down at the foot of the stone bed, staring at its work in eager expectation.

As the faint echoes of those climbing the hidden staircase reached the bear's ears, the statue started moving. First her eyes flung wide—milky things staring up at the shadowed ceiling. Then her mouth fell open, narrow lips parting so her transparent tongue could explore the opening with stiff, choppy movements. Her whole gore-splattered frame was still more stiff than supple, made all the more evident by her jerky attempts to rise from the bed.

Blood dangled from the tangled, still semisolid, clear strands of hair, which, like her eyes, had taken on a milky quality. With purposeful effort, she pulled her right hand forward and flexed her fingers. The bony claw cracked and popped like icicles falling off a roof. She repeated the same effort with her left hand. She stopped when her gaze rested on the bear, obediently seated at the end of her stone bed.

She made an effort to scoop up some of the congealed blood from her red-stained attire, cupping it to her lips, where she ravenously slurped it down. When she finished, she cocked her head, listening to the growing noise on the stairs. A haunting, wide grin shot across her still partially transparent, blood-splattered face, deepening its repugnant nature. And it grew only more so with the sharp teeth poking out like daggers behind her lips.

"How much farther?" Charles groaned as the procession climbed the tall flight of stairs. He was nestled between Corwyn and Hirim near the front of the group.

"Afraid you'll break a sweat?" Hirim asked.

"Afraid I'll die of old age before this gnome gets to the top." They'd been walking about a quarter hour, and while it should have taken them less time, they were still led by Josiah, whose smaller frame and cautious nature slowed everyone's progress.

"Patience, Mr. de Frassel," Josiah returned from the front of the line. "That is how the day is won."

"Well, the longer I wait, the closer to becoming an ice sculpture I get."

"Shh." Corwyn motioned for silence. "I think I hear something."

Everyone stopped.

After no sound followed for a short span, they collectively let out a breath, bringing a limited sense of calm.

"Can we keep moving before I freeze to this stair?" Charles wiped a fresh stream of snot with his mitten.

Again they continued their ascent. It wasn't much longer until they'd reached the top of the stairs and an oak door a few steps beyond. Though clearly aged, the door remained solid and strong. Each cautiously neared. None wanted to touch it or get too close, lest it look like a commitment to venturing into the opening.

"So, we go in?" Corwyn asked after their brief pause.

"Certainly, Mr. Danther." Josiah stood tall, bringing to his words what gusto he could. "We must be getting close to something. I can feel it in my bones."

"That's probably the cold gnawing away at your marrow," Charles mumbled.

Corwyn placed his hand to the door and pushed it all the way open. Flickering light sprayed out of the doorway like silvery dust.

"*This* looks promising," said Charles, who weaseled his way between a pair of legs and the door frame.

"Indeed," Josiah replied.

Corwyn led the way, flanked by two crewmen and followed by Hirim and the rest. Charles went last, joined by the remaining crewmen.

"How come there's light in here?" asked Hirim.

"This feels odd somehow." Josiah was immediately interested in the painted images on the wall on his left, pulled from the darkness by the sconces' cold light. The fresco portrayed a battle between what looked like priests of Asorlok and a collection of wild Nordicans.

"You're telling me." Charles fully stepped into the room. "This whole place feels like a crypt."

"What about it, Mathias?" Corwyn found the elf intently staring at another fresco. All the frescoes were connected, stretching across the chamber's walls like an unrolled scroll. "Are we getting close?"

"This whole place could be filled with secret rooms like this one," Mathias commented as he continued his careful study.

"Then keep searching." Hirim motioned for the crew to spread out. "You stay here and watch the door." He stopped four sailors—the ones who had followed behind Charles—from leaving the doorway. "If you hear anything from downstairs, you let us know."

"Aye, sir." One of their band, a Celetor with a cutlass in one hand and a sputtering torch in the other, became a watchful guard. Meanwhile, Corwyn and Mathias made their way to the altar, winding around the stone slabs and climbing the dais with care. Once they reached the top, each took a turn viewing the silver chalice.

"What do you think?" asked Mathias.

"That I'm not sure I want to touch it."

"Me either, but what could it be used for? Ceremonial?"

"Could be . . ."

"You don't think the chalice is what we're looking for, do you?" Mathias was about to pick it up when he was stopped by Corwyn.

"Look there." He motioned to a faint scratching of runes on the altar's surface beside the chalice. "What do they say?"

Mathias squinted as he read. "Ah . . . 'Hail' . . . 'Hail the Eternal King.'"

"Looks like there's a lid here of some sort." Corwyn held his finger above the altar, tracing out a square where a faint line disrupted the uniformity of its surface.

The others in the chamber wandered silently along the walls, mindful of their step and prepared for anything. Some crewmen studied the sconces; others ventured near the altar, curious as to what they could find. Others stopped to consider the granite slabs resembling common beds. Still more, like Josiah, were intrigued by the frescoes.

He carefully walked around the chamber, following the progression of the story. So far he'd seen a group of Asorlins fighting some Nordicans. Judging by their attire, it seemed to have been in some distant time. This flowed into the next image of the priests of Asorlok running several of these Nordicans through with gold-tipped spears.

The spears pierced into their chests and out their backs with a violent shower of crimson gore. Following this attack, the Nordicans slaughtered the priests with their bare hands. Some even were so feral they gnawed into the priests' necks like a wolf taking down its prey. Josiah shivered at the imagery, not due to its graphic nature—he'd seen depictions of violence before—but because of some other hidden meaning he didn't yet fully comprehend. This shadowy recollection hid behind the more orderly halls of his intellect, scurrying away from any attempt at drawing it out into the light.

"I think we found something." Mathias' words summoned all to the altar.

"Me too," came the words of the Telborian crewman who stared down at the blood-splattered granite slab—torch in one hand, cutlass in the other, and eyes awash with fright.

"What is it, Mr. Onuis?" Josiah joined the others at the dais. They were taking in the sight of Mathias and Corwyn peering into a hole they'd uncovered by removing a section of the altar's surface.

"I think you might want to see for yourself." Mathias' voice was flat.

"Well then, let us just see, shall we?" Josiah made his way through the group up the dais. Both Mathias and Corwyn stepped aside, giving the gnome room so he could bend his neck over the opening.

"My word." Josiah's face went monumentally white before quickly recovering. "Dear me, gentlemen, this *is* a peculiar quandary. Do you think *this* is the object we seek?"

"Hey!" Charles wormed his way through some legs but was stopped short of the altar. "Let me see."

"What about *this*, then?" Hirim stood where a few of his crewmen had gathered around a granite slab covered in a dried and partially frozen layer of blood.

"This is bad luck, Captain," said an old-salt Telborian. "It's the curse. The curse that elf's been talking about."

"Nonsense." Hirim's reply was as mellow as he could keep it. "It's blood—and fresh at that; something is in here with us, lads. Maybe even the same person who closed the door on us. It's no curse, but a real-enough threat. One that bleeds."

"Comforting," Charles murmured.

"I think we should be going," Corwyn told Josiah. "We should really find a way out of here and then come back once we—"

"You are giving up *now*?" The gnome shook his head in solemn disappointment. "Mr. Danther, I may be a meek man in many things, but I have not been known to leave an obligation unfulfilled. We came here to find the secrets of eternal life or some such boon as described on the map, and we have yet to find it. As the representative of Coggsbury, Elliott, Chesterfield, and Company, I believe we should soldier on. Keep our wits about us, and we will get out of this safe and sound."

"And I say it's time we start looking for an exit," said Hirim. The notion might as well have been a slap in the gnome's face. "There's nothing here, Josiah. This is a failed venture."

Josiah set his torch on the altar. "If we do find a way out of here—and we will, rest assured—there is no guarantee we will be able to find our way back inside. We have only now found a chalice in this apparently sacred room and . . ." He released a small grunt while shoving his dainty mittened hands into the altar's pocket.

"Josiah—" Corwyn started.

"Don't—" Mathias added simultaneously.

"This skull," he said, pulling free an aged human skull from the altar's hidden compartment. Dry and clean, it mimicked some gruesome trophy in the gnome's uplifted hands.

A roar echoed throughout the chamber. The men whipped their heads toward the noise, weapons raised. A large, blood-splattered white bear was rapidly climbing down the wall above the doorway like some bulbous spider.

The crewmen standing guard could do nothing but scream before the beast was upon them. Meaty claws slashed into the closest Napowese crewman. He fell to his knees in a crescendo of agony, clutching the contents of his abdomen as they spilled out between his red fingers.

"To arms!" Hirim bellowed.

He didn't need to tell his crew what to do; they already had plunged into the fray, coming to the aid of their crewmates. Some of them ditched their torches, focusing on their weapons instead.

Two Telborians, with a hearty heft, slashed home their blades only to hit something like stone rather than flesh. Undaunted and fueled with the fire of life-and-death combat, each struck once again before the bear rose on its hind legs. The crewmen's additional attacks were worthless. With each ineffective blow, the bear roared in mockery.

"It's not *natural*, Captain!" one of the combatants shouted in fear. "We can't even draw blood!"

The others had joined the fray, weaving in and out of the bear's reach. A downward strike of one paw raked the leathery skin of one of the Telborians along his neck and face. The force behind the assault knocked him to the floor, a stream of curses on his bloody lips. The other Telborian near him dared one last strike: a sharp lunge of his cutlass into the bear's chest.

Though he drove it true to its mark with all the strength he could muster, the point of the weapon halted when it touched the bear's hide. The sudden loss of momentum made the sailor trip and tumble backward, dropping his weapon as he tried righting himself.

The last thing he saw was a descending mound of ivory fur.

Those gathered around the altar could do nothing but watch the unfolding battle. Still holding the skull, Josiah focused on it as his mind raced for options of escape. The only way in or out was blocked by bloody and seemingly pointless combat.

He was trapped.

The gnome racked his mind for solutions, doing his best to drive the screams from his mind, and fixed his gaze on the skull. Empty eye sockets stared back at him in a far-from-natural manner. For a moment, he could imagine what his own skull would look like years from now . . . He pushed such grim musings from his mind.

Dry and cold, the skull was clearly human. A human who'd once possessed some rather odd teeth. They were in fact sharp fangs more in keeping with the maw of a wolf or some other large predator. The greatest of these fangs were the two incisors, larger and longer than the rest.

Focusing his mind on the skull, he thought he saw two greenish-blue pinpricks of light deep inside the dark sockets. The longer he peered into them, the more uneasy he became. Soon he could hear the faint sound of growling and snarling wolves.

He could smell fresh blood and hear the rending of limbs and a handful of guttural orders bellowed in the Nordic tongue. All these things flowed over him in faint echoes, intensifying the longer he held the skull. Soon, the din overshadowed his present reality, bringing him into a place where he never wanted to be again.

In horror, his hands loosed the ancient bone.

The skull hit the ground with a hollow clunk.

Instantly, he returned to his senses and the present danger—though he felt the blood hadn't returned to his face, while his eyes remained as large as belt buckles.

As Josiah contemplated the skull, Corwyn and Mathias started to leave the dais. Suddenly, from the darkness of the ceiling leapt a pale, blood-splattered woman. With her wild eyes and disheveled white hair resembling a clumsy bundle of hay, she gave the two men a dreadful start. Their fear only rose when she smiled.

Fanged teeth and large incisors glistened in the light while her opaline tongue luridly jabbed at them between her pale lips. Her flesh was so white it could have been marble. The parts of the woman that weren't a cold, lifeless white were splattered red with partially frozen blood.

"What now?" The strangled whisper barely escaped Mathias' lips.

"I don't know." Corwyn felt his legs lock in place. The woman's eyes held the most fascination for him. He noticed a faint circle of blue forming what appeared to be irises on the otherwise blank orbs.

"Ah . . . I think we should be leaving now, gentlemen." Josiah's voice was the weakest Corwyn had ever heard it.

As Josiah slowly started forward, he accidentally kicked the skull with his foot. It rolled onto Corwyn's boot. He dared a move to retrieve it, watching the strange woman all the while. As soon as the skull was in his hand, the woman's eyes plunged the depths of their cool hatred into him. Scrutinizing his movements, she glared and snarled as he turned the skull around to face him. Inside its sockets he saw aquamarine pinpricks of light. These strangely grew brighter while the rest of the room got darker . . .

In an eyeblink the whole chamber vanished, replaced with an empty, ancient Nordic village. Corwyn stood in the middle of it. But at the same time he knew he wasn't really there either, like being awake in a dream. Dirt roads and a handful of longhouses built of rough-hewn logs sat between earthen mound walls. It was a rustic scene, like many Nordic villages, only this one had the chieftain's house and served as the capital of the whole tribal landscape.

How he knew all this escaped him. He didn't know what to think. It felt so unnatural—so haunted with the workings of some kind of supernatural quality—he didn't know where to start.

"Hello?" he shouted in Telboros. He tried again with what he'd learned of the Nordic tongue.

Still nothing.

Gingerly, he walked onward, drawing closer to a stone well in the center of the village. He moved forward, scanning everything in sight while staying focused. He chanced a peek into the well when he'd reached it—nothing but water and a wooden bucket attached to a rough rope and the crank above.

He started when he heard a low clamoring of voices in the distance.

Frantically, he searched the sparse area, finding nothing. Uneasy, but unable to do much about it, he continued moving about the village, which consisted of only about seven longhouses.

His gaze stopped on a particular building of interest. A bull's skull adorned the overhang. From it dangled a wrought iron chain, which in turn was attached to a wooden sign. The runic words written on the sign came to him rather quickly: Mead Hall.

He approached the well-worn stone pavement outside the entranceway, pushing the thick door aside. Ripe air smelling of sweaty bodies and sour alcohol rushed at him with a stale slap. Inside it was dank and dark. What light there was streamed in from a few cracks in the walls and the doorway itself. Suddenly, a wild-looking woman stepped into the light, preventing him from going any farther.

Garbed in tattered furs and snarling like a lunatic, she had sharp teeth and an unnatural cold, white pallor. It wasn't the same woman he'd faced just moments before, but she was close in appearance. Her disheveled blond hair was so light as to be almost white, and her hands were bloody claws.

He wasted no time in running from the sight only to charge into a group of ten other figures—men and women who resembled the first woman in dress and appearance. All made an attempt to get closer, clawing and lunging with snarls and hungry growls. Inhuman creatures encased in human flesh—he didn't know what to make of them or his situation.

He did his best to stay clear of their attacks, but they drew closer and encircled him. Any hope of escape became impossible. Yet even while this vision continued, the din of battle from the chamber he'd recently left echoed once again in his ears. As the familiar grim sounds returned, he saw the circle around him part, allowing access to a tall, strong Nordican. He was the most bestial of all of them, clear blue eyes gleaming with an animalistic fury and sharp features molded over his pale white skin like jagged contours of chiseled stone.

This new figure, whom Corwyn took for their leader, bore identical traits to those of the woman in the marble chamber. Even his long white hair, sharp teeth, and sinister smile were a near-perfect match. Dressed in war-ravaged, fur-lined leather armor, the man appeared a warrior of some kind.

He lunged at Corwyn forcefully and struck him hard around his shoulders, locking on to them with an iron grip. Corwyn could do little more than try to move his arms and hands in an attempt to keep the death-dealing jaws from snapping at his face and neck.

He felt his arms growing weaker as the feral Nordican's face inched closer and closer. He could feel the impossibly cold breath issuing out of the other's mouth onto his cheeks and neck until finally the jagged teeth found purchase . . . and then it was over.

Corwyn was back in the chamber once more. He'd dropped his torch at some point, bringing the skull even with his face. The empty, naked bone still held the faint outline of his attacker's clear blue eyes and chiseled features. Whether it was the result of the added stress of the moment or the glimmering of some short-lived revelation, he wasn't entirely sure, but everything he'd read during the trip and the things he'd seen—even that odd saga he'd discovered—were now part of one clear picture.

"Run!" Corwyn moved as fast as his legs could carry him down the dais. As he did, the pale woman lashed out at Mathias, slicing into the arm of his jacket before he could pull away by ducking behind the altar.

The attack was as painful as it was swift; his whole right arm became drenched in a deep crimson. The woman's eyes then locked on Josiah. Corwyn turned just in time to see the gnome raise an arm in front of his face in some feeble attempt to block the coming attack.

Corwyn reacted in a heartbeat, stepping in front of the gnome with the skull before him. Upon seeing the uplifted skull, the woman hissed. With a rapid movement, she found a temporary opening around Corwyn. The rigid impact of her fist into the gnome's upper chest made a sound like snapping twigs. Josiah toppled from the dais, landing on the floor. This done, she focused solely on Corwyn.

"Pull back!" shouted Hirim.

The bear gave a victorious growl. Confident none would challenge it further, it lapped up the slain crewmen's blood. None could do anything but watch the horrific sight as they continued their slow retreat.

"Keep your head about you." Hirim's gruff words yanked a few back from the brink of madness. "We'll get out of this yet if we all keep our wits about us."

No sooner had he spoken than the woman attacked from behind.

Faster than the human eye could follow, she leapt from the dais, ignoring Corwyn, Mathias, and Josiah, and onto the back of a retreating Patrician crewman. The very same moment she landed upon him, her teeth were in his neck, ripping it apart even as a scream gurgled from the bloody mess.

"Gods of Light, preserve us," voiced another sailor, seeking safety with his back against the wall. But it was weak comfort. They could do nothing.

Fright froze their limbs while the woman gorged on blood, turning the elf's pale gray flesh to a dirty alabaster hue. Finished, she dropped him to the ground, licking her lips in savage delight. Her body had changed, becoming more flesh-like and losing its previous stony nature. It still possessed an unnatural white pallor, but her eyes had gained two powder-blue irises, which searched among the scattered, cowering men for her next victim.

8

Josiah surrendered a small moan while Corwyn gently slapped his cheeks. Charles still cowered behind the altar, face wet with perspiration. Mathias had regained some of his senses, having braced himself against the altar to keep from passing out, with a hand clamped around his wounded arm. He was focusing too hard on staying conscious to hear the gnome sputter back to his senses.

"How bad is it?" Corwyn asked Josiah. The skull rested beside him.

"I believe I can manage." Josiah met his gaze. The pain outlining his eyes made it clear he was lying.

"We have to get out of here." Corwyn kept tabs on the woman harassing Hirim and his men.

"Quite obvious, but how?" Josiah struggled to sit up.

"I don't know." He helped Josiah to his feet.

Josiah watched Corwyn retrieve the skull. "I would not do that if I were you, Mr. Danther."

"I think it might be the only hope we have of getting out of here alive." He turned the skull this way and that, deeply inspecting every facet.

"I was not aware we had any hope left."

"Hope is *all* we have left."

"Well, at least you will die happy then." Josiah found Mathias and Charles behind him. He could barely suppress a shudder upon noting the elf's ruined arm.

The crewmen had gathered around Hirim, their cutlasses leveled. Wild fear mixed with determination filled their veins and molded their faces. All stared the woman down. Her cold aura wafted over them like a misty cloud which even their fur-lined garments couldn't fully deflect.

"If we have to make a final stand, then let's do it right." Hirim tried to sound inspirational but wasn't sure if his words straightened anyone's backbone. All had accepted their fate. It was only a matter of heartbeats before it found them.

The woman's eyes spoke of the hunger driving her onward—a ravenous thing birthed of unnatural desires and fiendish compulsion. She smiled, and another man died. It all happened before anyone could react. With a tiger-like leap she'd captured a helpless Celetor before he could do little more than wiggle his sword in his hand. His weapon fell with a chilling clang, the young man's throat torn by her pale maw.

"Vampires," said Corwyn.

"Beg pardon?" The fear already in Josiah took deeper root.

The figure in the vision, the one he'd seen leading the other Nordicans, had been Rainier. He was sure of it. Vampires connected to Rainier in some way. The saga. The friezes. And those chains suspended over those basins . . .

"*Vampires?*" Charles was equally concerned.

Josiah stood to his full height, wincing from the effort. "I was led to believe their kind were extinct—if they ever existed at all."

"I wasn't sure they were real either. All the old tales I know say they died out a long time ago. But I guess some—or at least *one*—is still alive."

"Vampires." Charles repeated, staring at the altar.

"Think about it," urged Corwyn. "This bear, the woman . . . the promise of eternal life for those who came here . . . the bloodletting room . . . Vampires were said to be eternal, but they needed to drink the blood of the living. It was part of their curse. The curse of eternal life. *That's* Rainier's legacy and why this place has been shunned and forgotten for so many centuries. He's tied to all the vampires because he *made* all the vampires . . . He was their *king*."

"So the secret to eternal life is *vampirism*?" Charles hurriedly worked his mind through the angles, perhaps hoping for some brighter lining amid the gathering dark canopy.

"It would appear so, Mr. de Frassel."

"That really ruins my retirement plans."

"I think obscene profit is the least of our worries." Corwyn hurriedly studied the carvings on the altar stone he and Mathias had removed. "How are you holding up, Mathias?" The elf's wound appeared worse than he first thought.

"I'm still here." His speech was slurred and weak.

"Good," said Corwyn. "Just stay focused on that for now." He tried to remain as calm as he could. Giving in to fear wouldn't help his thinking. "This skull and chalice have to be important for some reason. If we can use them—"

"Attack!" Hirim's command bellowed across the chamber.

Josiah, Corwyn, Mathias, and Charles all watched the crewmen surround the woman. Corwyn noticed she'd changed even more. Her skin was more supple, like a normal woman's, and her body had filled out with added curves and smooth lines. Her muscles were still thin but looked more lifelike—more fluid than before. Her eyes had become a brilliant soft powder blue, her hair like white satin. But all of that was overshadowed by her full lips dripping blood past her chin and onto her breasts, which lay under the formerly white but now gore-splattered cloth.

"You better hurry," advised Charles. "Once she's done with them, we're next."

"You two bandage Mathias while I see what I can do here," Corwyn said, focusing again on the altar. "We're going to have to move fast."

Urged on by Hirim, the sailors fought against the vampire. Sword swings did little but slice her clothing. As with the bear, the blades didn't mar her fair skin. The vampire, for her part, seemed unconcerned about the chaotic dance of blades. Instead, she merely latched her hands and then mouth upon yet another victim.

Telborian blood splattered and sprayed. As more of it flowed into her, the silken whiteness of her hair and eyebrows turned light blond, then darkened to a soft strawberry-blond hue. Her eyes became darker—the powdery blue becoming a deeper shade until they looked like smoldering blueberries with a black pupil clearly dominating their center.

The other sailors fruitlessly roared and swung, growled, slashed, and stabbed. Dropping the Telborian with one hand, she took a swift step and latched on to another with the other hand, lifting him off the ground and strangling him with the same grip.

The sailor dropped his sword, desperately clawing at the pale wrist and arm holding him tighter than a hangman's noose.

"Let him go." Corwyn's strong voice filled the room.

At once the tumultuous back-and-forth ceased. All eyes were on Corwyn, standing at the top of the dais. He'd raised the skull overhead with the best card-playing face he could muster.

"Unless you want me to smash this, let him go." His eyes narrowed and mittens tightened about the skull. He could see the vampire understood what he was saying. There was even a glint of fear behind those dark pupils . . .

The sailor she held continued his weak struggles. Not satisfied he had her full attention, Corwyn strengthened the validity of his threat, lifting the skull backward as if making ready to smash it. The white bear raised its head, letting loose a low growl of warning.

The vampire dropped the crewman like a rag doll before bowling down those between her and the dais. A swift sprint and she stood one step below Corwyn, her stare laced with malice and insatiable hunger.

"So you *do* understand me." Corwyn held his ground. He knew if he flinched, he was dead.

"What are you doing?" Hirim kept one eye on him and the other on some of the crewmen helping the recently choked sailor to his feet.

"This skull is important to them." He kept his face hard upon the bloody woman. The bloody vampire. "It might be the only bargaining chip we have if we want to live."

"And if it's not?" Charles questioned. Corwyn noted both he and Josiah had tended to Mathias' wound with some shredded rags torn from their own and Mathias' clothing. Mathias seemed better for it. A faint tint of life still graced his cheeks, but it would be a miracle if he survived the trek back to the boat.

"Then we all get to die."

"Give . . . it . . . to me." The woman's words were slow and thick with a Nordic accent.

"Not yet," Corwyn bartered. "First, let us go. Then I'll give it to you." The woman's snarl was echoed by the bear's angry bellow. "Those are my terms." He remained defiant.

None dared move or breathe. Finally, when the sands of time had seemingly frozen, the woman choppily spoke something in an old Nordic dialect. The bear lumbered away from the doorway and the mangled corpses it had so recently enjoyed. Hissing, she retreated a step down the dais, moving to Corwyn's left. All the while she watched him like a wolf.

"Are you able to walk, Mathias?" Corwyn didn't take his focus off the woman, though his hands had started aching, numb from his tight grip.

"I think so," came Mathias' tired voice. "They did a fair job of binding the wound."

"Josiah, you and Charles are going to have to help Mathias out of here." Corwyn took one step down the dais, gaze locked on the vampire at all times. For once the halfling offered no snide rebuttal. Both he and Josiah moved to either side of Mathias and helped him down the steps. "Hirim, get yourself and your men out of here," he continued.

"What about you?" asked the bewildered captain.

"I'll be right behind you, but all of you have to get out of here first," he continued, descending another step.

"Each one of you take a fallen man and head down the stairs." Hirim snapped into action. "If you can, grab one of the torches on the floor. We're not going to leave anyone behind."

Acting on his own words, Hirim bent down and retrieved the fallen body of a young Patrician sailor. The elf still grasped his cutlass, pale gray face frozen in horrible agony. Hirim slung the body over his shoulder. The rest of the crew made their way through the doorway and down the stairs, two men carrying each dead sailor. The last two sailors, who'd helped revive their nearly strangled mate, gave the dreaded bear wide clearance. The bear watched all this in frustrated anger.

"Can't you go any faster?" Charles asked Josiah as both huffed and puffed on either side of the taller Mathias. They were the last leaving the room save Corwyn, who walked after them backward—skull at the ready like a shield.

"You are shorter than *me*, Mr. de Frassel. Any implied lack of speed on my part should first be examined upon your own brief stride." Josiah's face was aglow with the first signs of perspiration.

"Just keep moving." Corwyn followed with the vampire just an arm's length to his right.

He'd left his own torch where it had fallen. He didn't want any chance of unintentionally dropping the skull. "You're going to have to let us outside too—let us out of this place entirely," he told the vampire.

Continuing out of the room, he lowered the skull to his chest, allowing feeling into his arms once more. The woman spat out another snarl and darkly muttered Nordic words.

"Good."

Mathias' aides safely got him from the room and into the stairwell below. Giving as wide a berth as possible to the bear, Corwyn followed their path with care. The bear watched him pass, its hot glare burning into his spirit.

"I meant what I said. Let us go free and you'll get this skull back," said Corwyn, retreating past the old oak door and on to the top of the stairs. He raced down them faster than he thought possible. At their foot he met Mathias, Josiah, and Charles.

"Keep moving." He squeezed by them and into the frieze-covered hallway.

"You don't say," Charles said under his labored breath.

A massive growl carried down the stairwell. All who heard it shivered. Only Corwyn dared look back while Mathias, Josiah, and Charles made their way out of the secret passage. He could see the vampire and her ursine companion at the top of the stairs. Though they held their ground, he decided he wouldn't press his good fortune.

"Let's keep it moving," he repeated.

"Move it, gnome!" Charles snarled. "You too, bookworm."

Josiah and Mathias grunted, moving into the hall, following behind the other crewmen, whose sputtering torches were the only guideposts in the entrance chamber's cold darkness.

The vampire and bear followed.

Soon enough the crew had bunched around the closed entrance. Corwyn was closing the distance, still walking backward.

"Keep your word." His voice was soft and expectant, yet his eyes and face still maintained their serious demeanor. The bear and vampire stood on the last of the marble stairs, watching.

"Wha—" Hirim spun around at the sound of stone grinding against stone. The same door that had allowed them entrance and then trapped them inside now opened of its own accord.

"Keep moving," Hirim ordered.

Corwyn stood his ground, waiting for the rest to exit. He let Mathias, Josiah, and Charles walk past and finally out of the citadel before taking a few steps back himself. The vampire and the bear, though, followed him closely—their patience decreasing by the moment.

"Now, I'm going to just set this down and trust you'll let us go as we've agreed."

He'd made it to the doorway. This was the riskiest part of his plan. He slowly bent over and placed the skull on the floor. Two more steps brought him outside and away from both it and the entrance chamber.

The vampire and the bear remained still as statues. Only their eyes followed him, attending to his every detail.

"How are we looking out here?" Corwyn didn't turn his head for an inspection. Not yet. He needed to be sure before he retreated from the citadel.

"I've lost more good men today than I care to say." Hirim's voice was a dirge. He and the others had discovered the grisly killing field where the rest of his crew had fallen. "We'll give them a decent burial, by Perlosa."

When he felt safe enough, Corwyn glanced at the carnage. The bodies were rigid from the cold and even dripping with bloody icicles.

The vampire dashed for the door, blood lust on her lips. Everyone shouted in fright until Corwyn pulled out something from inside his jacket and halted the vampire in her tracks as she let out a blood-freezing scream.

"I thought as much," he said, holding out the skull's lower jawbone. "In case you didn't keep your word, I held on to this. Get back inside and let us leave here in peace. I'll throw this back to the beach when we depart. If you don't let us depart, I'll break it into pieces."

The vampire growled in defiance but in the end returned inside the citadel. The doorway closed behind her.

"Well played, Mr. Danther." Sweaty and drunk on adrenaline, Josiah was quite pleased he would live to see a new dawn.

"You don't think they'll still attack us, do you?" Mathias' voice was weak but still audible.

"No," said Corwyn. "They want this too badly to risk it."

"So now we get to keep the jawbone, huh?" Charles smiled.

"No. I intend to return it, just like I said." Corwyn made his way over to the two boats, where the crew were loading up the dead and securing them as best they could for the return journey.

"So we did all this for *nothing*?" A crestfallen Charles helped Mathias to one of the boats.

"That depends on how you look at it," said Corwyn.

"Josiah and Charles, join Mathias in a boat," Hirim interrupted.

"With the *corpses*?" Charles wrinkled his nose.

"Either get in with a corpse or become one. We're not going to come back for any stragglers. While Corwyn's barter might have given us some time, I don't trust those devils; the sooner we leave the better." Hirim started organizing the dead into rows, maximizing available space.

"Agreed," said Josiah, climbing into a nearby vessel with enough room for his smaller frame.

"So, what did we gain?" Charles stepped into the boat, taking a seat beside Josiah. Mathias found a spot in the other boat.

"Certainly not what we set out to do, that is for sure." Josiah was rueful.

"I can't help you there." Corwyn picked up the rope tied to the boat. "I'm just happy to be alive."

He pulled the rope with the aid of a few of the Telborian crewmen up to the lip of the snowy crater. The work wasn't as hard as he thought it would be, but he knew after the adrenaline and fear had worn off, he'd be sore in the morning. The soft starlight reflecting off the snow and ice would provide enough light for a safe return to the beach.

"But I wanted to live forever and be filthy rich," Charles sulked. "This whole trip has been a colossal waste, and now I have to go back without anything to show for it."

"You didn't really want to live forever, did you?" Corwyn gritted his teeth against the biting breeze stinging his cheeks, focusing on putting one foot in front of the other.

"Who *wouldn't* want to live forever?" Charles obviously thought the question was the most foolish thing he'd ever heard.

"Not me."

"*Liar.*"

"I think having a set span of years is what makes life worth living." He huffed as he tugged. "If you have endless time, things begin losing their meaning; life itself becomes cheaper if it's not allowed to have an end. It's the journey along the path from birth to death that's the most wonderful and worthwhile. And every journey has a beginning and an end. If life had no end, then it would cease being a *true* journey and therefore cease being worthwhile."

Corwyn cast a glance over his shoulder, noting Charles' crossed arms. "Think about what was being offered for eternal life," he continued. "She was a *vampire*, Charles. She doesn't *give* life, she *takes* it. It isn't eternal life she would have given you but eternal death. Nothing is worth that curse." This said, all further conversation ceased, leaving the crewmen, Hirim, and Corwyn pulling the two boats across the sparkling snow.

9

The coming dawn found all back onboard the *Phoenix*. The dead had been prepared for their funeral and would be tossed into the ocean after they'd entered friendlier waters. Those wounded had been treated. A sense of order and peace had found its way among the men, though all would feel even better once the frozen island was far behind them.

From where he stood on the forecastle, Corwyn could see a fair deal inland. The sky was the color of molten lead, giving everything a strange, unnatural cast. Josiah joined him on deck with some minor effort. He found only a few of his ribs were bruised, a couple were slightly cracked, but given he'd originally thought they were all broken, he'd endure the discomfort. By the time they returned to Breanna he'd be healed and whole once again.

"I trust this will make for a very interesting story." Josiah peered across the small stretch of icy water to the snowy beach.

Corwyn studied the jawbone clasped in his mitten. "Who would have thought this was what we were searching for?"

"Tragic and ironic," Josiah soberly agreed. "I wish to apologize for my rash actions in the citadel. My disturbing the skull must have caused that whole terrible series of events to unfold."

"I doubt it." Corwyn took in the gnome. "Those two devils were probably waiting to jump at us no matter what we did. If anything, you picking up the skull only sped things up."

"No matter." Josiah remained resolute. "It was unprofessional of me, to say the least, and certainly put this whole enterprise at risk."

"Was it worth the investment?" Corwyn's gaze swayed back toward the snowy beach.

"There is always an amount of risk in any venture. What was done in this endeavor was nothing new, save in terms of what we found for our efforts. It seems a pity we did not get to explore the rest of the citadel. Of the fraction we did manage to navigate in our haste, I am sure we have left many wonderful discoveries behind—historical and perhaps financial in nature."

"And probably more vampires hiding in wait or even traps or some other macabre things better left hidden. I doubt there would be *anything* beneficial for your investors."

"Perhaps you are right." Josiah pulled out his pipe and filled it with tobacco. "That matter aside, I would be most interested in hearing how you came to the bold decision you did regarding our recent escape. Not even Mr. Onuis could piece together what you did there in the end, and he was the *scholar* on the subject."

Corwyn continued staring at the powdery snow, watching it sparkle like diamond dust. "I saw something when I picked up the skull. It gave my mind the jolt it needed to put everything together."

"I see." Josiah put the pipe in his mouth and began digging inside his fur-lined jacket for his sparker. "I had an uneasy feeling when I picked it up too, but did not experience any visions attached to its possession."

"It was Rainier's skull. That's why they won't risk harming it," he said, lifting the jawbone heavenward for yet another examination. "I'm holding the jawbone of the one legends say was the king of the vampires, and now I'm about to give it back to them."

"You *are* aware you are under no real obligation to do so?" Josiah had finally retrieved his sparker. "None of us would think any less of you should you keep it . . . or even destroy it."

"I know, but I gave my word."

"So you did." Josiah worked his sparker, sending a handful of sparks into the bowl of his pipe until a small stream of smoke ascended. "In the very least we now know not all the vampires have departed Tralodren, for whatever it is worth."

"Your investors don't plan on trying to turn some profit on vampirism, do they?"

Josiah mingled a cough with a laugh—smoke spraying everywhere. "Heavens no. Morality and ethics are cornerstones to any business that wishes to prosper. We will do no such thing as trying to profit from such an accursed thing. This enterprise has simply demonstrated the lack of any beneficial gain on this venture. We therefore have to cut our losses and move on to other things. Such is the nature of free enterprise."

"Glad to hear it." Corwyn hurled the jawbone over the water. Both of them watched it skip over the waves like an oversized stone before tumbling into the dry, brittle snow.

"Ready to go home?" He started for his quarters.

"Never has Breanna been more attractive than now."

A moment later Hirim's deep bellow brought the anchor up and set the *Phoenix* moving away from the floating isle into warmer waters.

MAIDEN ROCK

Corwyn's reddish-brown hair fluttered in the breeze. He wore rather common garb for this venture: an off-white shirt, brown pants, and matching leather boots with a cherrywood lute slung over his back. He'd made his way for the Gulian Hills shortly after the *Phoenix* had docked in Elandor. After the recent events aboard ship, he needed some peace and quiet. Maiden Rock was just the place to find it.

The hermetic shrine devoted to Causilla housed a wonderful statue of the goddess, called "the Maiden," naturally enough. He'd visited the shrine fourteen years prior and welcomed a chance to see it again. While he never had the experiences others who visited said occurred, he did know there was a cluster of perpetually blooming rosebushes nearby. Some tales said the bushes had formed from blood lost from dying lovers, tears from those mourning their lost love, or even drops of blood from Causilla herself. While the tales were clearly more fancy than fact, he didn't doubt the flowers were special. If they kept a constant bloom year round, then they couldn't be natural plants.

For all these tales, though, the shrine had become an almost forgotten thing. Most in these hills were dwarves and didn't take much to Causilla; Shiril and Drued were their gods of choice. Anyone else in the area did what most do in the Midlands: hail Asora or another of the Light Gods as their own. Outside of bards, the single-minded adoration of Causilla fell to a scant, scattered minority whose numbers comprised mostly young lovers, newlyweds, and romantics.

Though dedicated to the goddess of love, arts, and beauty, Maiden Rock wasn't an easy climb. Sloping widely at the base, the hill was dotted with low-lying green bushes. As these thinned, shards of rock—like pottery pieces—splintered through the grass. The higher one went, the more dominant they became. As small pebbles and then larger stones appeared, the ground transformed into something abrasive and steep. While not the tallest of foothills in the area, it was still quite formidable, even with the thin game trail snaking around the rocks and greenery.

About a fourth of the way up, he noticed the landscape turning browner. Patches of color still caught his eye, though, and stout, stubborn bushes yet held their ground amid jagged overhangs. These larger ridges of stone resembled rough-hewn walls. Corwyn figured he'd be near the top by late morning if he kept his pace.

He'd traveled here on foot instead of by horse in order to slow down and perceive things from a more relaxed point of view. In truth, the hill was less than a day's walk from the small town of Tolan, east and south of the hills. A simple yet restful night in the wilds yesterday allowed him even further relaxation and time for thinking away from the crowds, music, and past adventures. When morning rose, he felt better than he had in weeks.

He'd begun his ascent at dawn after finishing his last crust of bread and hunk of cheese at the hill's foot. An hour later he found himself at his present location, slightly warm from the climb but excited to see the top. He took a moment of rest from his progress. The angle of the slope wasn't yet that steep, but increasing quite rapidly. Even so, there was enough of a change that he found himself catching his breath while leaning against a dandelion-speckled sandstone bulge.

As he rested, he felt some weight lift from his shoulders. Closing his eyes, he lifted his chin, letting the rising sun kiss his neck and face. More relaxing than a hot bath on the coldest of days, the warmth seeped into his bones and brain. It and the soft fragrance of the nearby honeysuckle provided a soothing sensation. Like a healing balm, it drew out the stress from his marrow and muscles. Once refreshed, he continued on. An hour later, he'd reached the last quarter of the hill.

He let himself get distracted by the soft chatter of songbirds perched in the bristly shrubs and spidery, short trees spotting the greener terrain. The grass here had started reclaiming lost ground, beginning to cover the hard rock once more. He kept up the pace. A few moments later he reached the top. The stony surface was almost completely taken over with soft, lush grasses, bushes, and even a few trees.

He made his way through a shoulder-high, erratic rise of earth, eager to lay eyes on the Maiden once more. This rise actually parted in the middle, forming a miniature valley. Passing through this pathway, Corwyn heard a soft melody sung in an unfamiliar language coming from ahead. Slowly, he moved his head around the exterior of the undulating, grassy mound to where it opened into the shrine beyond.

The first thing his eyes found was the shrine, focusing on the statue in particular. Depicting a fair Telborian maiden dressed in an elegant long-sleeved gown and carrying a small lyre in her right hand, the granite figure, now worn down from the elements, couldn't be missed. Supposedly inspired by Causilla, who one story said had been seen by the artist in the flesh, it rested on a circular colonnade's polished stone mosaic floor. Long locks of hair streamed down the statue's head, draping her shoulders and neck and adding to the figure's natural beauty. Even from his current distance, Corwyn was taken aback by the detail. He'd forgotten how amazing it really was—even after decades of weathering.

A smooth marble dome capped off the colonnade, covering the statue and the short gray marble bench that had become an altar before it. Corwyn knew from his previous visit that pilgrims' offerings were scattered about the top of the bench: faded flowers, tarnished trinkets of luck and various craftsmanship, small lockets, charms—even miniature ceramic figurines representing the ideal mate they sought—rested amid a myriad of other decaying and dusty things. From where he stood, he could see there hadn't been many visitors for quite a while. The trinkets looked old—even ruined in some cases. Around the colonnade grew the thick, thorny rosebushes. And like during his last visit, fat buds and deep crimson blooms covered the dense green leaves.

Near the colonnade, however, was something new: a woman. Fair looking—at least from what he could see of her back as she sat on the ground facing the bench—she continued singing her strange lyrical melody a cappella. With little else to go on, he assumed her a fellow pilgrim or maybe even a bard. He moved out from behind his hiding place. As he did, the woman stopped and turned to face him.

Probably no older than his own twenty-six years, she had short white hair, olive skin, and soft brown eyes. She wore a long-sleeved auburn gown with a yellow shawl draped about her shoulders. Standing to greet him, her soft smile invited him into her presence.

"Hello," she said, with a cheerful nod.

"Forgive me for interrupting." He carefully advanced. "I wasn't expecting anyone else up here."

"You didn't disturb me." The woman beamed, almost as if happy she'd been interrupted.

"That was a lovely song. I've never heard anything like it before."

"It's something I composed myself," she said, reclaiming her former seat in one fluid motion. This time, she put her back to the shrine, keeping her focus on Corwyn.

"I didn't recognize the language."

"You probably won't." She patted the grass across from her. "It's Dranarin."

"*Dranarin?*" Corwyn remained where he was. "That's a bit obscure, isn't it?" He didn't know of anyone who'd learned the ancient language of the dranors, let alone someone who could make a song out of it.

"Come on and sit down already. I'm quite tame, I assure you."

"All right," he said, sitting where she'd directed. "Are you a bard?"

"In a way. I love all the gifts Causilla's blessed Tralodren with."

"Now you sound more like a priestess."

"A *priestess?*" She laughed. "No, I'm not a priestess either, just a pilgrim looking for a spot to rest for a while. What about you?" Her eyes drew him into them like a moth to flame. He tried shaking off the effect as best he could by directing the conversation somewhere else. He didn't think he could capably talk about himself while she watched him with those honey-brown pools.

"How do you know Dranarin?"

"Hey," the woman said, feigning a disciplinary glare. "I asked *you* a question first."

"So you did." So much for steering clear of self-discussion. "I'm a pilgrim too, I guess."

"A bard?"

"Yes."

"What's your name?"

"What's yours?" he quickly countered.

"I asked *you* first." She playfully swiped at him with the end of her shawl. The finely woven tassels made a poor scourge across his chest.

"Corwyn Danther."

"Corwyn Danther . . . I've heard of you, I think. What do they say? 'Best bard in the Midlands'?"

"Something like that." Corwyn found himself blushing under her gleeful gaze.

"Modest too, eh? Well, how about that? Not too many bards you can find these days who'd be so humble. So, what are you doing out here?"

"I'm here to pay homage to Causilla."

"At *this* shrine?" She turned back to the colonnade, almost as if to make sure it was still there and hadn't fallen down while they'd been talking. "*Why?* No one really comes here anymore; it's lost its appeal to most."

"Sounds like you know a lot of things about a lot of things," Corwyn said and then wished he hadn't when he realized how foolish it sounded.

"Now *that*"—the woman's face parted wide in a smile—"was almost poetic." The two shared a brief chuckle.

"So, you were telling me why you came here . . ." she continued.

When he looked away from her gaze he felt like himself again. "This was where I first came when I decided I wanted to be a bard."

"When was that?" His focus automatically shifted back toward her. No matter how hard he tried, he found himself staring into her eyes again. Maybe they *were* honey: sticky pots of dark golden delight that didn't want to let him go for anything.

"When I was about twelve."

"You knew you wanted to be a bard so young?"

"Since as long as I can remember."

"You any good?"

"I've been told I'm good."

"But *are* you?" Her eyelids drooped as she pressed the matter.

He found himself speechless.

"You okay?"

"I'm sorry, it's just, you're so beautiful—I mean that in a good way . . . I, ah . . . what I meant to say—"

Her free-spirited laughter interrupted him. She covered her mouth in an attempt to stifle the lively eruption.

"It's all right." Some additional giggles escaped her lips before she got a handle on them. "I understand. No harm done."

"I just—"

Her hand was suddenly hovering over his mouth, her fingers barely touching his lips. "Shh. You're sweet." He could smell the aroma of wildflowers and lilacs drifting from her slender fingers. "I like that. Not too many men left today who are as forthright as you," she continued. "Don't worry. There's no need to explain anything. I'm really interested in your story, though, and would love for you to continue."

She withdrew her fragrant fingers from his lips.

"Not too many women like you in the world either," he said, shaking his head, attempting to free himself of the stupor that had enveloped him with the fragrance of her touch.

"No, there aren't," she agreed. "Please, tell me your tale," she continued, crossing her legs. "So, you obviously became a bard."

"I've been at it for about thirteen years now."

"Thirteen?" She was impressed. "Then you really *must* be good, or you're a sucker for punishment." She stopped, cocking her head in a curious manner. "What is it now?"

"I'm sorry," he said. "Just thinking."

"About what?"

"About how you remind me of all the stories about what a muse is supposed to look like."

"A *muse*?" She smirked. "Have you even seen one before?"

"No, but like I said, I've heard a lot of tales, seen some drawings, and I even know the old rhyme they teach in the bardic colleges."

"And what rhyme is that?"

> Thirty maidens to inspire and delight,
> By goddess' command, get up and take flight.
> Three to the South to plant seeds in the sand,
> Five to the Midlands—inspirers of man.
> Four more to the North, mixing beauty with ice,
> Six to the West, championing virtue over vice.
> Six more venture beyond the Boiling Sea.
> And six with the goddess forever shall be.

"So then who would *I* be?" the woman joked.

"Well, I guess one of the five in the Midlands." He played along.

"You know, they say a muse lives here . . . well, comes to visit from time to time," she said. "It's one of those old tales, I suppose, priests tell to keep people coming to a shrine. Course, why a muse would want to come to this old place . . . well, that's up for debate."

"I think there's some truth to *all* legends," said Corwyn. "That was part of the reason I came here in the first place. I've heard that story about the muse being here, too. Even one about Causilla herself appearing on occasion. I actually hoped it was true. I wanted to get Causilla's blessing, talk to a muse, or get some sort of sign that becoming a bard was right."

"But I thought you said you always knew you were supposed to be a bard?"

"I did . . . but if I'd a sign or encounter to confirm it, I thought—"

"That you were really on the right path," she finished.

"Exactly."

"It's a pretty common thought. But what happened with you? Anything—or anyone—show up?"

"It was just me and a few hours of silence until I finally got up and left."

"But you became a bard *anyway*?"

"I couldn't get away from it no matter how I tried," he confessed. "In the end the desire overpowered any lingering doubts." He suddenly recalled what the woman had been doing before he arrived. "I'm sorry. I've talked way too much as it is. I'm sure you want to get back to whatever brought you up here. I suppose I should get some time in as well before it gets dark and I have to head back. If I'm a disturbance—"

"Not at all. I could use the company, actually."

"I never did get your name."

"I never gave it."

"So—"

"Play something," she jubilantly insisted, motioning to the lute still slung over his back. "You wanted to know how I learned Dranarin, right? Well, I tend to tell tales better with musical accompaniment. And besides, I'd love to hear the famed 'bard of the Midlands' play."

"All right, if that's the only way I'm going to get answers," he said, removing his lute.

After tightening the strings and getting to a comfortable spot with the instrument resting on his lap, he strummed out a slow, rolling tune. Simple yet robust, the notes progressed in their dance. All the while the woman closed her eyes and listened. Swaying in a slow rhythm like a serpent with a charmer, she followed the entire tune until Corwyn brought it to a respectable end. When finished, her lush lips parted with an expression of absolute delight.

"That was *beautiful*, Corwyn," she whispered with eyes still closed as if reliving each note. "Do you dance?" Suddenly, she was on her feet, catching him by surprise.

"I'm not that good really," he said, pushing away the outstretched hands trying to raise him to his feet.

"Come on," she playfully insisted. "It isn't hard."

"I thought you were going to tell me *your* story now," he politely inquired in hopes of avoiding her latest request.

"I will in time . . . But if you aren't going to help me out, I'll have to dance on my own then." She took her shawl in both hands and pulled it forward, letting the rest cover her back, as if drying off after a bath.

"Now," she playfully commanded, "I want something up-tempo—filled with life. There's something I picked up from the dranors—"

"*Dranors?*" Corwyn looked up in surprised wonder. "You're going to tell me you actually learned it from a *real* dranor?"

"I'm not as young as I look."

"Then you wouldn't be alive either. They've been gone for—"

"Are you going to play or not?" she asked, arms akimbo.

"Fine," he sighed. Though truthfully any show of reluctance was halfhearted at best. He was incredibly curious about what she'd do next.

"So how should I play? An up-tempo beat, but what's the melody?" He fingered the lute trying to catch a chord or two to round out the evolving tune.

"Just follow my lead and you'll get the rest. Freeform will be fine." He noticed she'd placed a set of brass finger cymbals on her right index finger and thumb. Whatever type of dance this was, it would be quite unique; only Celetors used such instruments. Well, them and dranors too, apparently.

"Ready?"

"I suppose."

"Don't be so glum. This will be fun." She flashed some teeth. "Trust me."

"You don't have to do this. I'm more than happy to leave you to yourself. I was only making conversation—"

"But I want to. So please let me do this. I don't get to dance for too many people anymore." And with that she clapped her finger cymbals and twirled out her shawl. Corwyn started with a few chords he thought might work, balancing them with the emerging rhythm of her steps.

Cha-ching.

She sped up her pace.

Cha-ching. Clap.

Corwyn picked up the chords he needed, feeling the music flow into him—inspired by the dance and the woman performing it. His fingers seemingly had a mind of their own, playing what they willed apart from any mental commands. The pitch intensified, and so did the dance.

Cha-ching. Clap. Ching-ching. Clap.

In time, he wasn't sure if his fingers still strummed the lute or if it strummed itself. His eyes—and now mind—were focused solely on the graceful woman before him. The bright yellow shawl spun around her lithe frame like fire; the finger cymbals clapping away in time to her step punctuated her consciousness-snaring movement. Amazingly, she kept her eyes focused on him through it all, never breaking a sweat from her rapid, fluid motions.

Cha-ching-clap-ching-ching-clap-ching-ching-clap-clap.

His heart followed the rising rhythm. The whole experience went beyond words. The bending, twisting, small skips and jumps, twirling fabric, the colors, those soft brown eyes and olive skin . . . He became transfixed—amazed such a dance could be performed by anyone. It seemed too intricate, too perfect and refined for even the most gifted of dancers.

And then he stopped playing.

His mind and fingers could no longer communicate with each other, causing the wild strumming to cease midnote. He simply couldn't go on. He was too enraptured with it all—battling too many fantastical thoughts and ponderings. His heart pounded, and sweat covered his body in a layer of wet silk. The woman froze midmovement, viewing him with a playful expression as if she knew the answer before asking the question.

"Problem?" She rested her hands on her hips, eager to continue.

Corwyn shook his head, trying to pull himself back from the experience. "Ah . . . no . . . Yes, I guess. I-I couldn't keep up."

As she glided his way, Corwyn noticed there wasn't a drop of sweat on her. She didn't even appear tired. He wagered she could have gone on dancing like she had for hours—perhaps even *days*—without any difficulty.

"Well, it's a hard dance to keep up with, in truth, and you really weren't doing it justice anyway."

"I'm sorry. I just—"

"Shhh." Another slender finger found his lips. Once again the fragrant lilac and wildflower bouquet fluttered into his nostrils. He began feeling lightheaded. "You came here to worship Causilla." Her voice and manner had changed into something slightly more authoritative, yet still welcoming and charming. "Well so did I, but in a different way. Give me your hand."

Corwyn complied in a sleepy, trancelike state. The woman pulled him up, and the lute fell from his lap with a muffled thud.

"What are you doing now?" The words felt like syrup in his mouth.

"I don't want to harm you, only enlighten you."

"So you *are* a priestess?" His eyes widened. Even with his fuzzy mind, he still knew what was going on and could follow what she was saying.

"I'm a servant of Causilla. Now close your eyes. Go ahead and close them. You can trust me." He lowered his eyelids. "You can open them now."

When he did, his jaw dropped. She had changed in less than a heartbeat! The yellow shawl and auburn gown were gone. Now she stood in an ankle-length golden silk skirt with sides slit up to midthigh. Her white blouse flowed from her shoulders to the base of her ribcage, leaving her smooth, defined stomach exposed. Her sleeves billowed out, then banded about her elbows, leaving her forearms naked. The white puffs were sliced open into ribbons, revealing a shimmering silver fabric beneath. But this wasn't the only change in her appearance.

Her short white hair glistened like diamond dust and was spiked in all directions. Her honey-brown eyes still remained inviting and peaceful, but her lips were stained a brilliant red and gleamed like the skin of a dew-drenched apple. Anklets of gold, toe rings on her bare feet, rings, bracelets, and earrings finished off the rest of her transformation. To see her in such a state, when compared to how she'd looked just moments before, was beyond amazing.

"Who are you?" Corwyn finally managed to ask through his molasses-filled mouth.

The woman pulled him sharply to her chest, even with her face, nose to nose, eye to eye. "Five to the Midlands, remember?" Her red lips parted ever so slightly, and Corwyn could smell the familiar floral bouquet dancing on her breath. He could do nothing but stare dumbly at the two nutmeg planets across from him—the whole of his cosmos as far as he could fathom.

Five sisters also came to Midlandic shores:
Alanna and Ella—sights to behold.

Mortal minds to enlighten, inspire, and mold.
Hannah, Keely, and Lena the other three—
Delight of men and mortals be.

"I don't understand," said Corwyn.

"I was here when you came searching those many years ago. I saw you and was pleased with you, but you had yet to learn patience. You left before I could give you my blessing. Now, follow my lead." She took Corwyn's hands and began dancing.

She started with a simple, almost methodical, step. This soon increased into a steady allegretto prancing in time with the sound of a fiddle he heard ringing out its giddy notes from afar. He tried searching for its source while twirling.

"You won't find *this* band. Now keep in time, it's going to get a little faster."

She was right. Following the fiddle, a flute made its presence known. Higher pitched, it picked up the melody and carried the beat echoed in the couple's dance. Around and round they spun like a dust devil. As they did, he noticed everything about him had changed, radiating an unimaginable beauty.

In this enchanting haze he saw things he'd never be able to fully describe: a palace of splendor on top of a flower-covered hill where beautiful women and men played lyre and lute, flute and drum—frolicking in wild delight. A place of never-ending beauty and tangible love, a place he'd never see as long as he called Tralodren home.

The longer he danced, the more he felt himself becoming infused with a creative passion that rivaled everything he'd felt and known before. Ideas flashed in his head—images and colors. He heard songs older than the world's foundations and new as a babe's first cry.

Around they danced to the beat of a disembodied drum, thumping out a rhythm both unnatural and glorious. She let go of one hand and spun herself around him like a wild dervish.

The beat increased.

The dance became fevered—faster than anyone could dance without error. Yet he felt like he could go on forever—like he was prancing about on air instead of earth.

The song gained still more phantom instruments. A lute and pipes . . . and he saw things in a new light that intensified the colors of everything around him. The rocky earth became a rich ocher hue, the green an almost neon flare of verdancy. The sky blazed a sapphire light with white silk clouds melting away with the tears streaming from his eyes.

And still they danced.

Yips and yells jumped in: a frantic, invisible, jubilant host accompanying the music in time. And they spun. Gold and white, silver and brown, spinning like a top above the hill and shrine. Corwyn's breath fled his lungs upon seeing the flaming gold sun fall away with the azure sky and be replaced with the dark satin of night, peppered with the pinpricks of frozen crystal stars.

"Most mortals would let their lust for beauty consume them—control them—rather than learn to appreciate it and to nurture it in themselves and others. You, though, Corwyn, are different. You subdue your lusts even while moving to embrace me and what I represent: pure beauty and creativity made manifest through love.

"You're a rare treasure, for you grasp the true nature and power of our goddess. I knew this on your first visit, and if you hadn't run off before we could meet, we could have had this conversation fourteen years ago. Now you see the truth of things as few can or have. And that truth has drawn me to you." She pulled him close once more. He could smell a new fragrance about her like cinnamon, vanilla, nutmeg, and honey, mixed with roses and sweetened cream.

Finally, when he felt he'd die if he continued this mad event, everything stopped. His mind unlocking from the spinning, hazy whirlwind, Corwyn could for the first time understand what had been happening and what was being said. He dared a look below. They were high above the world, peering down at the clouds themselves like fleeting things beneath his notice. The silence of the whole setting was in itself grand and beautiful, as was the view: a blue sea with floating white islands of misty cotton . . .

"But why—"

The muse's lips halted his words.

His initial shock was overcome with delight. This wasn't the mere kiss of any fair woman, but the kiss of a divinity. It didn't carry with it a physical fire like with a mortal kiss, but rather a mental and spiritual blaze flaring across the parched landscape of his being.

Consumed with this passion, he again saw visions, but these were of himself and what he was going to do in the days and years ahead. Music and adventures, tales and companions—some he'd met already, some he would meet in times to come. All these pictures and still more flooded his mind, but the most powerful aspect of the kiss was the quaking overtaking his heart. He felt like he would explode from the creative energy screaming inside for release. New ideas for songs, tales, and more saturated his brain, embedding themselves in his skull . . . and then . . .

And then it was over.

Their lips parted.

He reached out for more, but the muse held him back.

After he opened his eyes, she said, "Know that Lena calls you blessed and has favored you. From this day forth I will be your patron. For love of Causilla and by her decree, I have come to you and done these things. Your heart is true and your love is pure. I'm more than pleased to be your patron." Lena released Corwyn to hover alone in open space.

"Wait," he said, reaching out with a desperate hand.

"We'll meet again. Have no fear." Lena's eyes sparkled brighter than the stars above them. "For now, you must rest. There's much to do in this life of yours. Much to see," she said while fading from sight like mist in a breeze. "And you only have a short span of years in which to do it."

"A short span?"

"Well, short compared to the way *I* measure time." She winked and was gone.

Unsure of what to expect next, he looked below for answers. He'd never forget the sight of Tralodren as the gods must see it for as long as he lived. Yet even while he observed the sweeping white mists, the clouds became blurry. He felt lightheaded again. In an attempt to push back such sensations, he closed his eyes. A moment later he found himself on the grassy hill beside the shrine.

Sitting up slowly, he noted his lute and walking stick resting beside him. Alone on the hilltop, he beheld the world once again in its familiar contrasts and hues. As he sat up fully, a white rose tumbled from his chest into his lap. He brought it to his nose. It smelled of vanilla, cinnamon, honey, nutmeg, and sweetened cream, mixed with the flower's own subtle fragrance.

He inhaled deeply and smiled.

WHERE DREAMS GO TO DIE

Fat drops of rain splattered off Corwyn's sopping brown cloak and onto the muddy road. The thoroughfare's normally hard-packed surface had turned into a soupy, meandering puddle, which he'd had the pleasure of sloshing around in for the better part of an hour.

Every piece of his outfit either hung against him or dragged him down as if he wore a coat of chain mail rather than his simple, light garb. Even his boots were filled with a shallow lake splashing about his toes with every step. He only kept the hood of his cloak up since it kept some of the rain from getting into his eyes. The roomy covering clung to his head. The drenched cloak also offered little protection for his cherrywood lute, which rested on his back, making him appear like a hunchback as he pressed on through the weather.

Alone in his travels, he trudged onward, hoping for a dry place with a fire where he could warm himself before he caught a cold or something worse. After an hour of searching the flat prairie, he finally spied an old building off the side of the road. It was still some distance from him, but close enough to get to before it got too dark. He was uncertain, though, as to what it was: barn, granary, an old home, maybe even an abandoned shrine. All that mattered at the moment were its four walls and roof sturdy looking enough to hold back the rain. He turned toward it with a fresh sense of urgency.

En route, he caught sight of a simple graveyard. Resting on the right of the road, in close proximity to the building, it was seemingly out of place in the surrounding terrain. He studied it for a moment in passing. Hemmed in by fieldstone walls, the manicured grounds were populated with surprisingly well-maintained headstones. It lacked a gate, with only a break in the wall allowing access.

He wondered how so many came to be buried here when he hadn't seen any sign of house or farmstead for quite a while. He let his eyes wander a little longer, studying the rectangular plot and the basalt statue at its center: a hooded figure with a set of keys in one hand and a measuring scale in the other—Asorlok, the god of death himself.

A low grumble from above brought his head heavenward. He redoubled his efforts. The old building, now clearly resembling a rough and common inn, lay a few yards away. He also noticed smoke rising from the stone chimney atop the shingled roof and illumination from inside. Illumination he knew, like the smoke, hadn't been there before.

The rustic building was pushing a hundred years if he had to guess. A two-story, medium-sized structure allowing for just about the right number of travelers who'd ramble through this part of Romain. And like the graveyard, it was well maintained. The worn oak door seemed inviting enough; more so was the slick-shingled overhang keeping the steps leading up to the entrance dry.

Corwyn ducked underneath and pulled the clinging hood from his head. Shaking his drenched hair, he let loose a shower of his own. He peered inside the old glass windows, noting outlines of people in the dingy glow of what could only be firelight. There weren't too many shapes beyond the glass, but enough to hint at some life in the old inn.

The door opened with a creaking grind. Before he crossed the threshold the warmth and smoky aroma of the fire embraced him. As his eyes adjusted, he noticed a matronly woman moving toward him. A Telborian of about fifty years, she was plump and rosy cheeked, resembling a loving mother.

"Well, aren't you just soaked to the bone?" Corwyn noticed her garb with slight wonder: a plain parchment-colored dress reaching her ankles with a red sash tied about her waist in a slipknot on her left side. If he didn't know any better, he'd have sworn she was a priestess of Asorlok. But he didn't see any necklace bearing the god's symbol. Maybe she was a follower instead.

"We better get those wet things off you before you catch your death." The woman's stubby fingers began removing Corwyn's cloak. He let her, seeing no reason to resist.

"Thank you," he said, trying to get a closer look at her as she slipped off the drenched garment and draped it on the back of a wooden chair. She moved the chair closer to the fire so the cloak could dry. As she did, Corwyn became aware of the people around the old hearth: a man and a woman who paid little attention to his arrival in the very empty common room.

"My goodness, you must have been out there for quite some time. You're just a walking puddle, aren't you? Best go upstairs to the first door on your right and you'll find some clean, dry clothes to change into, along with some towels. Then come right back down to the fire to drive off any cold you might still have in you."

"I appreciate your hospitality," said Corwyn, "but I don't have much coin on me. If I could take a moment or two by the fire—long enough to dry my clothes and wait out the storm—that would be all I'd require."

The woman chuckled, waving his words away by means of a shooing hand swipe. "You don't have to pay anything here. This is a wayfarer's inn and I'm happy to provide what service I can to those who've grown weary."

He'd heard tales of such places from other bards and travelers over the years but didn't know where they were located; in truth, none really did. As in most Tralodroen religions, those who followed Asorlok—Asorlins— were divided into different sects. Unlike some splits, there wasn't any ill will attached to their division. Since Asorlok was seen as a god of death, decay, journeys, and the afterlife, it was only natural his followers would find some of these aspects more to their liking than others.

Some worshiped the god as presented, entire and pure in his complete godhead. Others identified with him more as the god of travelers and journeys, for after all, life itself was a journey toward death and death a journey to the afterlife. These followers built roadside resting places to honor their god by helping those weary from travel. At least, those were the tales he'd heard, which apparently were true. Though who could have found this place on their own so far into the empty plains, he couldn't say.

"Now go get those soggy things off you." The woman made another effort at shooing him upstairs like a stray cat.

Corwyn felt a little uneasy resting in a place dedicated to the god of death, but realized he needed to be practical. He could either dry off here and wait out the storm or go back out in the muck and rain, trudging about for who knows how long until he might find another suitable place . . . *if* he found one.

He climbed the steps to the upper level, hoping to find some decent dry clothes. Although he wasn't too wild about changing into used clothing—which is what he was sure awaited him—he'd take what he could get, as long as it wasn't too shoddy and had a semblance of being clean.

He neared the top of the stairs and made his way to the first door on the right. Slightly ajar, it opened into a rather simple room. The only light came from a lone candle resting on top of a nightstand. A brass holder, overrun by melted wax, made sure it remained upright. Other than the nightstand and candle there were only a bed and a chair. On the bed rested a selection of garments, all folded in a neat pile and sorted by type: shirts, pants, belts, etc., resting alongside some folded towels. Moving closer, he caught sight of a shirt similar to the one he was wearing, along with a pair of pants he thought might fit.

"Just leave your wet clothes on the chair to dry." The woman's voice came up from below, startling him.

Closing the door, he tossed his outfit over the chair, then dried himself with a towel. He dressed in some haste. To his surprise, he found the pieces he'd chosen not only fit him like a glove but were newer too—as if stitched together a few days ago. He kept his boots, though, tipping them upside down and spilling out the small pool inside. He wasn't keen on the sparse selection of shoes—some wooden, some leather—nor with the one pair of rather tight-looking boots. Instead, he let his wet feet go bare, taking his boots and drenched socks along with him to the fire.

Downstairs, he smelled the welcoming aroma of mutton stew. He didn't know how he'd missed it earlier but supposed he'd been distracted by other things. His stomach groaned as he descended.

"Don't you look handsome now?" His hostess greeted him at the bottom of the stairs with a smile. Her eyes fell on the still-muddy boots clasped in his hand. "Couldn't bear to part with those, eh?"

"I've just broken them in."

"Then come to the fire and warm up."

"You sure this isn't going to cost me anything? I could certainly offer up something for the clothes and fire."

"It's all free for those who find their way to this inn. Now sit. I should have some stew ready for you soon." He did as told, not wanting to offend the woman after her kindness. This also was part of her religious service. Refusing her hospitality would not only be rude but possibly an insult to her beliefs. Corwyn found his way to the fireplace, joining the two others, who still hadn't shown much interest in his arrival.

"Hello." The two figures sat in opposite chairs, framing the hearth. He opted for a wooden bench between them, allowing an unobstructed view of the crackling logs. The man who sat at his right looked to have seen about seventy or so winters. He said nothing. The woman on Corwyn's left nodded politely. He figured her about thirty. Haggard and road weary, they sat around the fire in a half-awake, half-asleep state, which caused him some slight unease as he took ownership of the backless bench.

He placed his wet socks and boots close to the blaze and tried relaxing. After a few moments he felt the cold and moisture in his bones drying along with his drenched hair and skin like steam rising from a mug of hot cider. The sound of the rain on the roof, like horse hooves galloping down the road, was so hypnotic he didn't even realize he'd fallen into a similar trance of his own until a large wooden bowl, brimming with mutton stew, rested in his lap.

"Here you go," his hostess said from beside him.

"Thanks." The hearty aroma reminded him of his previous hunger.

"I'm sure you're famished, so eat up." She handed him a wooden spoon. "Might be good for you to get to know some of your fellow patrons, too." She stood at her full height again, a few fingers above five and a half feet. "Travelers to this inn are quite unique and have a good many tales to tell those who'd listen."

"I don't doubt that," said Corwyn. Stirring the stew increased his hunger. "So, I guess I can start with you," he addressed his hostess. "What's your name?"

"Molly Darkwode, priestess of Asorlok and keeper of this inn and the graveyard beside it," she replied with a curtsy.

"Corwyn Danther."

"Corwyn, eh?" A pleasant expression washed across Molly's face. "I've heard of you, I think. Some say you're the most famed bard in all the Midlands."

"Well, that's yet to be proven," he said, digging into his stew. He wouldn't resist the urge any longer. To his delight he found it quite delectable. There were carrots and parsnips, onions, and chunks of mutton. And there was something else . . . a combination of spices he'd never tasted before. "This is wonderful," he said between bites.

"Just something I've found helps those who visit get filled and whole before moving on again." Molly motioned at the two others gathered around the fire. "If you're a bard, then you should listen to their tales. I think you'll find them rather interesting." At that, she left him alone with his stew.

Corwyn peered over at the younger woman between bites. She gave him a weak smile. He returned the grin. Upon closer inspection, he noticed her dress looked slightly older than what he thought currently in fashion. Maybe she'd come in the rain and changed her clothes too.

"Is it true?" the young woman asked with a soft voice.

"Is *what* true?"

"That you're a bard?"

"Yes. I'm a bard." He sat a little taller on the bench.

"Then you must hear me."

"Why's that?" he asked, absently stirring the stew. He wasn't entirely comfortable with the desperation in her voice and face.

"I've been told bards like to hear tales and songs and then tell them to others to enjoy." The desperation hadn't left her eyes. Instead, it was joined by a swelling excitement, making for a very odd and slightly off-putting mix.

"Most do, yes."

"Then hear mine, please," she begged, leaning forward on her chair. He would have pushed the bench back with his sudden jerk, but it was rather heavy and didn't budge. Seeing his reaction, she sat back apologetically. "Please, I mean no harm. It's been so long since anyone has heard my song . . . I just want someone to hear it before I go."

A strange, icy pang jabbed his heart. He actually found himself pitying the woman. With a slow breath, he told himself to be still . . . for now. It would probably rain for a while longer—the horses on the roof hadn't even slowed to a trot—and he was still damp. What harm could there be in listening? In the very least it'd help pass the time . . . *and*, like Molly had hinted, he might learn something new in the process.

"Then please share your song." Instantly, the woman's face lit up, but the deadness in her eyes remained. For a long moment she said nothing, merely staring at Corwyn with the same overjoyed expression—motionless.

"Everything okay?"

"I-I just have to find a way to begin. I haven't sung it in so long I don't know how to start."

"How about we start with your name, since you've already heard mine." He took another spoonful of stew.

"I'm Jenna Gridley."

"Pleased to meet you, Jenna. What's your song about?"

"Well, it's a love song really." She blushed.

"Tragic?"

"I guess so."

"Those make the best kind." Corwyn grinned, swallowing more stew before resting the bowl on his lap and giving Jenna his full attention. "There's something about love and loss that endears a tale and song to the heart and makes it hard to forget." He watched her fidget with her hands on her lap. "Take a deep breath. Close your eyes. Forget anyone is here and sing your song." He glanced at the other man, but he remained stoic and apparently unconcerned with anything around him.

Jenna feebly nodded and did as Corwyn advised. She scrunched her eyes tight, then released them with a heavy, hard breath. Then she started to sing.

He'd heard many a song of love and sorrow, but none quite as elegant as this. The tone was earthy and grounded in personal experience; when it blended with the woman's high voice, the expression was wonderfully surreal.

The song enraptured him. He clung to every verse and followed the narrative telling of true love between a young man and woman who lived during the Shadow Years. The man was a warrior for the army of Gondad and had to follow the army in its bloody wars for many a year, leaving his love behind.

She waited for him, living on nothing but her love for the young warrior, for she couldn't eat or even sleep in his absence. The man, for his part, spurned the advances of the army camp wenches in honor of her, even though he wasn't sure he'd ever see her again. The war raged on; their love held true. Yet neither was fated to see the other alive again.

The young man died in battle, whispering the name of his love on his lips. The wind carried it to the ears of the young woman, who then knew her true love was dead. Heart stricken, she threw herself from a cliff so she could be with him in death because she couldn't bear being without him in life.

A tragic tale, and one quite common in most circles Corwyn frequented, but the song endeared itself to him. While the performance was very original, some other quality he couldn't quite place added much more than what the lyrics alone provided.

Jenna opened her eyes.

"That was quite lovely." He smiled. Another check on the older man revealed him the same as before. It mattered little to Jenna, though, who acted as if only she and Corwyn occupied the room.

"Thank you." She blushed.

"So, are *you* a bard?"

Jenna shook her head as if it was the silliest thing she'd ever heard. "Oh, I'm no bard, but I do have a song or two in me to sing. At least that's what my father always said."

"I'd say he was right."

Jenna's blush deepened with a smile. This one wasn't as meek—even showing a fair number of teeth. "Well," she said, rising from her seat, "thank you for listening. If you could perhaps pass it on in your travels, I'd be most grateful. I'm going to retire now. If you will excuse me."

"Rest well," Corwyn said with a nod.

Jenna stopped, swinging her still cheery face over her shoulder. "Gods bless you." She then made her way into the shadows and out of sight.

Corwyn continued ruminating over the interaction while he went for his stew. It had cooled during the song but was still warm and, oddly enough, even more flavorful than his last spoonful. His thoughts were interrupted when the older man suddenly spoke up.

"I have a tale for you too, if you'd be so kind as to listen."

Corwyn concealed his surprise. "If you have something to share, I certainly won't stop you. After all, it's great weather for it." He waved the spoon at the roof for emphasis.

"So it is." The man's voice was gravelly and worn like an old wheel rut ground deep into the road. "I have a myth to tell," he continued. Though more active than before, his eyes were as dead as Jenna's. In truth, Corwyn thought he probably looked the same to the man. After resting for a while, he'd found out just how much his soggy journey had taken out of him.

"About what?"

"It's an older myth, that's for sure. I doubt many, if any, have heard it but me." He shared a wrinkled grin. "Since I made it up, mind you."

"So, a *very* rare tale, indeed." Once he'd started speaking, the man was more at ease than Jenna. His manner was actually very engaging and grandfatherly.

"It has a meaning too," he continued while getting comfortable in his chair.

"The best ones usually do. What's it about?"

A mischievous sparkle flashed in his eyes before drowning in the previous dullness. "Just keep your horse in the barn. You'll hear it in a moment ..."

He figured the man was rehearsing the tale's spine—making sure all the points were in place—before starting. It was a common ploy for storytellers. Corwyn did it himself from time to time.

"Back when the world was still new, Dradin and Causilla visited a city each wanted to have worship them as their patron. This city was barely getting started, as most were in those ancient days, and each god came offering something that would advance the city into higher levels of civilization. These gifts, of course, were predicated on the understanding that the citizens would make the chosen god the patron of their city.

"This event wasn't new; it had been repeated in other cities by other gods. But this time Dradin and Causilla made a contest out of whose gift was the best for mortalkind. To ensure fairness, each god would present their gift and then let a mortal judge decide which of the gifts was best for the city, thereby declaring the bestowing god the victor. The honor of judging this contest was given to a simple sage said to be the wisest in the city and therefore the best suited to make such a judgment.

"The first to present their gift was Dradin. He offered to shower the city in knowledge and learning—to make it the envy of the world for the insight they'd all possess. He said he'd grant them all incredible amounts of knowledge and they would be as wise as gods in many things. This was a tempting offer, but the sage waited to hear what Causilla would counter it with. She, for her part, offered much too, saying she'd enrich the city with art: sculpture and song, illustration and painting, taletelling, and much more.

"This too was a very generous offer, for each truly wanted to have the city as their own. And while the sage was still a wise man, he didn't want to take a chance with his city and what he saw as a hard and possibly dangerous choice between the two deities. So he bided his time as best he could while he thought through each offer. Finally, the gods pressed him for an answer. They didn't understand why such generous offers would require so much deliberation. But when the sage told them his reply, both deities were amazed.

" 'You offer much, Dradin, for books and scrolls, and the knowledge they contain, are a good thing and needed for any city to thrive, but if there are no people in the city to read the books or apply the knowledge they bring, then of what use are they? While you do make a generous offer, I will have to decline such a gracious gift.

" 'You offer the arts, Causilla, and they too are wonderful. Towering statues of heroes gone by, drawings of family and friends, plays and songs and dances . . . But if there is no one in the city to enjoy the plays, to hear the songs, or appreciate the art, then what good are these things? So too your offer I must decline.'

"Each god was perplexed and asked the sage to explain himself, for they had never foreseen any mortal turning down their charity. The sage then explained his reply:

" 'Please take no offense at what I've chosen to say, great ones. I have my reasons, which I will now share. It occurred to me while pondering your offers I better understood the nature of the city in which I live—what makes it up and why any city can be called great or alive in the first place. For a city is not a collection of buildings or laws or art or knowledge; it is a collection of people. They are what make any city great. It's true just laws and righteous living improve and indeed prolong the successful existence of a city, but if there could be such a thing as laws existing without people, then there would be no city over which they could govern.

" 'While we could have great art or knowledge, what would they be without the blessing of people to enjoy them? For a piece of art is only an inanimate thing—little different than a tree or rock. A book or scroll is the same. A citizen, though, is far more important than these things and actually elevates these inanimate items rather than being elevated by them. And that's why I have to refuse both your offers. They do not add to the city's true worth, as its truest patrons are its people.'

"When the sage had finished speaking, both gods left in peace to think about what was said, while the city where the sage lived thrived throughout his lifetime and beyond.

"Do you understand the meaning?" The man's wizened face peered straight into Corwyn's with his strange dead eyes.

"I do." It would have been pretty hard not to miss such a blatant meaning, though he had to admit—even if it *was* freshly crafted—it made a good myth. With a little polish and tweaking to its rhythm and flow—

"Then it's yours. Use it well, for I never will." The man stood and made his way from the fire. "About time I go back to sleep too," he continued before stopping midstep. He turned back to Corwyn. His eyes locked hard upon him, reflecting the firelight like hollow glass balls. "Use it well." This said, he entered the flickering shadows and was lost to Corwyn's sight.

He ate the rest of his stew in silence and felt warm again. And with that warmth, a full belly, and the rain above, sluggishness overtook him. He didn't realize how tired he must have been until he felt his eyelids growing heavy. He thought he could hold out a while longer—thoroughly dry out before asking for a room for the night.

He was wrong.

He woke to a cold hearth. He was still on the bench. He marveled at how he'd managed to stay on it through his slumber. Thank Causilla for small favors. He could tell it was morning by the muffled bird chirps outside the building.

Rising, he stretched, discovering his body wasn't as sore as he'd thought it would be from sleeping in such an awkward position. He didn't see Molly anywhere, just a dark, silent interior that made the hair on the back of his neck stand up. How had this place lost so much of its life in only one evening? The door swung open, spilling in welcome daylight and forcing him to put a hand to his eyes.

"Ah good," said Molly. "I thought you might be up. I've made breakfast for you outside, should you care to take any. Hope you didn't mind sleeping on the bench. I was going to wake you, but you seemed so restful, and you needed the sleep, so I let you stay. It was a small miracle you didn't fall."

"I actually slept fairly well," he said as his hostess' plump frame came into full focus. "Causilla knows I've had far worse places to lay my head. But breakfast does sound good." He made an effort to straighten his crumpled clothing and ran a hand through his slightly tangled hair. "Just give me a moment to clean up and I'll be right out."

"There's some water in a basin—the last door on your left," she said, pointing to the stairs. "A fresh towel too, and anything else you might need."

"Thank you." Corwyn climbed the steps, dry boots and socks in hand. "When you're finished, you can join me in the cemetery."

Outside he found the new day much to his liking. The storm had freshened the air. Small songbirds in the grasses and stringy trees around the worn road and inn greeted him with playful song.

As he entered the cemetery, the wet grass licked at the dry but mud-caked boots and the cuffs of his borrowed pants. He wanted a closer look at the statue of Asorlok at its center. The figure wasn't as ominous as it seemed the night before. Indeed, any hint of darkness it might have harbored had been washed away in the rain. Now it just looked like a regular statue, worn from the elements.

Molly sat at the statue's base. A red cloth covered a section of the soft, damp grass encircling the sculpture. She rested upon the cloth alongside a platter of sausages, a hunk of cheese, and a round loaf of dark rye bread. She was reaching for a pitcher that stood in between all this food when Corwyn approached.

"Good morning." She cheerily poured what looked like milk into two wooden cups.

"When did you have time to make all this? I didn't hear or smell any of it."

"I cooked it outside, since it was such a nice day and I didn't want to wake you," she explained, returning the pitcher to its resting place.

"Are the others going to join us?" He took a seat on the edge of the cloth farthest away from the statue. While it might not have been as forbidding, he still wasn't in the mood to cozy up to it. It *was* supposed to be Asorlok, after all.

"No." She handed him a wooden plate, copper fork, and knife. "They've already departed."

"Strange place to have a picnic," he said, taking in the gravestones. Now that he was seated, they were level with his gaze, giving him the impression of being literally surrounded by reminders of death.

"I think it's a bit restful and reflective." She cut off a few pieces of cheese from the large chunk.

"How so?" He did his best to keep his attention on Molly and away from the headstones.

"There are very few places you can go that are unaffected by time," she said, offering him some cheese. Corwyn took a few slices. "You can walk through the woods but it's always changing, always moving and growing, because it's alive." She next offered sausages and a few slices of the rye bread, which he also received.

"But a cemetery is dead," he said before taking a bite of the bread. It was still warm and very good.

"Yes," said Molly, busying herself with filling her own plate. "Here time has stopped. There are very few places like it on Tralodren."

"And why is that good?" Corwyn bit into his sausage, discovering it was warm and flavorful venison. If anything could be said of his hostess, she certainly knew how to cook.

"It's good for reflection." Molly began eating as well. "Sages study dead things and learn from them. I think we can and should do the same from time to time."

"Study *corpses*?" He almost choked at the notion.

Molly chuckled. "Not corpses, but ideas. They study dead ideas, nations, even years long past, and learn from them. I think it wise we look back and think about the days that were and see what we can discover and learn from them so our days to come might be brighter."

"Forgive me," he said, taking a swallow of milk—and cold milk at that. "But I've never heard of Asorlins being so philosophical."

"Not all of us are. I'm of a sect that sees Asorlok as the god of journeys. For life is one long journey toward death, which is itself just another journey into what lies beyond. It's like I told you last night: I keep this small inn as a resting place for those on their journey and maintain the cemetery beside it. That's what my beliefs have led me to do. Other Asorlins have different ideas about what Asorlok wants and pursue those agendas."

"I see," he said, biting off more bread. "So why don't you wear the Silver Cross like all the other priests do?"

"I'm of a slightly different conviction than my fellow Asorlins. I wear it only when certain occasions call for it."

Corwyn washed the rest of his curiosity away with another swallow of milk. "So, who's buried here? What town, I mean? I didn't see any on my travels."

"Not too many anymore, that's true enough. And as you can see, it's filled to near capacity anyway."

A quick survey reminded him of how many graves were present. He'd missed in the rain how they filled every available spot. "No villages nearby then?" He renewed his focus on Molly.

"Not for many a mile."

"So then, who's buried here?"

"Those who came to find their way here."

"I don't understand."

"This is a special cemetery. It houses the dead who found their own way to it."

"You're starting to get cryptic on me now."

"Yes, I am, aren't I?" Molly pointed out a headstone left of Corwyn's shoulder. Following her direction, he peered at the worn marker and the writing carved upon it.

"Jenna Gridley? But I just spoke to her last night, and this headstone looks like it's been here for fifty years."

"Seventy-five, actually."

Suddenly, a rather unpleasant thought captured his attention. "So those two people I talked to last night . . . were they—"

"Not in that way, but they were dead." Molly's answer was far from comforting. "Don't worry about trying to make sense of it," she added, taking another draft from her cup. "It won't change your path anyway. You're not destined for this graveyard and those like it."

"So you killed them and I was talking to their *ghosts*?"

"Nothing of the sort." She motioned for calm. "Peace, Corwyn. I'm not as black blooded as some would have you believe. Those here kill themselves long before they're buried, and then find their way here." Seeing his obvious confusion and discomfort, Molly changed the topic. "What happened to you last night with those two patrons?"

"I was sitting by the fire and they spoke to me."

"What did they say?"

"Jenna"—he shot another glance over at her tombstone—"wanted me to hear a song she'd composed, and the other—"

He stopped. He couldn't recall the man's name.

"He never gave you his name, but you can find the headstone of Devin Jilth if you go wandering near the eastern corner of the wall."

"Well, he wanted to tell me a myth he'd made up." Corwyn's appetite was gone. He may have had an open mind, but this was still an uneasy matter to be discussing—and in a *cemetery* of all places.

Molly looked Corwyn straight in the eye. He felt the touch of that gaze all the way into his spirit and started inching further away from her. "They and many like them have waited for a long time to share what they've kept locked inside."

"I beg your pardon, but—"

"I'm not here to harm you, Corwyn. I'm trying to teach you something, if you'll let me. Where do you think the greatest wealth lies?"

"I suppose the greatest wealth would be what the dranors collected in the greatest of their capitals."

"A creative answer but not the best by far, nor the truest." She pulled out a small copper coin emblazoned with the mark of Romain: a stylized lion wearing a crown and standing on its hind legs looking to its right. The obverse bore the profile of Jacob III, Romain's king. "This is just a hunk of metal, like all the coins we use. It's a means of exchange—nothing more. It only has value because a good many of us ascribe value to it. Should you take it into a strange and wild land where they don't welcome it, you'll find how impractical it is. For you can't use it as protection from the elements, it doesn't keep you warm, you can't even eat it. It's simply a means of exchange because we say it is. It has value because we say it does.

"Here"—she indicated the cemetery—"are greater treasures than the world can fathom. Here you'll find poems, songs and tales, ideas for new weapons and defenses, new inventions to ease the toil of mortalkind, and many, many more amazing finds. They're here just waiting for someone to use. Sadly, many who had been given these ideas let them die with them instead of sharing them."

"So, this graveyard is the richest spot on Tralodren?"

"Not only this graveyard, but *all* places where people have died before they've had a chance to share the ideas they'd been given." Molly stood, dusting stray rye crumbs from her skirt. "You weren't expecting a philosophy lesson today, eh?" Her pleasant smile melted all previous concerns away.

"Not really, no." He joined her on his feet.

"I think you'll benefit from this insight, however," she continued, motioning to Jenna's gravestone. "When Jenna was buried, she was dead years before that. That song she shared—and she had a few more—was a seed she carried and needed to plant outside herself to grow. But she didn't, and it, and the others keeping it company, remained locked away until she died." Staring at Corwyn with a serious eye, she asked, "Do you understand?"

He wrinkled his brow at Molly's claim. "I didn't expect I'd ever hear an Asorlin taking about the importance of *life*."

"Just because you're awake and moving doesn't mean you're alive. Many people are awake but never embrace the fullness of living. Those who don't live while alive end up leaving behind a rich trove of treasure for others to exploit."

"You mean their unplanted ideas and dreams? So that's what you do here, then? *Exploit* those treasures?"

Molly's expression remained calm and inviting. "My order is misunderstood, but you already know that. What I do here is twofold. First, I help travelers on their journeys, as with you and yours. Second, I guard over this cemetery and give rest to those lying here. However, only those who wish to have their seeds sown after death wind up here and at similar localities, as Asorlok wills."

"So no one is ever actually buried here?" He studied the cemetery once again, working his way through the varying thoughts swirling inside his skull.

"No, they find their way here *after* death, Asorlok willing, and then to people like you. Though people die and their spirits pass on, not all ideas perish easily; they struggle for a chance to be born. I tend those ideas, passing them on to those who can give them life so they too can achieve a sense of purpose in the world."

"So it wasn't really Jenna who I spoke to last night, nor Devin . . ." He watched Molly closely as he put everything into place. "It was only their *ideas*—the song and the myth. It was *part* of them, but *not* them."

Molly nodded. "They wanted a chance to pass on these ideas and dreams. Fear and other obstacles, whether self-made, imagined, or real, hindered them while they lived—but they wanted to have their seeds scattered in order to grow after death. Some were given to you to sow last night. They're a part of you now as much as your own ideas are part of you." She started cleaning up what remained of their picnic while Corwyn studied the statue of Asorlok with a renewed interest, fascinated by the keys in his right hand. The fourteen keys legends told opened the fourteen gates to the afterlife.

A god of journeys . . .

"How many more are here? How many more ideas and dreams?"

Molly had nearly finished her work when she found Corwyn's face. "More than you can birth in your lifetime. You took your fill last night. Best you move on with your own journey."

He fell silent, pondering a while longer. How long, he didn't know, for this place felt timeless somehow. But when he did begin registering the passage of time, he noticed Molly was gone, along with the food and red cloth. Based on the sun, it was getting closer to late morning—well past time he returned to the inn. Inside he found Molly behind a long counter lined with a handful of stools. A bundle of red cloth and a hat rested in front of her. Corwyn's walking stick leaned against the counter next to them.

Again, the inn remained an odd thing. In the morning light it seemed a hollow shell—a castoff memory slowly fading through time. Even the air felt dusty and ancient, wizened from lack of use. Yet the sensation wasn't sinister. Rather, it was exciting. There was a hint of stumbling into a forgotten room or hidden ruin still glimmering with the prospect of finding some lost treasure nearby.

"I suppose you'll be on your way now."

"How long was I out there?" he asked.

"Long enough. I packed a little something for you." She placed a hand on the cloth-wrapped package before her. "I got your gear ready for your trip, too. If you start out now, you should make it to a village by nightfall."

"So, are *you* real, then?" Corwyn drew closer to the counter.

Molly shared her now-familiar and comforting maternal grin. "Real enough for you. When I do die, I'll be in Sheol working with my fellow priests in service to Asorlok. For now, I tend to mortalkind and their needs as best I'm able." He knew he wasn't getting any more out of her on the subject. And did it really matter anyway? He supposed not.

"I didn't have a hat when I came," he said upon noticing one placed among the items on the counter. "The gear's mine. So is the walking stick, but—"

"You have one now," she said, handing it to him. The hat was woven of prairie grass, with a cylindrical crown and a wide brim expanding out around it and curving up more on the sides than the front or back. Two thin strands of leather fell from inside the crown as he took it from her—a chin strap.

He placed the hat back on the counter. His attention focused on the clothes she'd let him borrow. "I only slept in these one night. They shouldn't be soiled—"

"Keep those too. It's the way of this place. Those who come, should they need new clothing, take up what others have shed before. I'll wash what you left and get it ready for the next traveler who finds his way here. I thought you might like a hat, though."

Corwyn paused, his gaze going from Molly to the hat and back again. "Try it on." She motioned for him to do so. He gently placed it on his head. "It suits you." She shot him a crooked grin.

"I think you're right," he found himself saying, much to his amazement. Oddly, it fit him perfectly and somehow made him feel better about the journey ahead, though he didn't quite know why.

Molly handed him his walking stick in one hand, gear in the other. "You have many more things to do, I'm sure, before you die. Folks who live life, like you, often do."

Corwyn gratefully took the items. "You sure I don't owe you anything?"

She shook her head. "You've done more than enough for those who needed your aid. Good journey."

He tipped his new hat toward Molly and made his way out the door. He'd cleared the porch and started down the road when the temptation for one last look got the better of him. Turning, he found nothing but a wide expanse of flat plains. The inn and the cemetery next to it were gone.

He wasn't the least bit surprised. Molly had said he'd found the inn ... or had the inn found him? No matter, it was gone now, and he wasn't going to try to figure out the workings of Asorlok and his priests. He had enough of a time keeping abreast of his own religion and beliefs. And it wasn't getting any earlier, either. If he wanted to get anywhere by nightfall, like Molly said, he'd have to get moving.

Before him the sun-brightened road stretched onward. Walking stick in hand, new hat on his head, Corwyn continued his trek. The birds shared a sweet melody as the inn faded into a pleasant memory. As he walked, he hummed. It was an old song about a tragic love affair between a soldier in the army of Gondad and the woman who loved him.

CHARITY FOR HALFLINGS

"Stupid waste of time." Fredrick's caustic words seethed in the pleasant early evening air. Corwyn strode beside him, walking stick in hand. Though a foot taller than the dwarf, the auburn-haired bard made sure he didn't outdistance his friend.

They were traveling Riverford Way: a dusty, wheel-rut-worn dirt road that flowed out of Romain, the capital city of the kingdom of the same name. It wove through the Grasslands of Gondad into the southern portion of the kingdom, where it became lost in a mixture of trails, smaller footpaths, and a handful of other roads on the outskirts of Romain's influence. The road took its name from Riverford, the first town outside the royal city, to which Corwyn and Fredrick were returning after their fruitless search for some ruins a fair distance to the south.

"So the ruins weren't that impressive," Corwyn confessed. "At least we were able to see more of the land." He was enjoying the soft wind tickling the grass on either side of them. Every so often an unseen bird would take up another part of the soft melody that had traveled along with them since early morning.

"There's nothing here but grasslands, Corwyn," said Fredrick, waving his hand across the landscape. "Grasslands and farms. And those ruins weren't even *ruins*." He shifted the weight of the pack on his back, grumbling inaudibly into his beard.

Fredrick was right. The trip back, like the one to their destination, wasn't much of a sight. A few clumps of trees popped up here and there in lonely clusters, but other than that, they saw nothing but fields of tall grass and dull brown road.

"Well, yes, they *were* actually ruins." He tried for some optimism.

Fredrick's orangish-brown eyes shot him a glance as if he were a father correcting his son's folly. "They were two piles of rock and a pillar. Two *small* piles. That's not what I'd call a ruin."

"What would you call it then?"

"A rock dump." Like all dwarves, Fredrick had gray skin, a charcoal sort of hue, and was a bit stocky, standing just below five feet. A hill dwarf from the Rollandheim Clan, who made their home in the hills of the same name nestled around the eastern edge of the Diamant Mountains, he constantly wore a serious face.

"I suppose we should reach Riverford by tomorrow night if we can keep up a good pace." Corwyn focused back on the road.

"Well, at least we didn't get into trouble."

"I said you didn't have to come with me. You could have stayed back at the inn."

"I came to protect you. You know that. Until you learn to take more care in these exploits of yours, someone has to keep you breathing. Besides, if you allow strangers to dress you, it just proves how *much* you need my help." Corwyn still wore the hat and the rest of the clothing he received from Molly at the wayfarer's inn, swapping them out as needed for performances.

"I told you how I got them."

"I know. That's what worries me. How do you know she didn't get them from corpses? She could have looted that graveyard you told me about and then just piled it up.

"That's your problem. You're too trusting. You could have been chatting with some murderer or one of them folks who like snuggling up to dead bodies, but you just trust them all the same."

Given the reaction after he'd shared his story about Molly, Corwyn was glad he'd kept the matter of meeting Lena to himself. It was more personal anyway—something he probably wouldn't share with anyone for some time, if at all.

"The hat might be a bit much," he admitted, tapping its brim. He'd grown rather fond of it, to Fredrick's obvious displeasure.

"That might be an understatement." Fredrick snorted. "You look like a pirate. A *halfling* pirate."

"Better than a sour dwarf."

"That a jab at how *I'm* dressed?" Fredrick wore a dark green long-sleeved tunic with brown pants and cordovan shoes. On the left of his wide chestnut belt a silver loop held his mace. A sheath for his dagger was on the right.

"No."

"If you think you're so funny, you can carry this backpack all the way to Riverford." Fredrick shifted the pack's weight with a huff.

"I wouldn't dream of upsetting you," he teased.

Fredrick let out another huff of hot air, rustling his braided mustache. He kept his full beard shorter and rounder than those of his fellow clansmen. Even the braided, green-tipped strand dangling over his chest was modest.

It seemed they were ready for a change of topic. "You up for a show again?"

"What? Out here?"

"Why not? Riverford, Spole, or even Romain would be fine places for a performance."

"*Spole?*" Fredrick snorted snidely in protest. "It's a *village*, Corwyn. Hayseeds and sheep. You really think you can get any coin there?" He shook his head. "Riverford would be better, but not by much. At least they have a decent tavern hall for putting on shows."

"I'm thinking about promoting my name in the area. We haven't been this far into Romain in a while, and with my recent absence things need some stirring up again."

"Your recent *vampire* absence?" Fredrick raised an eyebrow.

"Yes, *that* absence."

"Pity the halfling lived through it. That must have made a long trip back home."

"Longer than I cared for. At least *I* got dropped off on Talatheal. *They* had to go all the way back to Breanna."

"Maybe you should skip the small-potatoes crowd and head right for King Morgan himself. I'm sure he and Egrain would like the entertainment, and it would shoot you up the ranks, if you're worried about having been knocked down a peg or two."

"No, not yet. I'd rather be asked by the king than invite myself."

"Dreaming big, eh?"

"Why not? You tend to get what you expect."

Fredrick grunted. "So, you're for Riverford?"

"If we get there at a decent hour and there's a place to have performances, sure." Corwyn waved to a dirty farmer walking a field of wheat. The same returned the gesture before continuing his inspection. Out of the corner of his eye he saw Fredrick shaking his head in obvious disapproval.

"And if it's a hayseed pig stall?"

"If we can't get a decent place, then we'll move on to Romain, I suppose. But I want to have at least one performance in the area before wintering in Haven."

"Well, the others will want to do something. They're probably getting bored out of their minds while we've been off chasing old wives' tales. And it's not like coins are falling out of—"

"You're still mad about the money, aren't you?" Corwyn stopped and faced him.

"What do *you* think?" he asked, crossing his arms. "They said it would be filled with treasures."

"Oh come on, Fred." Corwyn rolled his eyes. "You didn't buy that part, did you?"

"*You* certainly bought the idea of ruins being out here quick enough," Fredrick countered, eyes as stern as stone.

"*That* at least sounded plausible. There are a lot of ruins all across this region. You can't expect them to all have treasure though—not when they're so close to civilization. They're bound to have had their fair share of looters over the years."

"So why go if not for profit?"

"There's more to ruins than just digging for coin."

"Oh no, here we go again." Fredrick rolled his eyes with a low moan. "The talk about how one travels and explores to learn and develop a better understanding of themselves and the world about them."

Corwyn said nothing, merely stared.

"*What?*" Fredrick lifted his hands in surrender.

"You don't think we learned anything today?"

"Sure we did. We learned to not trust people who say they know where some ruins are and then take your money."

"You didn't learn anything from the surrounding terrain or the travel itself?"

"Only that we should have paid for horses or maybe a coach or wagon. The trip took too long." He resumed his walking.

Corwyn sighed and joined him. "You know, if you don't start learning to enjoy life, you're just going to get even more sour with age."

"I'm a dwarf. Don't expect too many miracles."

The rest of their walk was a rather quiet affair. Night found them near a small grove of lanky maples. Fredrick continually muttered into his beard while he finished making his makeshift bed. Corwyn had already established equally simple accommodations and reclined against a tree, hat cocked low over his eyes.

"Should be a nice night."

"Still can't believe they don't have anything but farmlands out here." Fredrick finally finished his task. "You'd think they'd put in a hamlet here or there. It doesn't seem to be an efficient use of all this open space."

"They're farmers. Be thankful they and the others like them are out here, else you wouldn't be able to get all that rye bread you enjoy."

"I'm sure I'd adapt if there was ever a shortage." He lowered himself against a trunk and into his simple bed.

"I think it's quite enjoyable."

"This from the man who thinks searching for rock dumps is rewarding," Fredrick continued, adjusting himself into a comfortable position.

"Good night, Fredrick." Corwyn let the chirping crickets and occasional rustling leaves lull him into a restful slumber.

A twig snap and an intrusive, nasally voice woke him.

"Stand and deliver your money or your life." Corwyn opened his eyes, peering up into the moonlit surroundings at what appeared to be six or seven short figures standing at the base of the spindly maples.

"Corwyn?" Fredrick asked from beside him.

"I'm awake," he assured him.

"I said stand and deliver, vermin." The nasally tone was punctuated by the impact of a crossbow bolt hitting the trunk just above Fredrick's head. He rose with a growl, mace in hand. Corwyn slowly made his way to his feet, easily towering over all the other figures. Their hooded visitors stood even shorter than Fredrick.

"Keep your ground," the nasal-voiced figure snapped at Fredrick, "or you'll soon find yourself like the dog who chased the porcupine." Corwyn subtly motioned for Fredrick to keep back. He couldn't see much about or around the cloaked figures. And if *he* couldn't, he knew Fredrick couldn't either.

"You're *highwaymen*?" he asked the one he believed first addressed them, assuming he was their leader.

"Not just *any* highwaymen. You have the pleasure of being robbed by *Jarnelle's Blackguards*, the most *dashing* and *deadly* brigands to claim this territory as their own." The one who'd first spoken stepped closer. Corwyn assumed it was Jarnelle himself. He couldn't make out anything under the hood but did see the reloaded crossbow aimed in their direction just fine.

"Now kindly hand over your valuables and you can return to your slumber with your lives intact." Corwyn could hear the wicked mirth in the other's tone. He also detected something else about the way he was speaking Telboros.

"You're halflings."

"*Halflings?*" Fredrick shook his head with disgust. "We're being robbed by *halflings*? This is so humiliating."

"No," Jarnelle snapped. "Your outfit is humiliating." A low murmured chuckling erupted among the others behind Jarnelle, further elevating Fredrick's ire. "Hand over the valuables, or we'll take them from your corpses."

"Get behind me, Corwyn." Fredrick boldly stepped forward, right hand gripping his mace. "I'll have them running home to whatever rock they crawled out from under before they can—"

As one, the halflings focused their crossbows on him.

"No, Fred." Corwyn placed his hand on the dwarf's shoulder, pulling him back.

"Don't be stupid," Fredrick growled, never taking his eyes from Jarnelle. "There could be more out there than we know."

"You don't know that—it's too dark to get a clear count."

"Exactly." Corwyn focused again on Jarnelle and the crossbows. "How do we know you won't kill us if we cooperate?"

"You have my word as a gentleman." Jarnelle gave a courteous nod.

Fredrick snorted. "The word of a *halfling*? That's about as good as wearing armor made of meat and trying to defend yourself from starving bears." A frigid stillness followed his words. It was jagged like a shard of glass. Corwyn could feel the tension cutting into them. Tension, he imagined, causing some twitching in the small halfling fingers resting on triggers.

"We shall see who mocks whom when this is over, you disgusting mound of hair and dirt." Jarnelle's voice grew increasingly nasal as it swelled in rage, his accent even more pronounced. "We may be thieves, but we still hold to what made our forefathers great—like bathing."

Corwyn could imagine Fredrick's knuckles whitening around the handle of his mace. He applied more pressure on his friend's shoulder in compensation, praying it'd be enough to keep him in place.

"Now, start handing over your valuables. We haven't got all night," Jarnelle said in a slightly calmer voice.

Neither Corwyn nor Fredrick moved.

"Oh dear." The halfling inched closer, bringing his crossbow nearly right on center with Fredrick's nose. Corwyn could feel Fredrick's whole body readying to pounce. "Do your ears need cleaning with a good blast of bolt?"

"You can't take them all in this darkness," Corwyn repeated. "You're bound to get a bolt stuck in you somewhere, and you know I'm not the world's best healer."

"Don't remind me," Fredrick muttered.

"I'm running out of patience, gentlemen, and losing my willingness to let you live."

Corwyn shot Fredrick a quick glance they'd often shared on both the road and the stage. It said for him to follow Corwyn's lead. Fredrick gave a small nod and Corwyn released his shoulder.

"I'm afraid we don't have any real valuables to hand over."

"Don't give me that." Jarnelle's tone grew crasser. "We can all see you have coin by how you dress. You're not one of these dirty hayseeds, so hand it over . . . *now*." The other cloaked halflings drew closer, surrounding Corwyn and Fredrick in a semicircle. He counted ten. Though their cloaks hid much from view, their crossbows were in plain sight—steel-tipped bolts twinkled like deadly stars in the moonlight.

"We have a smattering of coin." Corwyn moved into what he knew Fredrick would recognize as his performance voice. It wasn't overly dramatic, but nuanced and polished in certain ways, making it easier to effect a desired emotional response from his listeners. "But there *is* something more valuable than anything else we carry on our person."

"And what's that?"

He paused, giving the impression of someone struggling against sharing anything else.

"Corwyn?" Fredrick jumped in right on cue with the perfect measure of rising anger and concern.

"What good is it if we're both dead?" He made a show of replying, making sure the sense of absolute surrender lingered on the edge of his voice.

"Whatever it is"—Jarnelle was clearly losing patience—"let's have it."

"It's in my shirt pocket," said Corwyn.

"Check his pocket." Jarnelle motioned to Corwyn with his crossbow. A halfling at Jarnelle's left followed the command. The height difference was rather comical. If another had passed by, they easily could have thought they saw a small child robbing an adult.

"Hand it over . . . slowly." This halfling had a froggy voice, further adding to the surreal nature of the event. His face was still hidden, but Corwyn could see the hint of a scruffy, flabby face bobbing in and out amid the hood's shadows. He also couldn't help noticing the tang of sour wine and the odor of stale tobacco.

"Very well." He did as told, reaching inside his shirt pocket and slowly retrieving a folded piece of parchment.

"What are you doing?!" Fredrick was angrier and more concerned, even stepping toward Corwyn for good measure.

"Shut up, hairy." Jarnelle jabbed his crossbow in Fredrick's general direction before turning to the froggy-throated halfling. "Bring it here."

The other did as ordered, fetching the parchment from Corwyn with his left hand while keeping his right on the crossbow; finger on the trigger, he backed away until he'd rejoined his comrades. Jarnelle snatched the parchment away and unfolded it with one hand, keeping the crossbow in his other still pointed at Fredrick.

"So, what is this?" Jarnelle inquired after a rapid glance.

"A map to some ruins," Corwyn answered flatly.

"Big deal. Now you're just wasting my—"

"Ruins we were told were filled with treasure," he quickly added.

"Shut up already!" Fredrick pretended to be fuming.

"No, *you* shut up! You mop-faced, soiled-rag-wearing cave dweller." Jarnelle sneered under his hood. "Your friend's trying to save *both* your lives, and you're making it harder for him to keep us from filling you full of bolts."

Jarnelle studied the map again, turning it about in the moonlight. "Seems to be not too far from here." He peered up again at Corwyn, apparently studying him rather closely. Corwyn could see a faint glimmer of a face under the hood. It appeared clean shaven, dark eyed, and lined with the years of a hard life.

"Maybe a day at the most." Corwyn studied the situation carefully, constantly tailoring his performance.

"Riches, eh?" He could see the outline of the halfling's deepening smile, along with a black domino mask. He assumed the others were wearing the same. There was little need for such a disguise, though. It couldn't be hard for the authorities to find a group of people half the size of the general population.

"All yours if you let us go," he continued.

"Why not kill two birds with one stone?" Jarnelle motioned the other halflings forward. "Empty their pockets of any coin."

The others eagerly rushed them. Their small hands pilfered what they could from the backpack resting against the trees. Two others watched and waited behind them—weapons ready for any retaliation. These other halflings shared the same sickly sweet and rotten smell of sour wine and spent tobacco, with one or two reeking of fresh ale.

"You sure I can't—"

"No."

Fredrick sighed in bitter frustration, resigning himself to his fate, all to the best of his acting abilities. He let the two halflings on either side of him dig through his pockets, patting him down to make sure they hadn't missed anything. Corwyn submitted to the same.

"I'll give you your lives, but not on a full coin purse." Jarnelle folded the map and placed it under his cloak.

"You're more than fair." Finally, the halflings stopped their groping.

"Oh please," said Fredrick as the brigands finally left him as well. "These are halfling thieves we're talking about. Not that there's much *difference* between them and halflings who *aren't* thieves, mind you."

"You could learn much from your friend." Jarnelle motioned for the others to leave. "How to dress, for one thing. Especially that hat. We'll leave you with it since you understand good fashion sense."

Corwyn nodded in humble appreciation. "You're too kind."

"Yes, I am," Jarnelle gloated. "So, I leave you two with your lives, as promised. And *you* have given me a rich trophy, it would seem. A fair trade, yes? Don't follow. No bold actions, and you'll see the dawn once again. Fare thee well, gentlemen." Corwyn watched the halflings scatter like black mice into the night. After they were out of sight and earshot, Corwyn and Fredrick relaxed.

"Now, you have to admit that was better than beating them up." Corwyn grinned.

"Better for *whom*?" Fredrick started rummaging for his gear, which had been scattered along with Corwyn's among the trees. "I would have enjoyed kicking those little slugs around."

"You were pretty convincing."

"It's not hard pretending you're angry when you already are."

"That and you've gotten a lot of practice over the years." He joined Fredrick in his efforts. The piercing glance told him it was time for a change of subject. "We should probably put some distance between us and them before they find those ruins."

"I didn't like losing my coin either." Fredrick had packed up almost everything and was making ready to leave. "*Or* getting groped by that pack of vermin."

"You couldn't have taken them, Fredrick. You couldn't see how many you were facing, and they probably knew the terrain better than either of us, too. Besides, we have more in Riverford. A lot more than what we gave to them."

"It's still lost coin."

"Then think of it as charity."

"*Charity?*"

"Charity." Corwyn stood. He supposed they'd taken enough rest to sustain them until the next village.

"For *halflings*?" Fredrick held his gaze, uncertain of what to make of such a statement.

"Can you think of anyone who needs charity *more* than halflings?" He adjusted his hat and started for the road. "Looks like a nice night for walking."

"Well, at least the map finally did do us some good." Fredrick came up beside him. "I can almost picture the little twerp's face when he sees his ruins in all their glory." He shifted the weight of the pack on his shoulders. "That'll give me a warm night's rest when we're in a nice inn in Riverford.

"You do see what I mean now about you having to change your wardrobe? If you start getting compliments from halfling highwaymen, you might want to rethink your sense of style."

"You could have a point there." He did his best to keep his focus on the road, fighting off the rising smirk.

"What do you mean *could*?"

They continued walking. Fredrick muttered something into his beard, shaking his head. Finally, Corwyn's smile broke free, brightening his spirits as they journeyed into the night.

SELLSWORDS AND SNAKE OIL

1

Hammond made his way through the tall grass behind his barn. The late afternoon sun washed over the swaying tawny stalks, giving them a bronze cast and covering the rest of the world in an amber hue. With grasses equal in height to a man, the wild prairie of the Grasslands of Gondad was a rich and still somewhat unexplored part of Talatheal. To many, Hammond's farm represented one of the last spots of civilization before the ancient grasslands reclaimed the landscape.

Hammond himself was a middle-aged, sun-kissed Telborian. He kept his balding head covered by a wide-brimmed straw hat. A farmer like his father before him, he'd just returned from his fields, eagerly anticipating the evening meal with his wife. He'd worked up quite the appetite. But before he went inside, he wanted to do a few last-moment chores in the barn while he still had light.

Like many in the area, he and his wife did their best to be self-sufficient. They kept livestock beyond their two oxen for plowing: chiefly a cow, some chickens, and a few pigs. These they kept in a separate pen beside the barn. Any of life's necessities they couldn't get from their fields or animals they bought in town.

He'd nearly reached the one-story building when he heard a strange noise. His knees locked. He hadn't heard anything like it in his thirty-plus years in the plains. It was low and animal-like but with an eeriness that made his spine tingle.

Turning, he noticed rustling in a section of the tall grass. Straining his eyes, he couldn't see anything among the fields, and he forced his held breath to resume.

The rustling stopped.

He waited a few moments before convincing himself to continue with his chores. He'd taken only a few steps when the noise continued.

In a flash, he whipped his head around, his eyes narrowed, searching... The stalks were still. He felt cold beads of sweat on his forehead, matching the ones already present on the back of his neck. Then came a low, body-trembling growl. He took a step back. The growl was closer this time, the unmistakable sound of something nearly upon him.

He still couldn't see what threatened him. He retreated another step. He had a pitchfork and sickle in the barn. If he could get to them in time, perhaps he might be able to put up a fight and scare the thing away. As he turned to run, the thing in the grass leapt straight for him. He only saw it out of the corner of his eye—long enough to fuel his feet with a fire they'd lacked even in his youth.

His hat flew off in his dash.

"Marion, bolt the door!" he shouted to his wife, hoping she'd hear him inside the house some five hundred yards away.

He knew with even his brief glimpse the creature wasn't going to be stopped by any sickle or pitchfork. More like a good lance or sword. Altering his course in midstride, he prayed to whatever god would listen for strength and protection. He also prayed Marion had heard him and done as ordered. He wasn't about to head back—he only continued to race onward, hoping for the best.

It was early evening when Fredrick and Corwyn entered Plainsview. The reddish-umber sky had turned the clouds into velvet waves, aiding the night's hold over the surrendering day. The pair had been on the road for the better part of the day, making their way to the small village which sat between the wilds of the Grasslands of Gondad to the west and the more cultivated lands making up the hamlets, villages, towns, and cities of Romain to the east.

It'd been a few weeks since they'd made their way off Riverford Way, favoring rural thoroughfares and villages over more populous locales. Because of this decision, Corwyn had let go the other musicians he'd previously hired, much to Fredrick's dismay. He wasn't quite sure why Fredrick stuck around. Corwyn didn't have any real plans for doing large shows the farther west he traveled.

He planned to spend his summer in the grasslands, searching for something from the Imperial Wars. What he might find there he didn't know. It could be a "rock dump," like Fredrick called the last set of ruins they discovered, or it could be something truly of note. For now, he simply enjoyed the journey. Soon these modest villages would be hamlets and then nothing more than sporadic farmsteads, if anything, and then the wide-open plains would spread out for miles.

Plainsview was nothing really of note: a small scattering of wooden structures resting around a central village square with a few smaller buildings spaced around the outside of this timber-and-plaster cluster. Without any walls to protect it, the village lay open to the sprawling swath of fields and grazing lands surrounding it. A simple wooden sign swung back and forth on rusted chains attached to an equally worn post at the village's entrance. Stained a reddish brown from years of exposure and painted neatly in Telboros, it declared the village's name and its population of three hundred.

Fredrick curled his lip in passing. "Hayseeds," he muttered beneath his breath.

Corwyn ignored the remark. He'd known Fredrick long enough to realize when to let things slide and when to take him to task. While the people in the village weren't well off, they were far from backward savages. He also knew the dwarf didn't really dislike the people who lived there, but rather the lack of coin the townsfolk would be willing to part with if they performed anything here.

"Tonight we should have a nice bed to sleep on," said Corwyn. He was delighted at the prospect of having a soft place to rest his head. The past two nights they'd found rest in the open stretch of land beside the road.

"One without lice, I hope."

"You could have stayed back at Riverford with the others," Corwyn reminded him, as he'd done on several occasions since they'd left.

As they walked along the hard-packed dirt streets, a couple of residents greeted them with polite grins. Others nodded their suntanned faces, tipping their wide-brimmed hats in passing. The odd wild child bubbling with laughter and boundless energy scurried about here and there. These children soon found others, who joined them in running up and down the street and between houses, shouting and screaming while they went.

Other than this, Plainsview remained relatively silent. The few shops present in the village along the main street were closed. The street continued for a few more yards before branching off into a handful of pigtail curls that composed the residential streets.

"There we go." Corwyn focused his attention on a slightly shabby two-story building. Another worn sign swayed over the doorway. This one was also written in Telboros, though not as neatly as the previous sign. It declared the building Plainsview Crossing. "I hope they have some rooms."

"And some edible food," added Fredrick.

As they drew closer, they could hear the sound of people. The inn doubled as an alehouse and food hall for most of the population, who, when they grew bored on their own parcels of land, could come and have a home-cooked meal and fellowship with the local community. Corwyn had seen plenty of such examples in his travels.

"Well, something smells good," he said, enjoying the fragrant wafting of meat and other savory aromas emanating from within. Once they were inside, the noise transitioned into a rumbling ambiance, mingling with spikes of soft laughter and bawdy cheers. Here and there, scattered among ten round tables, sat what he guessed were a good portion of the townsfolk—some with hot meals, others with mugs of ale.

Farther in, near the back, others sat along the wall on single stools. These ate their meals facing knotted wooden panels, seemingly content with the modest degree of privacy. The rest gathered around a bar—a fair number of men and women leaning against and sitting near it, eating food and downing drink.

"Hungry?" He already knew the answer before asking.

"Starving."

"Let's get a room lined up before we eat," he said, making his way to the bar. He placed his walking stick against it, catching the eye of the middle-aged woman working behind the oaken counter. Wide hipped and attractive in a maternal way, the short, graying Telborian reminded him of his encounter with Molly in another inn not long ago. But the resemblance lasted only for a moment.

"What can I do for you?" Her smile was stained from years of tea drinking and a few odd evenings with the pipe, but her face was plump and jolly.

"My friend and I need a room for the night and a meal."

The woman looked from Corwyn to Fredrick in an approving manner. "You can have the one on the right at the top of the stairs."

Corwyn reached for his coin purse. "How much will I—"

"Don't worry about that right now," she said, raising a plump hand. "It will be taken care of tomorrow—a fair rate, I assure you."

"Thank you." Corwyn didn't press the matter, even though he could feel Fredrick's hot stare urging him to do just that.

"You won't need a key either. We don't have any reason to lock our doors here," she added with a reassuring smile.

"Probably nothing worth stealing," Fredrick muttered.

The woman pointed out the way up the flight of stairs at the back of the room. "You can go there now if you like. It's all ready."

"Get me an ale," said Fredrick. "I'll go put this backpack away and be down in a moment." Corwyn watched the dwarf make his way for the stairs. He knew Fredrick wouldn't admit it, but he could tell he was getting tired from constantly lugging the backpack since their encounter with those halfling highwaymen a few weeks back. But although Corwyn offered to take it for a time, Fredrick had always refused.

"I suppose you'll be wanting something filling after a long day on the road," said the woman, drawing his attention back to the bar. "You're already getting close to skin and bones. If you don't get something to help hold you down, you just might blow away."

"We can't have that now, can we?" Corwyn grinned. "How about a mug of ale and . . ." He searched for the sign smaller inns usually kept posted near the kitchen, informing travelers of what meal options were available.

"Took the sign down to freshen it up. It's time for summer dishes."

"Do you still have cider?"

"Sure do."

"Spiced?"

"No problem."

"Okay, then hot spiced cider and a tankard of ale." Corwyn tried to get a sense of the menu by investigating some nearby patrons' plates. "What's a good dish you'd recommend?"

"Well, we do have a fresh run on jackalope."

"Jackalope sounds wonderful."

"Two of the same then?"

He unslung his lute from his back. "Yeah, though could you put extra bread on one of the plates? Rye bread, that is." The woman nodded and left for the kitchen.

Corwyn placed his lute beside his stool, feeling better with the weight off his shoulders. He adjusted his walking stick against the counter, then turned fully around, arms resting on the edge of the counter, taking in the room once again. Trained over the past fourteen years on how to read a crowd, he knew Fredrick wouldn't be happy. These people were hardworking, pragmatic folk not too keen on parting with coin—should they have any—for a simple evening's entertainment.

He removed his wide-brimmed hat and set it on an empty stool beside him. Fredrick would have the other empty stool to his right. He rarely sat anywhere else if given the choice. Corwyn continued to think and observe until Fredrick's voice roused him.

"Did you get my ale?" He watched the dwarf approach the empty stool he'd left for him.

"That was fast."

"It was just a backpack," he replied, taking his seat.

Besides dropping off the backpack, he'd also shed his weapons. Fredrick had long held a strong conviction of the pointlessness of wearing armor and carrying weapons in safe public places. He'd often said people who kept their armor and weapons when there was clearly no need for them were either being showy and cocky or looking for trouble.

"What did you get for food?"

"Jackalope." He turned back round, facing the counter.

"Extra bread?" Fredrick's orangish-brown eyes offered an inquisitive gaze.

"Of course. How does the room look?"

"It's livable."

The woman returned with a piping-hot wooden mug of spiced cider and an amber-frothed tankard of ale. "Your dinner should be out shortly." She set the beverages in front of them, her years of service giving her the wisdom to know who would drink what, and departed for the kitchen.

"So, what have you got planned for tomorrow?" Fredrick took a draft from the tankard, getting some of the foamy head in his mustache, then wiping it away with the back of his hand.

"Get some supplies and head off into the wild." Corwyn took a sip of his steaming cider. It was still too hot to take a full drink, but from what he could taste, he knew it was almost just the way he liked it. Before he could say any more, the door was flung open and a wide-eyed man rushed inside.

"It's a *monster*!" His shout strangled all other conversation into silence. "I saw a *monster*!" His flushed face was wet with sweat, and his chest heaved. "There's a monster loose in the prairie!" the man continued through huffing breaths.

"This should be interesting," Fredrick said under his breath while the two watched a slender older man rise to try to calm the newcomer.

"Take a moment to breathe," said the older man, who turned and addressed the rest of the patrons, saying, "We'll give Hammond a moment and then look into this matter, but let's not jump to conclusions before we know the facts."

"Who's the older man?" Corwyn asked the woman behind the counter. "Your mayor?"

The woman nodded. "Bryan," she answered, keeping her face on Hammond. "Oh, that poor Hammond," she continued more to herself than anyone else. "Must have been something quite frightful to get him into such a state."

"Don't even think about it," Fredrick warned Corwyn.

"Think about what?"

"Monster hunting."

"Aren't you jumping to conclusions a bit?" He knew what Fredrick was thinking. They'd been traveling together too long for him not to. "Let's just hear what's said." Then he added a logical argument even Fredrick would have a hard time countering. "We still have to eat our meal and rest from the road. Think of it as entertainment while we fill our bellies."

"Fair enough," he grudgingly accepted.

After taking a moment to catch his breath, Hammond began telling his tale. All kept silent while he spoke, not wanting to miss a single detail. "I was outside by the barn, looking to finish up for the evening, when I heard a rustle in the grass. I thought it was an animal at first and so paid it little mind. But it grew louder, and the sound it made . . . And when I heard the roar of the thing . . ." Hammond's face went white and he found it hard removing his tongue from the roof of his mouth.

"Take all the time you need." Bryan patted Hammond's shoulder.

Hammond nodded, his strength already returning and his face regaining some color. Soon enough, he got his tongue back under his command. "It came out of the grasses and it had to be the ugliest thing on Tralodren. It was large too—about ten feet long and at least half that in height. I wasn't armed and didn't think I could fight it off anyway. So, I did what I *could* do: run. I'd hoped the beast would follow me and leave Marion alone, but I didn't look back once I crossed the creek and made my way into the village." Murmured conversations quickly bloomed across the room.

Bryan raised his hands for silence. "Let's not get too dismal in our outlook. I suggest we select a group of men who can be trusted and are able enough to go and look into the matter. Perhaps together they can take care of this without much trouble."

"A wise idea." A strong new voice drew all eyes to two armored men entering the common room. Both were Telborians of average height with brown hair and rugged, tanned faces. Each was armed with a short sword at his side. In many ways, they were the spitting image of what most folks would think of when the word *hero* came to mind.

"You've nothing to fear now that we're here." This comment came from the slightly older of the two men as both stepped further into the inn.

"And who are *you*?" asked Bryan.

"I'm Victor, and this is Thomas." Victor motioned to the other man. He too had a strong face, but with green eyes and an open-faced helmet covering much of his head.

"Forgive our intrusion, but we couldn't help overhearing your conversation." Both men moved to stand before the mayor and Hammond. "We've been traveling the grasslands and other parts of Talatheal, searching out this very creature."

Fredrick jabbed Corwyn with his elbow. When he bent closer, Fredrick whispered, "This all seems a little odd, don't you think?"

"Maybe a little." Corwyn's suspicions were piqued. "But let's give it time."

"Have you now?" Bryan shared Fredrick's slight unease, but his tone remained diplomatic. "So, what has brought you two to Plainsview?"

"The hunt," Victor returned. "We've been following this blight demon now for—"

"*Blight demon?*" Hammond's eyes swelled in fright.

"Aye." Victor nodded. "The creature you saw had to be a blight demon."

"How do you know?" Hammond was now more curious than fearful.

"Was it like a great serpent with the head of a wolf and four arms like a man's and legs like a centipede's?" asked Victor.

Hammond's face went white. "I saw a *demon*?"

"Not just *any* demon." Thomas' mellow voice filled the room. "But one known as a cruel creature carrying curses to all who'd strike at it, and even blighting the land it lives in for sport. No normal weapon can stop it, for the weapons of mortalkind are useless against those of cosmic origin. That's why we carry enchanted blades." Thomas gave the sword at his side a quick pat. "With these we've seen many a blight demon fall into Mortis."

Fresh murmuring erupted among the patrons.

"You *believe* this?" Fredrick had finished his meal, freeing his full attention for the discourse.

"I'd be more inclined to believe it if I could see them in action." Corwyn still worked on emptying his plate. "Though they are pretty polished with their presentation. It's almost like I'm watching a play."

"Yeah, they *are* laying it on a bit thick." Fredrick's eyes squinted. "And I, for one, would like to see those swords."

Corwyn swallowed. "So then you agree. We should go with them when they go after this blight demon."

"I never said that." Fredrick's defenses rose along with his furrowing brow.

"But this is something of interest, wouldn't you agree? And," he added in softer, tempting tones, "it would keep us at least one more day from the grasslands."

Fredrick sighed. "Yeah, I suppose we could. And you'll need someone to protect you too, since you'll probably carry little more than that stick of yours."

"I've never seen a demon either," Corwyn added, taking another draft of cider. "Should be interesting."

"*Vampires* not interesting enough for you?"

"Good people." Victor's raised voice and hands hushed the rising din of conversation. "We're willing and able to help you rid your village and fields from this threat. As I've said, we've done it before, and we have no qualms about doing it again. We only ask for a room and some food to sustain us while we search out and ultimately defeat this foul threat. There would be no risk to your lives and by the same time tomorrow this blight to your property and livelihood will be eliminated.

"What say you?"

The room fell silent while all eyes found Bryan, who weighed the matter in his thoughts. After further internal debate, the mayor acquiesced to the two men. "You have the permission you need to stay in this inn and be given some food and supplies, provided you hunt for this creature, and you allow some other men to serve as witnesses with you on your hunt. Should we face a similar threat again, it'd be wise to have others who know how to contend with it."

Victor nodded. The hard look of the warrior melted a bit, helping him appear friendlier, more approachable. "A very generous offer. We accept. Let us get unpacked and then we can begin talking with you and those you wish to have accompany us." Thomas, who had followed Victor, was already making his way for the bar. "We'd also like to speak with the man who first saw the demon, to learn what we can."

"What room might you have for us?" Victor addressed the woman behind the counter.

"Top of the stairs and second on the right is yours," she replied, pointing out the direction as best she could.

"Thank you." Victor departed, Thomas at his heels. "We shall return momentarily."

As they passed, both Corwyn and Fredrick sized up these traveling heroes. Corwyn couldn't speak for Fredrick, but something was slightly off to him, and it didn't stem from anything he saw. Both looked every bit the part they professed. It was something else missing . . . But what?

2

"Seems the whole village has turned out," said Corwyn.

The two of them sat on their stools, backs resting against the counter, waiting for the demon hunters' return. Since their arrival, word had spread like wildfire within the village. The inn was now standing room only.

"They were pretty full of themselves," said Fredrick.

"They *were* fairly confident." Corwyn wasn't bothered by the half-hour wait, enjoying the people watching. Fredrick, on the other hand, wasn't as patient.

"*Cocky* is more like it."

"Maybe a little," he conceded. "But sellswords have to appear capable if they want to get paid."

Fredrick eyed Corwyn in disbelief. "It was practically *dripping* off them. Still seems a bit odd," he continued. "These two guys show up shortly after that farmer starts yammering about some creature . . ." He focused back on the stairs. "What's taking them so long?"

"Relax, they'll come down when they're ready." No sooner had he spoken than the sound of approaching footsteps filled the air. "We'll have our answers soon enough."

"I hope so, because their weapons didn't look any different from any other swords I've seen." Fredrick joined Corwyn in watching bodies gather at the foot of the staircase. "Did you notice their armor and swords weren't marred either?"

"There's some wear, but they did look rather clean. Course, if their armor and swords are enchanted, they might not get nicked and dinged like regular armor and weapons, I suppose." The crowd around the stairs parted, allowing Thomas and Victor—now free of armor and weapons—to pass. "Would you even know an enchanted weapon if you saw one?" He watched Victor and Thomas walk past.

"I might . . . given the right conditions."

Victor and Thomas waded through the bodies to the front of the room, where Bryan and Hammond waited. Even without their armor the two men made a fairly heroic impression. Both wore simple tunics, pants, and leather shoes—common dress among fabled warriors. Their attire was not too different from that of the populace of Plainsview, though their clothing was cleaner and newer. A simple-looking copper headband encircling Thomas' head remained the only difference between them.

When the demon slayers made it to the center of the room, the mayor and Hammond rose to greet them. Silence fell over all assembled. This lingered until Victor's strong voice arose.

"Good people, I see word of our arrival has caused this inn to swell with a great many bodies." Victor's voice sounded like the gold-tinted timbre of a practiced politician. "Let me say firstly that there's nothing to fear. We've tracked these creatures all over and dealt a swift death blow to each and every one we've encountered. Your children, wives, and crops will be safe and secure." Pleased murmuring arose, then quickly faded when Victor continued.

"For the benefit of the newly arrived, I am Victor, and this is Thomas. As I've said, we have been successful in the tracking and killing of these blight demons for many a year. We have gained our success by mastering the use of the enchanted weapons and armor we carry for these hunts. Tomorrow, if you'd have our help, we'll travel to where this demon was seen, track it down, and slay it before evening."

Victor turned to Bryan, who spoke to the two men loud enough that the rest of the assembly could hear him. His voice wasn't so golden, but rather the fatherly tone of a friend whom many had, no doubt, come to trust.

"And if we'd have you, then what would you have from us other than what you've already stated?"

"We'd only ask what we have before," said Thomas. "That we be given provisions and a place to rest our heads while we're in Plainsview."

"Nothing else then?" The mayor's white eyebrows framed his studious dark blue eyes.

"Nothing else." Thomas' kind face deepened in its sincerity.

Once again, murmuring erupted across the room.

"Sellswords." Fredrick muttered the word in disdain.

"Sellswords who don't mind getting paid in room and board." Corwyn watched Victor and Thomas with greater interest than before. "Now *that's* a bit odd, don't you think? Most fight for coin only and would have few qualms about asking these people for gold or silver to do their work. I wonder why they aren't pressing the matter."

"Maybe they know they won't get much of anything out of them if they squeeze." Fredrick glanced Corwyn's way. "You still want to go with them?"

"Yes. It'll be something unique for sure."

"Just thought I'd give it one more try." He couldn't hide his disapproving frown. "You might change your mind one of these days."

The mayor lifted his hands for silence. "I've already said if we're going to allow these men to help slay this monster, then we want to have some men accompany them," he continued. "Not only to witness the deed but to learn how to protect the village should another demon appear in the future. I'm willing to pay their terms and let them have their hunt, but I wonder who of you will be willing to accompany them on it?"

The room fell still.

"We will."

Fredrick and the rest of the room found Corwyn's raised hand.

"And here it comes . . ." Fredrick muttered.

"And who are you two?" Bryan asked.

"I'm Corwyn Danther and this is Fredrick Grenze."

"Corwyn Danther." Victor's eyes lit up. "I've heard of you. A bard of some repute, if the stories can be believed."

"The ones based on reality can be. You probably shouldn't put too much trust in the rest."

"You'd really want to watch us work?" Thomas' hands adjusted his headband while seemingly sizing Corwyn up. "You think you can handle seeing the horrors we've come to deal with?"

"Sure. I might even learn something useful."

"Okay," said Victor, sharing a sideways glance with Thomas, who tweaked his headband again. After the two men's wordless exchange, Victor continued, "Just make sure you stay out of our way when the danger comes. We can't vouch for your safety. It will take all our concentration to hunt the blight demon. We can't divert any of our efforts to watch out for your welfare."

"That's why *he's* coming along." Corwyn gestured to Fredrick, who merely grumbled into his beard.

"You aren't from the village, though," Bryan continued. "I need two people from the village to join the hunt. People who'll still be here after you've all left."

"I'll be present," Hammond spoke up. "They'll have to follow me to where I saw the creature. I'll stay with them the whole time."

"So you will," said the mayor. "Who else will volunteer?" There was soft muttering and descending eyes, but one hand raised above the gathered heads.

"I will."

"Ganatar bless you for your courage, Harold," Bryan commended the tawny-haired, bright-faced young man.

"Then it seems we're decided." Victor took charge of the room once again with ease. "Thomas and I will speak with Hammond for a better idea of where to start, and then address those who will accompany us on the morrow's hunt."

"So, you're really Corwyn Danther?" Victor gave Corwyn's hand a hard shake. The bard, Fredrick, the two sellswords, Hammond, and Harold had managed to find a table of their own.

"Yes," said Corwyn. With most of the action at an end, the crowd had thinned and quieted. Given what had been shared, he figured most had anxiously beat a trail for their homes to make sure everything remained safe and sound. He couldn't blame them.

"From what I've heard, I'd have thought you were taller and more rugged." Victor grinned. "I guess you can't believe everything you hear, eh?" He then eyed Fredrick. "I haven't heard much about you, but welcome." Fredrick took the hand he offered with a strong, forceful grip. His gaze was watchful, but not too threatening.

"He's a fellow I just can't seem to shake." Corwyn tried smoothing over some of the dwarf's rougher edges with light humor. "He also plays in the band when we perform."

"So he's a bard, too?" Thomas seemed reserved, like he was thinking deeply and had to focus just to keep abreast of the conversation.

"No." Fredrick took Thomas' hand and offered him the same shake and look he'd given Victor. "I play a few instruments, but I'm not a bard."

"I see. So you're a musician then." Corwyn thought he saw relief in Thomas' face. "What instruments do you play?"

"Pipes and flute mainly."

"And who are you?" Thomas asked Harold.

"Harold," said the young man. "I help out in Jeffrey's leather shop."

"It seems you're a man not easily frightened, if your eagerness to volunteer is any indication," said Victor, taking his seat. Everyone else followed his lead.

"I don't know about that," said Harold, face flushing. "I thought if someone was going to volunteer, it might as well be me. I don't have any kids or even a girlfriend."

"I don't think it will get that grim," said Corwyn.

"No, it won't," Victor agreed. "We'll do the hard work, and if you keep a safe distance, you'll be able to see all you need and won't even twist an ankle."

"You'll have no complaints from me," said Hammond. "I never want to see such a monster again."

"I've never seen a blight demon before," said Corwyn. "Can you tell me about what you saw?"

"Only that it must have been from the Abyss; such a thing isn't natural in the least. It had the stench of evil all about it." Hammond's face paled.

"What do you mean?" he pressed gently.

Hammond shook his head, the pallor of his visage increasing. "It's something I'd rather not revisit."

"Nor should you," Thomas butted in. "Blight demons are a terrible sight to behold, and we'll not have you relive such a horrid thing. Time enough to see it dead on the morrow. For now, let your minds be at rest."

"Laying it on a bit thick, aren't you?" asked Fredrick.

Victor's eyes narrowed slightly. "What do you mean?" His look wasn't angry but certainly discerning, like the gaze of a card player trying to ascertain his opponents' hands.

"Oh come on," Fredrick half snorted. "You've been preening the whole time—ever since you walked through the door. I'm surprised you get any work to begin with. You're probably the showiest sellswords I've ever seen."

"But sellswords would want money." Hammond's voice was small. "These men have merely asked for some supplies—"

"Because they know you folks don't have two coppers to rub together."

"We make our living on the kindness of others in return for our actions, that's true," said Victor. "But not in the way you might think." This time Corwyn noticed a hint of anger behind Victor's green eyes when they burned into Fredrick's face. "We're wandering warriors who are trying to stop a grave threat to innocent lives." Corwyn watched the sellsword deftly move his gaze around the table, the emotional footing of his words hitting home all the harder with each individual visual exchange. He showed no hint of anger, only strong conviction. Corwyn was impressed.

"These blight demons are a real threat and have done great harm in many places. We'd sooner stop them than find ways to earn food, supplies, and shelter. It's a truth we live by our swords. However, it's truer to say we live by our actions, helping the poor people oppressed by these demons."

"Well, I for one won't hold anything against you," Hammond said with conviction.

"Thank you, friend," said Victor. "Can we move on now to other matters?" There remained just enough condescension in Victor's voice to make Fredrick's beard hairs bristle, but he let it drop, much to Corwyn's amazement. "The night will be over soon, and we have a few more things to discuss."

"So what's the plan on how to catch this thing?" asked Fredrick.

"We'll have Hammond lead us to where he saw the demon tomorrow morning and then track it from there."

"That's it?" Fredrick was unimpressed.

"Pretty much." Thomas was nonchalant, focusing his attention on Corwyn more than the dwarf. "We track it down and dispatch it to Mortis."

"So you can kill it with just your enchanted weapons?" Corwyn was intrigued by the concept.

Victor nodded. "It's the only way you can kill a blight demon this side of the Abyss. Pity the poor fool who tries any other way."

"How did you come by your weapons and armor?" Corwyn jumped at the opening given him. "That certainly has to be a great story."

Victor and Thomas exchanged a glance. "I think I'll let Thomas tell that tale," said Victor.

"Well," Thomas began like a man accustomed to telling a good story, though he still seemed preoccupied as he spoke. "We received our weapons and armor from the same wizard who taught us the nature of the blight demon. It was about five years ago when we came upon the first demon—and it nearly took us to Mortis right then and there. Had it not been for that wizard's aid, we wouldn't be here talking with you today."

"A fortunate turn." Hammond was clearly invested in the story already.

"Indeed. Had it not been for Elias, we wouldn't have been able to help as many as we have."

"So this Elias gave you these items?" Corwyn sorted through Thomas' story, making sure he understood everything being said. It had been part of his training. Many things in a tale went unsaid, and good bards heard these things as well as what was spoken, understanding what was really being conveyed in its entirety. Such insight could often enrich a bard's later performance.

"Yes, he did." Thomas seemed to lose his train of thought when he brought his attention back to Corwyn but quickly regained it. "He wanted to, since he'd grown too weak and old to use them in battle. Upon seeing the threat these demons posed, we dedicated ourselves to stopping their scourge over Talatheal."

"I've never heard of blight demons before," Corwyn continued. "Where do they come from? I thought demons and other cosmic races were all kept from Tralodren by divine decree."

"True," said Victor. "But a few have found their way around the decree, it seems, focusing on Talatheal to work their evil."

"Talatheal only?" He grew even more curious than before. "Not *all* of Tralodren?"

"Yes, that's the odd thing," Victor continued. "They can only come here through a weak spot in our reality in Talatheal. At least that's what Elias discovered. I don't know why, but something in certain areas draws them out of the Abyss. So we've been tracking them down the best we can and taking them out as soon as they appear. In fact, Thomas and I had a feeling we were getting close to one when we arrived at the inn and heard Hammond's story. Seems we got here just in time."

"Yes," Hammond enthusiastically agreed. "And I'm glad you did, too."

"Us, too. You don't want a blight demon hanging around any longer than necessary."

"We'll need to hear your story, though, Hammond, if you're able to share it." Victor gripped Hammond's arm when he saw the pallor returning to the farmer's face. "We don't need you to relive it, friend. Merely share what led up to and followed it—and let us ask you a few questions."

Hammond nodded grimly. "I'll do what I can, if it will help."

"Thank you." Victor motioned for the woman behind the counter to come take their order. "However, Thomas and I have been on the road all day and have yet to have any halfway-decent meal. Once we've eaten, we'll hear what you can share. Then, tomorrow, we can all make our way to your farm and dispatch this demon before noon."

"You seem pretty confident of that," said Fredrick.

"Experience is a good teacher," Victor coolly replied as the woman approached the table and started taking their requests. Everything they ordered would be free, of course, thanks to the benevolence of the mayor and townsfolk.

While they ate, another villager found Hammond and told him that his wife was reported to be fine but worried about leaving for the village lest the blight demon find her on the way. To his further relief, Victor assured him both he and his wife would be safe until the group arrived tomorrow. How he could be so sure of this, Corwyn had no idea. Nor did he really explain when asked. But it clearly calmed Hammond's fears, giving him the confidence to make the return trip home in the dark. Corwyn and Fredrick, along with the two sellswords, left to take their rest shortly after the farmer's departure.

3

The next day Hammond and Harold were waiting outside the inn before Corwyn and Fredrick even made their way down. They'd both arrived at dawn—eager for, if a little fearful of, what the day would hold. That fear, however, lightened after Corwyn and Fredrick joined them.

"I hope they *can* deal with this demon before noon," Hammond fretted. "It was hard to leave Marion alone knowing that thing is still out there."

"I just wish they'd hurry up and get out here." Fredrick kept his eyes pegged on the door. "I *told* you we didn't have to get up so early, Corwyn. They're *still* not ready." He crossed his arms with a huff. "We could've had breakfast while they were preening."

"You'll survive." Corwyn watched the dawn's soft fingers wrap the buildings and sky with a warm glow. He hadn't brought his lute with him, leaving it in their room, but donned his hat and attire from the day before, walking stick included.

"Oh, don't worry about food," said Hammond. "When this demon's been slain I'll be more than happy to entertain you all in celebration."

"Course, we have to find and kill the thing first." Fredrick started tapping his boot in a frustrated rhythm. "And that would mean we'd have to have our two demon slayers here to do it."

The door opened, and Victor and Thomas emerged. Each was finishing a rather large sweet roll as they joined the others. Both were dressed again in their full armor, swords strapped at their sides.

"Good day," Victor greeted those gathered with a partially full mouth. "Are you all ready?" He finished the last of the roll with one ravenous bite.

"We've *been* ready," Fredrick growled while Thomas consumed the last of his substantial pastry with obvious delight.

"Sorry for the delay," said Victor, wiping his hand on his pant leg. "Doris, our kindly innkeeper, wanted to give us something to keep up our strength before we left. She didn't want us fighting on an empty stomach."

"How kind." Fredrick's face transformed into a stony scowl.

"I thought so," Victor agreed, moving into their midst. "So where's your farm, Hammond?"

"This way."

"With any luck we should be done with this deed before late morning." Victor followed Hammond, Thomas right beside him.

"Let's hope so." Fredrick took up the group's rear. No one said anything more until they arrived at Hammond's farm.

"So, you ran from this spot here?" Victor asked Hammond, who'd led them close to the area where he'd first seen the demon.

"Yes," Hammond nodded sheepishly.

"Nothing to be ashamed of, man." Thomas gave the other's back a hearty slap. "You could do little against such a creature, and you did well to warn your wife and run for your life. If you'd tried to face it, you'd be dead now."

"You say it came out of the grass?" Corwyn was making his way toward the very spot where the demon emerged. "I don't see any signs of something as large as this demon coming through here."

"I thought the same myself," said Hammond, joining Corwyn at the edge of the prairie. "But I can't deny what I heard and saw."

"Well," said Thomas, joining Corwyn and Hammond, "that's the mystery of the blight demon for you: they don't leave much of a trace behind if they don't want to, and very little even if they do."

"Really?" Corwyn found the news unusual, but with what he'd experienced of demons and magic these past few months, he'd become more open to a whole host of possibilities.

He could see his question unsettled Thomas, but only momentarily. "Really." He observed the flash of a faraway, concentrating look in Thomas' face before it returned to its previous expression.

"Then how do you track them?" He held his ground, seeking to understand the other's unease. He didn't like the fact Thomas seemed uncomfortable with the question. Of course, part of him thought it was possible that Thomas was a fan of his. Victor had mentioned hearing about him before. He supposed it wasn't too much of a leap to assume Thomas shared the same interest. But that still didn't explain the sense of something else being slightly off . . . Something he still couldn't peg down, no matter how hard he tried.

"We do so with the skillful training Elias gave us," Victor said, disrupting the tension.

"Well then"—Fredrick motioned Victor forward into the tall grasses—"have at it." Victor squatted, searching with his hands and eyes. Thomas joined him in studying another part of the same area.

Harold watched this all with intense energy, not wanting to miss anything. "What are you doing?" He tried to get a better view of the sellswords' actions by shifting his position.

"We're checking for the small signs we've been trained to locate." Victor didn't stop his investigation. "They'll tell us how long ago the blight demon was here and if it might still be in the area."

"I see," said Harold, increasing his concentration on the two men and their work.

"Do you see this?" Thomas asked Victor.

"Yes." Victor noted the spot Thomas indicated with interest. Though it appeared to be an ordinary patch of ground, the two sellswords treated it like a sacred find.

"Then it can't be far away." Thomas rose. Victor joined him.

"If it isn't far away," Fredrick wondered aloud, "shouldn't we *smell* it or *see* it or something? Don't demons make noise? I thought they're supposed to stink too—brimstone, right?"

Victor shared another nonverbal exchange with Thomas. "Not necessarily," Thomas said at last. "They're known to be experts at hiding, even in plain sight."

"Then are we in danger now?" asked Hammond, fear tinting his voice.

"No." Victor began scanning the area around them with a steely gaze. "Not yet."

Hearing this, Hammond drew closer to the rest of the men, the color draining from his face.

"He's here, though." Thomas drew his sword. "We'll find him."

Victor also drew his sword as both he and Thomas made their way into the grasses. "He won't be hard to find." Before the tall stalks nearly swallowed them whole, Victor turned, saying, "Wait here."

"But we're supposed to witness the event," Harold protested.

"It's too dangerous," said Victor, resuming his course, disappearing among the grasses. "I don't want to have to worry for your safety when we're contesting with this demon." Harold made a step for the grass, then abruptly stopped and sighed.

"*This* is fun." Fredrick's pessimism was darker than usual.

Thinking to reduce some of the tension, Corwyn found Hammond. "So, you farm wheat here?"

"Yeah." His question caught the man off guard. "I've had this land for years. I got it from my father and his father before him—all the way back to King Phillip."

"So you're the descendant of serfs?"

"Yes, but now we're freemen." Hammond's posture improved with his statement. It was something to be proud of, for in historical terms, the freedom afforded folk like Hammond was still somewhat new.

"I think that's one of the best things to come out of the Telborian kingdoms." Corwyn's words further straightened the farmer's spine. "They really have learned a good lesson from the other independent cities."

A noise rose from the grass. "All of you keep back, we've—"

A terrible roar devoured the rest of Victor's words.

"The demon!" shouted Hammond as everyone's attention was captured by the violently swaying grass.

"What do you think?" Fredrick asked Corwyn, keeping his gaze locked forward and drawing his mace for good measure.

"It's too early to tell." Corwyn remained focused on the shaking grasses. There were more shouts from the sellswords. Corwyn supposed they were swinging their swords. None of them could really see what was taking place. Then came the horrid sounds: pain-filled, bloodcurdling screams and howls. But the thing making them still couldn't be seen. Finally, it shot out above the grass in a wild spasm of agony.

"Drued's sweet beard!" Fredrick cursed.

The blight demon was just like Hammond had described: a wolf-headed, serpent-bodied, human-armed thing with the legs of a centipede on its lower serpentine half. The sight both repulsed and intrigued him. It was something so amazing and yet so unnerving that any other time, Corwyn would probably have been tempted to run. But at the moment his legs and feet were frozen in place. This gave him some time for focusing on those four muscular arms ending in deadly claws as well as that maw of sharp teeth. The demon appeared wounded, and all could plainly see the marks left by sword blows and the blood dripping down its arms and body.

The blight demon's cruel eyes spotted the others with a hot rage. It made a drunken lunge for them but didn't get far before Victor jumped onto the demon's back. With a mighty effort he drove his blade up to the hilt into the demon's hide. The force of it and Victor's weight slammed the demon to the ground. He pulled his sword free with a heave, letting the demon thrash about in its death throes. This thrashing and crashing resulted in it landing outside the prairie grass, where it eventually fell silent.

"Is it . . . ?" Harold couldn't finish his question.

"Yes," said Victor, giving the demon a kick with his boot. "It's dead."

"And before lunch, too," added Thomas, exiting the grass with a weak, lopsided grin.

"You two don't seem any the worse for wear," Fredrick observed. And in truth, they didn't. Not a single drop of blood could be found on them. Only their swords were coated in red. They didn't even appear winded from their efforts.

"Like I said"—Victor patted his armored chest—"the armor keeps us safe." He cleaned his blade by wiping it on nearby shorter grass. "I wouldn't worry too much about missing anything, Harold. You won't be bothered by any of this fellow's friends."

"Why's that?" Corwyn asked, still amazed by what he'd witnessed.

"We sealed the fissure it escaped from," Thomas explained.

"I didn't hear anything," said Harold.

"You wouldn't have," explained Victor. "The process is silent—which makes it all the more dangerous when the fissures appear. People often don't know they are there until it's too late."

Fredrick started making his way for the slain demon. "What do you plan to do with it now?" He was still taken by its appearance.

"It will rot rather quickly." Victor inserted himself halfway between Fredrick and the demon, blocking his path. "Once life has left the body it's taken, and the fissure it used to enter our realm has been closed, the body dissolves into nothingness."

"I've never heard of such a thing before." Fredrick, filled with disbelief, was pushing past Victor for a closer inspection. But before he could get any further, a cry of pain rose from behind them. Investigating the cause, all saw Harold slumped on the ground, clutching his leg.

Corwyn ran to his aid, instantly noting the crossbow bolt sticking out of his lower left calf. "He's been shot."

Fredrick hurriedly joined Corwyn's side, the others following, forming a living shield around the downed villager.

"Can you stand?" Corwyn extended his hand.

"I think so." Harold tenderly took it. Hopping on his good foot, he let the other dangle free, cringing through clenched teeth all the while.

"We can take him inside," said Hammond, "and tend to him there."

"Here." Corwyn gave Harold his walking stick, which he gladly accepted. Together Hammond, Corwyn, and the stick managed to help Harold hobble toward Hammond's home.

"Who fired at him?" Fredrick walked alongside them, scouring the place for any hint of hidden trouble. "Can't be sloppy hunters."

Victor and Thomas silently took up the rear, their own eyes darting about with a strange nervous energy. Just then another bolt shot through the company, narrowly missing Victor's shoulder before sinking into the ground a short distance ahead of him.

"Make a run for the house!" Corwyn supported Harold with his shoulder, helping them increase their pace.

"We'll secure the way," said Victor while he and Thomas accelerated their mad dash.

"Can you make it?" Corwyn asked Harold.

"Yeah." Harold's sweaty face had paled, but his eyes still held a fire. Together they made it to the door of Hammond's home without further incident.

"Here," he said, helping Harold inside. Fredrick took up the rear, slamming the door behind him. All heard the telltale thud only a few heartbeats later of another bolt embedding itself into the door's exterior.

"Hammond?" Marion made her way into the main room, her face a mixture of surprise and uncertainty. She'd come from the bedroom, the only room apart from the main area, which served as the house's kitchen, living room, and dining area.

"Marion!" Hammond ran for her.

"I heard screams. Is the demon dead?" she asked, unsure of what to make of her husband's strong embrace and the gaggle of folks gathered in her home.

"Yes." Hammond finally released her. "It's dead, but not all the danger has passed."

"What do you mean? My goodness." Marion's brown eyes noticed the bolt sticking out of Harold's leg. "Harold, are you all right?" She hurriedly made her way to his side.

"He should be okay." Fredrick was already inspecting the area with experienced eyes. "But you better have rags and water handy to wash the wound when I pull this thing out—and a chair."

"How did this happen?" she asked no one in particular.

"We don't know," said Corwyn. "But someone out there was using us for target practice."

"In *Plainsview*?" Marion was flabbergasted. "I don't believe it."

"This bolt is real enough," Fredrick returned. "I still need that chair."

Hammond grabbed one from around their table. "Water and those rags," he told his wife. "We'll have time to sort this all out after we've attended to Harold."

Marion grabbed a wooden bowl, filled it with water from a pitcher on the table, then ran off to the bedroom. A moment later they heard the sound of tearing fabric. When she returned, Harold was seated, his wounded leg resting on Fredrick's shoulder as he squatted next to the young man. The dwarf's thick hand gingerly tested the bolt's shaft, seeking a good grip.

"This is going to hurt some," he cautioned, "but it'll be over quickly." Harold clenched his teeth and scrunched his eyes. Fredrick gave a fast yank on the bolt. Harold let out a yell, then fell silent. Everyone watched the blood seeping from the wound.

"Where's the water and rags?!" Fredrick demanded.

Marion put them in his hands, then turned back to the ashen-faced Harold. "Why would anyone attack Harold? He's one of the nicest people I've ever known."

"That's a good question." Corwyn focused on Victor and Thomas. Both had stationed themselves near the door. "You two know anything about this?"

"Why would we know anything about some madman with a crossbow?" Thomas was more nervous and distracted than usual.

The small window in the room, close to the table where everyone had gathered around Fredrick and Harold, shattered as another bolt flew through the plate glass. The bolt pierced the table beside the pitcher of water.

"Gods of Gray, Light, and Dark," Fredrick cursed, shaking bits of glass from his head and beard. He was careful not to let any shards into the wound he'd finished cleaning and just started binding with some of the torn bed linen.

"My window!" Marion exclaimed.

"Get away from it," said Corwyn, but they were already on the move. Hammond assisted in moving Harold, pulling back the chair as Fredrick balanced his leg, taking care to keep the bandages he'd nearly finished dressing from coming loose. Both chair and Harold came to rest against the wall beside the broken window. It was then Corwyn noticed a piece of parchment wrapped around the bolt's shaft. He yanked the bolt free from the table, then joined the others.

"What's that?" Hammond watched Corwyn unroll the parchment.

"The answer, I hope, to what's going on here." He began reading aloud. "'To those inside. We wish you no ill. We only want the two scoundrels you harbor in your walls. Release unto us Jarn and Gavin and we will leave you in peace. Should you not release them to us, we'll be forced to take more drastic measures to secure them and cannot guarantee your safety. You have a quarter of an hour to decide your actions.'"

"*Who* do they want?" Hammond shared the others' confusion.

"Jarn and Gavin," Corwyn answered.

"Never heard of them," said Harold.

"There, that should hold you." Fredrick finished his work on Harold's leg. "Sounds like bounty hunters to me." He grabbed another chair for Harold to rest his leg on.

"Bounty hunters?" Marion wrapped her arm about Hammond's waist. "What would such men be doing in Plainsview?"

"I think I might have an idea," said Corwyn, fixing Victor and Thomas in his sights. The sellswords exchanged another silent sideways glance.

"What are you getting at? You aren't saying . . ." Hammond followed the gist of Corwyn's logic, as did the others, who all turned to the sellswords.

"What's *really* going on?" Corwyn asked Victor and Thomas.

"I suppose it's little use pretending any longer," said Thomas, removing his helmet.

"Shut up!" Victor snapped.

"No." Thomas rested the helmet under his arm and removed his copper headband. "We knew we couldn't keep this up forever."

When Thomas removed the band, the two warriors' semblance changed. No more were they men of hard muscles and deeply tanned skin, but softer city-dwelling folk with pale complexions and tired expressions. Thomas transformed into a middle-aged, green-eyed, bookish fellow. Victor's tired brown eyes were lined with anger, which did little to improve his thinning black hair and lined face. Marion gasped at the sudden change, but the rest of the men held their amazement, letting it show only with a momentary flash in their eyes.

"The blight demon isn't real either, is it?" Corwyn's voice was low and purposeful.

"No." Thomas shook his head. "I'm Gavin, and he's Jarn. We're bards from Romain."

"*Knaves* is more like it." Fredrick's rebuke stirred up fresh anger in Jarn.

"We make our living the best we know how. No one gets hurt, and we keep as much on the level as possible."

"On the *level*?" Fredrick raised an eyebrow. "How can someone deceive another honestly? How do you dupe someone and keep your integrity?"

Neither Jarn nor Gavin had an answer.

"Why are these bounty hunters—if that *is* who they are—asking for you?" asked Corwyn.

"They have to be bounty hunters," Fredrick added. "If they were Remani, then these two would be dead already."

"They must have been sent from Romain," said Gavin. "A while back we duped a noblewoman there. Jarn pretended he was royalty and got her to fall in love with him. Course, before the wedding came, we took what loot we could and made our way out west into the wilderness."

"No one gets hurt?" Corwyn refashioned Gavin's words into an accusatory barb. "She's sent bounty hunters after you."

"And you were going to play *us* for fools too?" Hammond's rage only grew the more he heard. "I *trusted* you—we *all* did—and I even invited you into my home, and here you were playing me for a fool with this whole blight demon lie, looking to fatten your purses and backpacks with the blessings of this village. I should string you up myself!"

"Hammond, peace," Marion entreated. "Fighting won't solve anything right now."

"Maybe not, but it would make *me* a lot happier." With further pleading and coaxing, Marion finally cooled Hammond's heart and head, allowing Corwyn to continue.

"How did you create that creature anyway? Something like how you changed your appearance, I'm guessing."

"With this." Gavin held up the headband. "We've been using it for years."

"Why don't you give away *all* our secrets?" Jarn sniped.

Gavin faced Jarn somberly. "I don't see any way out of this or anything we can do at the moment. We're already found out; why keep up the charade?" Jarn's jaw locked under his friend's chastisement.

"We got it from a wizard," Gavin continued.

"Elias?" Corwyn was quickly threading things together.

"Yeah." Gavin played with the headband as he spoke. "That was one of our first jobs. We took this with us and have been using it ever since. All you have to do when you wear it is concentrate on what you want to appear, and it happens. The more believable you can make your thoughts and the harder you concentrate, the more real it seems to be."

"So then where *did* you get your weapons and armor? Or were they stolen, too?" Fredrick joined the inquisition.

"We *paid* for these," Jarn returned. "And no, they aren't *enchanted*. But the circlet wasn't doing much good in the hands of that old wizard either. He only used it to trick young women into his bed."

"So what I saw was an illusion?" Harold mused aloud.

"Yes." Gavin nodded cautiously. "The first time Hammond saw it, we were hiding in the grass, and the second time we put up a good fight and made you think it was slain. It would have rotted away while we ate lunch and been gone before we went on our way."

"Because there's a limit to the circlet's influence," Corwyn surmised.

"Yes," said Gavin. "It only works well in close proximity to the person or people you want to dupe."

"Maybe when you're done answering their questions, you can tell them your life story, too," Jarn mocked. "This isn't getting us any closer to getting out of here."

"Sure it is." Fredrick smiled a mirthless grin. "All we have to do is open the door and toss you out."

"And condemn us to *die*?" Jarn seethed.

"Sounds fine by me."

Corwyn stepped closer. "You really think this woman would want you dead rather than alive?"

"I don't know," said Gavin. "If we aren't killed, they'll probably take us back to Romain and Lady Stephanie's house."

"Where she could have us killed in her sight." Jarn's sardonic tone only thickened the tension in the air.

"Are you sure it's Lady Stephanie and not Elias who sent these men after you?"

"We've heard Lady Stephanie swore revenge," Gavin explained. "And Elias is dead."

"And no." Jarn jumped into the fray before anyone else could. "We didn't kill him. He died of old age a few days after we left."

"We don't really know if these men *are* bounty hunters," Corwyn told Fredrick, "or even how many men there might be."

"Who else *could* it be? Even *they* think it's plausible." Fredrick indicated the deceitful sellswords.

"You don't have any other ideas who this might be?" Corwyn asked the bards.

"Why do *you* care?" Jarn raised an eyebrow.

"Because these people have no qualms about hurting innocent parties to get to you, and I for one don't want to be at the lethal end of a crossbow bolt simply because I happened to be standing next to one of you." The firmness in his voice stilled Jarn's caustic tongue.

"Why are we even debating this?" Fredrick's irritation was clearly growing. "They've confessed already, and we don't have all day here. Let's just throw open the door."

"We can't go back. Please," Jarn begged.

"You can't go back to face the consequences of your actions?" Corwyn took a good, long look into Jarn's soft brown eyes. He still couldn't escape the thought he kept missing something. But what? "Why shouldn't we let you reap what you've sown? You almost succeeded in tricking some villagers out of their hard-earned provisions, got an innocent man wounded, and made sport of another for your gain. Why should we help you do anything but get what you've earned from your escapades?"

"Because we can make it worth your while." A velvety smoothness slathered Jarn's words. "We can pay you handsomely."

"You'd try to buy us off?" Hammond was disgusted.

"You wouldn't have to farm anymore," Jarn calmly continued. "You help us get out of here, and we'll make sure you get your fair share."

"You must think me a real idiot to fall for that," said Hammond. "You may have fooled me with that demon of yours, but you can't trick me a second time."

"You can't—"

"Enough of your whining already." Fredrick stomped forward. "Are you going to get out there or do I have to throw you out?"

"Okay." Gavin lifted his palms, pushing for more time and calmer heads. "Hear me out here. All you have to do is buy us enough time to let us escape, and we'll use the circlet to make it appear like we're giving up. We'll lead whoever is out there away from you. That way you'll be safe, and we'll at least have a chance."

"Right." Fredrick sneered. "And a halfling likes to do an honest day's work."

"You can watch us from the doorway," Gavin hurriedly returned. "You have my word."

"The word of a knave?" Fredrick snorted. "I'd be better off trusting a fox guarding a henhouse. Why not let them get what's coming to them?"

"Sounds fair by me," Hammond added. "They should answer for all the innocent people they've made fools of and stolen from."

"Let's not get too hasty now," Gavin cautioned. "At least think about my idea."

"To run and hide?" More color had returned to Harold's face along with some steel in his voice. "Seems to me that's *all* you've *been* doing."

Jarn's mouth opened, but Gavin stopped him from speaking. "We actually worried you might catch on, Corwyn." He focused solely on Corwyn, keeping his voice cool and even. "When you said who you were, we both couldn't believe we'd have to pull off one of our best performances in front of a well-known bard. I'm surprised we did as well as we did. But that doesn't change what we did. All I can do is plead with you, one bard to another, to have mercy on us and let us go on our way."

"If you run now, you're going to keep running for quite a while, maybe forever," said Corwyn. "Why not give up and deal with the consequences of your actions?"

"Because it might *hurt*." Jarn's retort jabbed into the heart of the conversation. "I've kind of grown attached to my head and I'm not really keen on losing it."

"And that's what you think awaits you?"

"Most certainly," said Gavin.

He could understand their reluctance if what they said was true. But he wasn't so sure if it *was* the truth and continued searching their faces and frames for tells. Since he was obviously going to be part of the final choice involving their fate, he wanted to be sure he had all the facts . . . and understood them correctly.

"Even if you escape these men today, they aren't going to just give up so easily. What kind of life will you live if you have the specter of capture and a possible death looming over all your days?"

"A longer one," said Jarn.

"But you'd be jeopardizing the lives of everyone you came across, like us today. Harold here is the first of many in that line. If that bolt had been aimed a few inches higher . . ." He let the unfinished thought linger.

"It seems like you've afforded us little freedom then," Gavin flatly observed. "Is this how you all feel?"

The rest concurred.

"I see."

"And hand over the circlet, too." Fredrick stuck out his hand. "We don't want you playing any tricks either." The two bards held their ground. "You can hand it over, or I can take it." The prospect of roughing up the bards put a sinister twinkle in Fredrick's eyes the two clearly found disheartening.

"Fine," said Gavin, surrendering the circlet into the dwarf's eager palm.

"And now out the door." Fredrick shoved himself between them and the door. He opened it with a mocking smile. "Here you are."

Both inched near the lip of the sill, striking an awkward balance between the wild outdoors and safer interior. "Well, we haven't been stuck full of bolts yet," Jarn muttered. "This is promising."

"Remove your armor and weapons." A deep voice came out of nowhere, startling the two men. For a moment they remained still. "I said remove them." The command came again, but with an edge of steel letting the two know the speaker would be willing to back up his words with hard action if they didn't comply. The bards did as ordered, steadily shedding their armor and weapons.

"You weren't too hard to track down," the same voice continued. "We lost your trail outside Romain for a few days but found it quickly enough. All we had to do was follow the tales of these two sellswords slaying demons, dragons, and ogres. You really should have changed your ruse. It might have given you more time to get out of the kingdom."

"I told you," said Gavin.

"Shut up," Jarn grumbled.

"Now walk out . . . slowly."

Gavin shared one last pleading glance with the others in the house, hoping someone would have a change of heart. They didn't. Hanging his head, he followed Jarn outside into the late morning.

"Now." The voice gained a face—the stubble-speckled, hard-lined face of a balding Telborian emerging from a patch of low-lying grasses at the edge of the front yard. "Walk this way."

Hammond, Marion, Corwyn, and Fredrick watched Jarn and Gavin make their way to the medium-sized man, who kept his crossbow leveled at the bards. Before they'd cleared five steps, six rough-looking Telborian men appeared behind them from their various positions around, behind, and near the house.

"Keep walking," one of the other bounty hunters flatly advised. All carried crossbows, each loaded and ready to shoot at a moment's notice.

Jarn gave Gavin another silent glance. Gavin nodded. Suddenly, both men burst into a run. They didn't get more than ten feet before they were struck with bolts from behind. Three bolts hit each bard. Three bolts aimed with deadly precision for their vital organs. Gavin and Jarn were dead before hitting the ground.

"Idiots," said Fredrick. Corwyn shook his head. "Wait, you're actually *sorry* they got what was coming to them?"

"They deserved to reap what they'd sown, but while they lived they still had a chance for mercy." He watched the bounty hunters approach the bodies, making sure they were dead. After a few kicks, they tied their hands and feet.

"But who would have granted them mercy?" Hammond comforted his wife, who had buried her face in his shoulder after witnessing the others' demise.

"That's probably what *they* thought," Corwyn mused.

"We have no ill will toward you." One of the bounty hunters addressed those in the doorway before gathering up the bards' arms and armor. "We've got what we came for."

"Where will you take them?" asked Corwyn.

After sliding the swords into his belt, he put the rest of the armor into a brown sack. "To Romain. While our client would have paid us more for them alive, she'll be just as satisfied with them dead." The gruff bounty hunter slung the sack over his back, then flung a gold coin in Hammond's direction. The farmer almost missed catching it out of sheer surprise.

"For the window." The bounty hunter nodded, as if he were a friend repaying a simple debt.

None spoke, merely watched the seven men make their way east. The two bodies they carried between them hung like a couple of freshly slain deer. When the last of them had faded on the horizon, Marion went inside, voicing a strong desire to prepare lunch. Hammond followed to check on Harold. Only Fredrick and Corwyn remained standing at the door.

"This might come in handy." Fredrick was playing with the circlet in his hands. Corwyn said nothing, keeping his gaze off in the distance. "Let it go, Corwyn. There's nothing more that could have been done. You said it yourself: they reaped what they'd sown."

"I was actually hoping they'd find a way for a second chance."

Fredrick snorted. "Maybe I should give *you* this circlet. It would conjure up something more believable than a reformed knave. Hey—"

Corwyn watched in amazement as between eyeblinks the circlet vanished from Fredrick's grasp. "Those worthless liars! It was all just another lie." He joined Corwyn in inspecting the flat expanse of prairie. "If those two *don't* get hunted down and—"

"Let it go." Corwyn rested a hand on Fredrick's shoulder. "There's nothing we can do about it now."

Fredrick sighed, releasing the fresh rage in the process. "Well, at least now I can finally get something to eat." When he stepped back inside, Corwyn didn't follow. "You coming?"

"I'll join you shortly." He kept his attention on the swaying grass. Once certain Fredrick was out of earshot, he prayed. "Watch over them, Causilla, and bring them to the truth before it's too late. Show them the right road to walk . . . for everyone's good." He then shut the door and joined the others.

THE FORGOTTEN

The summer heat didn't faze the hobgoblin, nor the handful of goblins behind him that Corwyn led through the Grasslands of Gondad. Their chain mail shirts jingled as they ran, reminding him of the scant distance between him and them. Swords drawn, they kept their eyes on him, eager for a misstep. But Corwyn wasn't about to give them such satisfaction.

Grass as tall as a man, if not taller in some spots, revealed Corwyn's trail better than fresh snow. His off-white shirt clung to his lean frame with large, sopping blotches under his arms and along his spine and upper back near his shoulders. His left hand strangled the neck of a cherrywood lute, while his right encircled a worn walking stick that swung back and forth at his side. His wide-brimmed hat was held tight to his head by leather straps tied snugly under his chin. Nevertheless, it often tried lifting free of his sweat-soaked head as stray swipes of grass struck his head and face.

He heard the hobgoblin shout a few phrases in his guttural tongue. Corwyn didn't speak Goblin so could only guess at what might have been said—none of it encouraging. His head pounded from the tsunami of blood crashing around his temples. His lips were dry, his eyes stung from the constant stream of sweat dripping into them, and his lungs were an inferno trying to set his whole torso ablaze. He couldn't go on for much longer.

The grasses continued whisking by like lashes of a whip, snapping at him as he barreled through. He was so busy concentrating on staying upright that he didn't notice the drop.

Down he fell, rolling in a somersault which took him all the way into the center of a rather large coulee. He found himself resting on his side, in pain from jagged bits of rock that had pummeled him during his turbulent descent. While he may not have been too clear on what just happened, one thing was certain: he couldn't run anymore. It felt like simply standing would take every last drop of strength. On the plus side, for the first time in a long while he couldn't hear the goblins' pounding heels. Instead, a deep calm hovered over everything.

He slowly forced himself to roll over on his back so he could get a better view of where he'd come from and his surroundings. He could see his pursuers eyeballing him from the coulee's lip. Each resembled a cruel statue. Swords in hand and chain mail shimmering in the sun, they seemed ready to pounce. He wondered why they didn't. Given his present situation, everything favored them rushing right for him.

Instead, he watched the goblins looking around the coulee with less-than-pleased expressions. They spoke more and then fell silent until the hobgoblin's deep voice rang out, producing a small echo from the coulee below. "You'll wish *we'd* gotten you first," he said in Telboros before sheathing his sword and backing away.

One by one, the goblins followed.

"Thank you, Causilla," Corwyn said in a small, haggard voice as he tried taming his furious breathing. He had no idea what the hobgoblin meant but would take any good turn he could get.

Gazing into the cloudless sky, he made a mental assessment of his body as best as the angry drums in his head allowed. Everything felt in working order—just sore and bruised from his recent tumble. He probably could stand without much difficulty but decided instead to close his eyes and rest a moment. He wasn't too sure of where his walking stick, hat, and lute were, but he was alive. The rest was secondary. Exhausted, he fell into an immediate slumber.

He woke to the late afternoon sun beating down upon him. He felt a little better, but still stiff from his run and sore from his fall. In sitting up he could tell he was bruised and tender in a few places. The blood rushing to his head caused a brief dizzy spell. When it cleared, he could see he remained where he'd fallen; the goblins were probably far away by now . . . he hoped.

Struggling to stand, he surveyed the coulee. The tall grasses were held back at the lip of a ridge around an oval-like enclosure. The ground on which he stood was a hard, rocky soil, affording only the most stalwart of greenery to take root—a thick emerald sward. This same green carpet ran up the sides of the coulee and down into the center, where the middle bowl of the depression cradled a clear pond. Around this pond mingled a mix of sugar maple and cottonwood trees.

The pond beckoned to his dry throat like a sweet oasis. On his way, he came across his walking stick. Retrieving it, he spied his lute a few feet away lying face down on the grass. Amazingly, it remained in one piece. He grimaced while squatting to turn it over. The back had suffered a few nicks, which could easily be repaired, and the front was unharmed. The strings and bridges and even neck and pegs weren't any the worse for wear.

His spirits lifted, he continued for the pond. Though partially enclosed by the fair-sized trees, he spied an opening on the side where he'd fallen, allowing easy access. The trees weren't the thickest he'd seen—nor the sturdiest either—but they were doing their best where they'd taken root.

His footsteps tangled in the sporadic seedlings and grass poking through the dead leaves. When he reached the pond's edge, he set his lute and stick beside him. Squatting, he observed its rocky bottom some ten feet below the clear water. His reflection revealed small scrapes and cuts around his face, but he didn't see anything serious that wouldn't heal in time. Resting on his knees, which didn't cause as much pain as he'd feared, he began slaking his thirst. Finally satisfied, Corwyn dunked his head beneath the water. Feeling much better, he slicked his hair back and took another look around. He figured the coulee was under half a mile wide, the pond and trees being more or less in its center.

He also noticed something that appeared to have been made by mortals in the opposite incline. Leaving his walking stick and lute, he made his way around the pond. The tall, wide structure was quite clearly chiseled long ago into the rocky ground around it. It was not more than eight feet in height but about six feet in width. He was at a loss for what it could be.

Dark from the grass and soil which had nearly swallowed it, the rectangular structure reminded him of a large plank. If he wanted any answers, he'd have to dig them out. But since it wasn't something he felt up to at the moment, he retreated back to the shade of the trees. As he did, he reviewed what had led up to the terrifying chase.

He and Fredrick had been making their way through the grasslands when they'd found some ruins. Corwyn thought they dated to the Imperial Wars. Since this was the reason he'd entered the grasslands in the first place, he went to investigate. Of course, he should have known something wasn't right about the ruins, which were clean and in tolerable repair. Fredrick had been leery, but Corwyn chalked this up to his less-than-optimistic appraisal of most situations.

Still, the shorter grass leading up to the buildings, and then the wide circumference of cleared land around them, should have been another warning, if he'd taken the time to pay closer attention. If he had, things might have gone differently. Instead, he pressed on into the ruins and started exploring. He then quickly discovered they were inhabited by a small tribe of goblins, who took to Fredrick and him like a swarm of hornets.

Fredrick shouted to run. Corwyn didn't argue. He didn't know what happened to Fredrick after that, only that along the way, the dwarf said to split up and let him take care of some of the goblins. He promised to join Corwyn afterward. That had been hours ago—even longer now that he'd slept more of the day away—and still no sign of him. For a moment a terrible thought whispered in his ear. He shoved it aside, focusing instead on his present situation, and reminded himself how little he could do for Fredrick at the moment.

Corwyn rested his back against a maple. The peaceful setting helped greatly in clearing his mind. He could wait for a while. He'd need more rest and to get his bearings anyway. Once Fredrick showed up, they could return to their original itinerary: getting through the grasslands before the end of summer and arriving in the towns and cities of the western part of Talatheal before fall set in.

As he mulled things over, he realized some alterations to the plan were in order. He didn't have any provisions to get him through the next day, let alone all the way he'd planned on trekking. He'd dropped almost everything he'd been carrying during the chase. He wouldn't part with his lute until he absolutely had to and only kept his walking stick in case he needed it as a last-ditch weapon.

This left him quite literally with nothing but the clothes on his back. In the middle of nowhere, he wasn't sure if he'd be able to get any aid. Backtracking might take them to a small village before they got too exhausted from lack of food and water, but that might also bring them right back to the goblins. If they pushed south, they might come upon some villages, too, but Corwyn wasn't sure how soon or if that would even happen. Traveling west would yield the same result. The north would take them eventually into swamps and marshes filled with all manner of creatures. Many of them were just as bad as or worse than the goblins. There had to be an answer. He simply wasn't seeing it yet.

He didn't know how long he sat there thinking but soon discovered he'd dozed off. He'd taken more than a catnap. The sun was spilling its lifeblood across the western horizon. He felt somewhat better, though still stiff and sore . . . and thirsty. Returning to the pond, he took his fill. As he finished, he thought he heard a faint whisper over his shoulder. A quick turn revealed nothing but silent trees. Taking up his stick and lute, he returned to the strange structure on the hill he'd spied earlier.

Resting the lute beside the hill, he grabbed the staff with both hands and poked around the structure's center. To his surprise, large clumps of grass and dirt fell away, revealing what looked like sturdy stone in the midst of the new depression. He continued, careful to not get carried away and pound too hard, lest he damage something in the process.

He dug away the finer, more persistent patches of damp earth with his fingers. The stone he'd uncovered was marble. It once would have been a gleaming white, before being soiled into its present shade by its swarded shroud. Clearing away more dirt and worms that mingled with some clinging roots, he discovered the profile of a lion's head carved into the stone. The regal-looking creation wore a crown and stared off to the right.

"Gondad." Corwyn could barely speak above a whisper.

He stared at the crest of a once-great empire that had ruled nearly all of Talatheal and many other parts of the Midlands. This was exactly the sort of thing he'd been searching for. He studied the stone slab carefully. It almost looked like a door. Of course, it could just be a simple piece of art—something symbolic rather than an actual portal leading deeper into the hillside.

Weighing the matter, he realized how dark it had gotten. If he wanted to do anything else, he'd have to hurry. He noticed the slab was cut separately from the rest of the marble, creating a door frame. Tapping it with his stick summoned the telltale sound of a hollow chamber beyond. Putting his shoulder to the door, he felt a small movement. Gritting his teeth, he pushed harder. He felt the door move inward and didn't stop until he'd finally managed an opening large enough to squeeze through.

The darkness of the opening invited him forward while a stronger chill accompanied by a damp, earthy tang filled the air. Looking heavenward, he noted the declining day had faded even more. Darkness or daylight, he'd still need a way to see inside and didn't have any torches. They'd been shed with the rest of his provisions. But catching sight of the trees brought an idea.

Rushing back to the copse, he took hold of a gnarled branch on an elderly cottonwood and ripped it free with a cracking pop. Satisfied, he set one end of the branch on the ground, clamped his foot over it, and pulled back on the branch's other end. There was some additional cracking and popping until it finally split into two fairly even halves. He inspected the pieces before placing them to his side. He then busied himself with collecting as many leaves as he could from the area, pooling them all in his shirt, which he'd untucked to convert into an apron for the task.

Once he'd gathered a mound, he carried them to the open door and dumped them inside. He repeated this activity two more times and then, on the fourth return trip, brought the broken branch and a handful of twigs and smaller branches. These too he dumped into the doorway and then made his way inside.

Beyond the door, the fading illumination streaming in from outside outlined the messy results of his efforts. While he couldn't see it, he sensed a great deal of space around him, more than enough to call for closer investigation. Staying close to the doorway without blocking its light, he began building a fire, using the leaves and twigs for kindling. In time he added the two branch halves, which really got the fire going.

With the firelight Corwyn understood he was in the midst of a chamber. He could see the ceiling about two feet above his head and a brick wall about eight feet before him with two passages extending to his left and right. Nothing of any significance could be seen insofar as relief images or text. He'd have to go farther into the darkness for answers.

He decided to build another fire in the passage on his left. He moved to the edge of the firelight and there built up the foundation of the new fire before tossing a blazing stick into it. When the fire crackled into life, it revealed an awesome sight: a life-sized marble statue of a Telborian warrior standing on a square granite block a few feet from him. The granite block added two feet to its stature, making for quite an impressive display and allowing less than half a hand's breadth between the ceiling and the statue's helmeted head.

From what he'd learned over the years, he determined the statue wore the garb common to a Gondadian soldier. Around the statue, a three-foot-wide circular path made of dark brick matching the walls caught his attention. The longer he stood before the statue, the more an uneasiness bubbled in his gut. But even as he tried making sense of why, another whisper caressed his ears. Like before, a quick survey of his surroundings revealed nothing.

"I have nowhere to run," he addressed the darkness in Telboros. "I'm sorry if you thought I was trying to bring any harm to your tribe," he continued, making a great effort to wade through the pitch-dark sea swaying beyond the firelight.

"I'm completely unarmed and not a threat." There came a scraping sound from the darkness of the hallway opposite him. "That you, Fred? It's a poor time for a joke."

A wave of chilled air sloshed around his ankles, standing the hairs on his legs and arms to attention. His joints locked and remained so until he was confident he was alone and the chill had completely faded.

Retrieving a burning piece of wood from the fire beside him, he gave it a good, hard toss. He watched it land at the edge of the darkness in the right-hand passage with a spray of sparks. The feeble illumination didn't help reveal what lay beyond.

Returning to the statue, he made his way behind the stone warrior, then he froze again. Before him stood a bloodied and battered soldier—a more battle-weary and life-sized version of the statue beside them.

The figure stared at him with weary, sorrowful eyes, then vanished. It happened so fast he wondered if he'd actually seen anything at all. He waited for a few moments before deciding to move on.

Pushing ahead, he arrived behind the statue. The diminished firelight washed all in a swimming puddle of muted color and swaying shadow. He could clearly see there wasn't anything of interest and continued his circle until he stood once again in front of it. There was nothing there. No markings or pieces of artwork of any kind anywhere. He decided he'd brave the other hallway. The fires wouldn't keep going forever; he might as well make the most of the light.

As he carefully pressed beyond the firelight's reach, he heard something. He recognized the noise as the sound of battle—a very large battle. The clanging swords and screams of dying and warring men were horrid echoes of an absent, violent scene. He stopped and kept his eyes fixed on the darkened hallway. When finally the noise grew too great, he clamped his eyes shut and thought of better things.

Silence rapidly ensued.

He could hear Fredrick's voice in his mind calling the place cursed, saying he should get out of there. But he wouldn't know for sure until he'd seen the other hallway. Taking a deep breath, he marched into the corridor, stopping only for a moment by the fire for another burning stick.

By the glow of his working torch, he found the hallway longer and narrower than the other he'd explored. Straight and unadorned, it seemingly had no purpose whatsoever. The walls were of the same plain brick and the ceiling was the same height as at the entrance. Once again, a cold encompassed him as he came to another dead end. Shaking the frigid flutter from his mind, he stretched out his hand. The brick felt cool and clammy but yielded no insights as he moved along the dead end up to the wall joining it on his right. When again he saw movement out of the corner of his eye, he turned to investigate.

"Causilla, preserve me." There before him stood a handful of Gondadian warriors who looked even more harrowed than the one he'd seen before. Somehow, though they should have been hidden in the darkness, they shone with a shimmering phosphorescence, which added another uneasy aspect to their already-frightening nature.

Silent and still, they looked not only at him but *through* him with their cold eyes. His heart approached a rapid gallop and his mind raced for ways to escape. Blocked in by the five figures, he could do little but stand in place. He'd been a bard long enough to know about ghosts but wasn't quite sure how to deal with them.

"What do you want?"

None of the five responded, only continued boring through him with their vacant stares.

"I'm not here to do any harm," he continued. "I'm just taking a look around." Again, they were unmoved.

He braved a step forward.

Nothing.

He took another, this time adding, "I'm going to leave now." His last step brought him right before the apparitions. For a moment he felt lost among their bloody, translucent faces. "If you'd be so kind as to let me pass, I'll simply be on my way." He did his best to mask his unease. All five acted as if they didn't even know he was there.

"Okay then." Testing a developing theory, he moved his hand in front of the closest warrior's face. While his hand passed back and forth, the warrior's gaze remained fixed. Taking more courage, he decided on something bolder. He thrust his sputtering torch forward. Not only did the warrior not react, but the firelight made his body grow dimmer—almost like mist fading before daylight.

"They're not real, Corwyn." A soft female voice seemed to come from behind the five warriors. "They're phantoms. Just walk through them. You'll be fine."

He took a deep breath and stepped forward. As promised, he passed right into and then through them. He felt a faint burst of frosty air as he did so, but nothing else. Finding himself on the other side, he glanced over his shoulder.

The hallway was empty.

"See?"

Searching out the voice, he found a friendly, smiling face. "What are *you* doing here?"

"I could ask the same of you," said Lena, drawing closer. The smell of vanilla, cinnamon, honey, nutmeg, and sweetened cream overtook the chamber.

"I didn't expect to see you again." Corwyn was enraptured by the muse's soft, olive-skinned face. He'd forgotten how dominating her beauty really was—even in this limited firelight.

"I'm your patron," said Lena, playfully ruffling his hair, "and I'm here to help you."

"Well, I could definitely use some help."

"You hungry?"

About a quarter of an hour later the two were sitting outside near the stone doorway while Corwyn stuffed himself with a chunk of cheese, two warm turkey legs, a loaf of bread, and even a small jug of cider Lena had managed to fit into a sack she'd produced upon their exit. "I guess you *were* hungry."

Suddenly he realized how gluttonous he was being. "I'm sorry," he said, hurriedly picking up a half-eaten loaf of bread. "You want some?"

"No." She shook her head. "I brought it for you."

"Thank you again." He spoke while picking the second turkey leg clean.

"And you're welcome again." Lena unleashed a playful smirk, wrinkling her nose. "So, what in the world are you doing out here in the middle of nowhere?" She offered to take the spent bone from him, as she had with the last leg he'd eaten.

"I was looking for ruins of the Gondadian Empire." Corwyn felt awkward relinquishing the bone, but Lena had insisted when he'd balked at first, and so he honored her wishes. She placed the bone into another sack with the rest of the refuse she'd taken from him.

"Seems you've found some."

"Yeah." He took a swig of cider. "But it isn't exactly what I thought it would be."

"Oh?" Lena looked at the half-opened door. "What did you *think* it would be?" The starlight mimicked the soft, occasional glimmers from her spiked white hair and the diamonds in her jewelry.

"I don't know," he said, tearing off another piece of bread. "Something that would help me get more information about Gondad."

"And being greeted by dead soldiers wasn't interesting enough for you?"

"That wasn't what I had in mind."

"Well, you certainly came unprepared," she replied, regarding the ground around him with a disapproving eye.

"I lost most of what I had when the goblins started chasing me." Suddenly his eyes grew large. "*Fredrick?* Do you know what happened to him? He said he'd catch up—"

"He'll be here soon enough. Which leaves us time to chat." She smiled once again, instantly alleviating his concerns. "I saw you running and then fall." She squatted beside him. "How are you feeling, by the way? Still sore and tired? Anything broken?"

"You *watched* me fall?" He found it hard to get angry in Lena's presence. Already her natural perfume was making his head spin. "What kind of patron *are* you?"

She patted him on the cheek. "The best patron you'll ever have." It wasn't condescending but more caring and maternal than he expected.

"You *do* make some good food." He lifted the small jug of cider, offering a toast before finishing the rest with a large gulp.

"I had a feeling you were in trouble and finally found you just about the time you fell into this place."

"So *you're* the reason why the goblins haven't come back yet?"

"No," she said, pointing to the partially open doorway beside them. "*That* is."

"So they're scared of it?" He glanced over his shoulder. "I can see why."

"Can you?"

"Are you *joking*?" Corwyn half laughed. "They're ghos—"

"Phantoms. Those were *phantoms*, not ghosts." She stood.

"And how is that different?"

"If they were ghosts, you probably wouldn't be here talking to me right now," she answered in a serious tone while putting the small jug into the other sack with the rest of the refuse. He didn't know if he liked it when Lena became serious. It was like Fredrick becoming optimistic and perky.

"But you would have protected me from them, right?" he half teased, hoping it was the case.

"I'm not a god." Her seriousness lifted. "But I do keep my eye on you from time to time."

"Well, I'm glad you do." He rose to his feet, dusting stray crumbs off his lap and chest. "While it's a nice stop for a rest, I don't think I want to stay here longer than I have to."

"It's safe, but not as serene as you might believe." Lena obviously wasn't satisfied with his efforts and dusted his shoulders and straightened his shirt. While he'd grown accustomed to her touch, he couldn't escape the awkwardness of having a divinity acting so personally with him.

"What do you mean?"

Lena snapped her fingers.

Instantly, the whole coulee changed from peaceful to unsettling. In the midst of what had been an empty depression, with only the pond and the trees breaking up the terrain, now stood a host of men. He recognized them as more of the Gondadian warriors he'd already encountered. And like those warriors, these were bloodied and scarred in both body and armor. They stood around the whole of the depression like a ghastly forest, their eyes forever staring blankly ahead.

Their semitransparency and sickly illumination only added to the grisly nature of their visages and wounds. If this wasn't unnerving enough, a swarm of whispers crept around the place. Like the voices of hundreds of men, the whispers all muttered their own unique messages, which were lost as they mixed with the rest. Churning amid these indecipherable words were the clashing of swords and the banging of shields. All combined, it made for a rather eerie cacophony.

"*This* is what kept the goblins away. I took the liberty of keeping them hidden, since I thought it might be a bit unsettling."

"You were right." He tried to keep his fears in place, reminding himself of Lena's presence and the protection it implied. Though knowing he'd recently sat down in the midst of these figures without a care in the world—even falling asleep beside them—still sent a shiver through his frame.

"So, what *are* phantoms?"

"They're splinters of dead people's souls who have become strongly attached to Tralodren for some reason and haven't been able to fully move on to Mortis."

"But you said they weren't ghosts."

"They're not. Ghosts are mainly spirit and soul who have stayed behind—for a whole host of reasons. Phantoms are more or less a *piece* of the soul—a strong memory or emotion—that ties itself to a place and stays there."

"So these aren't really men but the *memories* of men?"

"Memories of men that have been anchored here since their deaths. Think of them like echoes or signposts."

"Signposts?"

Seeing he wasn't getting the analogy, Lena snapped her fingers, and the whole ghastly company, along with their eerie chorus, vanished.

"Phantoms aren't real. Only *impressions* of the dead person, birthed from a strong emotion or thought upon their death. While others moved on to Mortis and then the realms beyond, these stayed behind."

"Are all of them birthed in trauma?"

"Some are, but there are those who have been birthed of love, and still others who have been birthed of hate or fear, or a whole host of other emotions."

"So why are *these* phantoms here?" He faced the partially open door once again. "What's this place about?"

"It's an unfinished tomb," said Lena, following Corwyn's gaze. "It was meant to be a sacred spot, holding the ashes of those fallen in one of Gondad's wars."

"Why was it unfinished?"

"Thousands of years ago all the grasslands and much of Talatheal was the territory of Gondad, which grew into a mighty empire with colonies established in other lands to further spread its glory. And while this was all well and good for Gondad, it stirred up strife with other nations who were growing at the same time."

"The Imperial Wars," said Corwyn.

"One of the topics you did well in at college, I recall." His face showed his surprise at the comment, but she continued before he could say anything. "The wars were long and bloody, as you already know, and took a hard toll on the population. It had been the tradition of Gondad and its people to honor those who'd fallen while fighting for their nation. However, while the last few years of the Imperial Wars raged on, many in Gondad faltered in their support. They began blaming the king for all their problems rather than trying to better the situation and even took to scorning those still fighting for their protection."

Lena waved her hand, and the doorway lit up with a shimmering white illumination. The dirt and debris covering the stone edifice fell away, like dust shaken from a rug. Corwyn was taken aback by the finer detail revealed—even more so by the white glow clinging to it like starlight.

"Like I said, this was supposed to be a place of remembrance, honoring the warriors who died in a decisive battle. But the people saw the war and those who fought it as something unworthy of remembrance. Their bodies were burned and their ashes placed beneath the statue you saw inside, but no honor or thanks were given for their sacrifice." Lena grew disheartened. Again, Corwyn found the sight unsettling. "They were forgotten along with this tomb. It was never finished. Gondad fell soon after. In the chaos, everything else was lost."

"And these phantoms are still here because of *that*?" he asked, inching closer to the door.

"In a way, they never left." Lena joined him. "Their final thoughts were focused on not having their deaths be in vain—that they counted for something and would be remembered, honored, and appreciated, not just by the ones they had left behind, but by all of Gondad. And so they still remain."

Corwyn stood in deep thought, with only the chirring of crickets interrupting the stillness of the moonlit evening.

"They made it to their final rest though, right?" he asked at last. "They're not stuck somewhere between realms?"

"No," Lena assured him. "They all have their afterlives. This is something different." Lena's face became a mixture of sobriety and melancholy. "These phantoms are a reminder of what was supposed to be done and never was." She put her hand on the cold stone, lovingly caressing it. "The phantoms are for the benefit of the living—a reminder to correct the errors of the past. By not honoring those who'd fallen, even if the Gondadians felt the war was no longer right, they hurt only themselves."

"Are you saying they *cursed* themselves somehow?"

"In a way. It's a foolish thing to try and forget your past. For how else can you learn and do better if you don't know what's come before and what can be done differently in the days ahead? By not honoring those who had fought on their behalf, they cheapened their lives and the service they provided, and this sowed seeds of discontent between those who'd stand for Gondad and those who lived off of and in the empire."

"So how can these phantoms be put to rest?"

"Honor them."

"How?"

"I'm sure you can think of a way."

Dawn found Corwyn busy composing on his lute. Lena was sitting nearby, her bare feet crossed. He'd been feverishly working since finishing his meal. Though he was inspired, it still took work, which he was happy to see approaching its completion. He sighed deeply, then found Lena, whose soft smile gave his weary body and mind some much-needed comfort.

"You didn't have to wait."

"You didn't have to stay." She rose and walked his way. "And you didn't have to put together this song, either." As graceful as ever, she took him by the hand. "Come on," she said, pulling him to his feet. "You need a break."

Corwyn relented, letting his lute slide from his lap. "So do you really watch me *all* the time?"

"Like I said, I keep my eye on you, but I'm not constantly looking over your shoulder." She took a teasing stance. "Why? You think I should check up on you more often?"

He smirked. "I wouldn't mind."

"You've grown more comfortable with me since last we met."

"Maybe." He didn't want to think about that right now. He may have been doing better than when they'd first met, but he was still fighting to stay on task. "But I *did* have to write this song," he continued. "It was important."

"That's what I like about you." The pleasure radiated from her honeyed eyes. "So, you finished it?"

"I think so, but I'd like your opinion."

"I'd be delighted," she said, taking note of the growing dawn, "but let's first get you set up for getting out of here." She made her way inside the tomb. "And before we do that, we'll have to clean out the mess you made with your fires."

Using only his hands, boots, and walking stick, Corwyn did a decent job of cleaning up the mess. He got most of it cleared away, save for a few sooty smears where his boots had pushed the spent wood out the door. To aid their efforts, Lena summoned light from the very bricks, making it feel like they were working during a bright summer day rather than in an empty tomb.

As he worked, Lena busied herself with dictation. Using her delicate finger, she carefully transcribed the words of Corwyn's song on the empty walls to greet visitors on entry. Her slender digit moved over the stone like a frenzied dancer but left behind words carved deep into the brick. Even more amazing, the words weren't in the modern Telborian tongue but the ancient language of Gondad. By late morning, their work was finished.

"There." Lena stepped back from the gleaming wall, admiring a dedication poem of her own she'd added below Corwyn's lyrics. "That should just about do it."

Corwyn stood at the doorway, observing their results. "I think this is as clean as I'm going to get it."

Lena made a casual inspection of the area. "I think you're right." The delight shone on her face when she caught his eyes. "I really like your song."

"You think it works?"

"Oh yes. I think it's very fitting," she replied, shepherding him outside. "Let's get out and away from here." As they departed, the artificial light faded. Corwyn placed himself at the door and made ready to push it closed. The effort brought a raised eyebrow from Lena.

"What are you doing?"

"Closing the door."

She crossed her arms while a playful smirk frolicked across her lips. "You didn't think you opened that all by yourself, did you?"

"I did," came his sheepish reply.

"You may be in good shape, but you aren't *that* strong. Stand back." She motioned him away and made for the door. He watched her shut it with ease. "There"—she dusted her hands—"that should do it."

"So you helped me with the door, too." It was a statement of fact, not a question. "Just how long *have* you been here? Why wait until you did to show yourself?"

"I wanted to see what you'd do next." She dusted Corwyn's shoulders. "You're a very interesting man." Her eyes twinkled. "I like that. Now, we need to do something about your outfit and give you enough provisions until you reach your next destination."

"You don't have to do all that. Though I *am* wondering how Fredrick's doing."

"He's fine and will be here soon enough. Trust me." Her hand came to rest on his shoulder, silencing him. "Now, let me do what I need to do. I'm your patron, and I can't have you going off looking like you're some refugee or have you wandering around in the grasslands slowly starving. Where were you going to go after this anyway?"

"I don't really know for sure. I'd thought of trying to get all the way to Wave's Rest."

"Wave's Rest? That's a great idea."

"It is?"

"Sure," she replied, already lost in thought. "Now you'll need at least enough food to get there, and money to pay for a place to rest, and some new clothes for the journey . . . How about this?"

She snapped her fingers.

Corwyn found himself wearing a new pair of pants and shirt with a large sack bulging with what he thought was food at his feet. He also felt a weight on his belt. Upon investigating, he discovered a coin purse stuffed to near bursting.

"I . . . thank you."

"You're more than welcome." She gently kicked the brown sack at his feet. Beside it rested a bulging new waterskin. "That should be enough to last you to Wave's Rest—with a little something extra for Fredrick too. And you should have enough coin to take care of anything else you might need once you get there."

"I've still never heard of a muse doing this before," he said, feeling the heft of the coin purse on his belt again in amazement.

"I told you. I'm your patron. You'll figure it out eventually." And with that Lena's smooth lips and soft, honey-brown eyes cast away any further concerns. He felt himself not only at peace with everything but entering into the familiar territory he'd experienced when they'd first met on Maiden Rock.

"So, you ready to sing your new song?" She handed him his lute. Corwyn hadn't even seen it in her hand or anywhere near her a moment before.

"Yeah." He tentatively took hold of the instrument.

"I think you'll need an audience for that." Another finger snap brought back the phantoms. With them also returned their haunting, semicoherent murmurings and the dim clash of sword, shields, and dying cries. He wasn't as unnerved as he'd first been but wasn't overjoyed at experiencing their presence again either. Taking a deep breath, he began strumming the lute. Once he had a solid feel for things, he started singing:

'Tis centuries now since Gondad fell, but some things still remain.
Take ear, my friend, to what I sing, of heroes who sought not fame.
Though oft they fought in wars not sought by those behind her walls,
Gondad was stayed by those who laid their lives down at her call.

In ancient days the battles raged over all the lands then known.
Through all this darkness Gondad stood; its brilliance forever shone.

'Tis said brave men went out to fight a battle for their king,
Men who served and died, for whom few cried, and of whom now
I sing.

Their deeds lost and hidden now for many a span of years,
Forgotten embers and well-spent ash, their lives like Gondad mirrors.
But for one brief moment they brightly shone for all to plainly see.
'Tis forgotten now, an ancient thing, but some memories will
not flee.

Join me now in honoring those who bore the greatest cost.
To keep their city and nation safe, they let their lives be lost.
Dutiful men who were spurned in life, now hear this anthem true:
Whatever was good of old Gondad was owed in part to you.

Many were those who soon arose who wanted to forget
Your noble deeds on bloody fields, which your kinsmen did regret.
Fire sped your spirits on, but no honoring did they do,
And so it falls to this humble bard to sing a song of you.

No more to rot in memories old, you need not linger here.
You've served your king, kith, and kin; of that you need not fear.
You may've been spurned in ancient days, but now your tale is told,
So linger not as a forgotten lot, and this memorial now
take hold.

Suddenly, Lena's amazing voice rose in harmony with his own. Her
heavenly singing added a new level of beauty to the final verse.

Offering one's life for another's is quite noble and true.
And so, great warriors of storied yore, I sing to honor you.
Henceforth all men will hear of how you bravely did your deed;
By your example many should tread, lest this lesson we
not heed.

And with the last note still fresh in the air, Corwyn watched the phantoms' glazed-over stares become sharply focused upon him. He wasn't afraid. It wasn't with hatred they sought him out, but with what he imagined was appreciation. A moment later they vanished.

"Well done." A delighted Lena gave him a side hug.

"So, they're gone?"

"Yes, all of them. You gave them what they needed. Now they can finally leave and be at peace. And now you should be on your way, too. Wave's Rest is a long way from here."

"Yeah," he said, slinging his lute over his back. "But what about Fredrick?"

"Corwyn?" The familiar timbre of Fredrick's voice pulled his attention to the opposite side of the coulee. There he saw a shorter gray-skinned figure moving his way.

"Fredrick?"

"Who *else* do you think it would be in this godsforsaken prairie?" he huffed while transitioning into a light jog.

Corwyn chuckled and turned back to Lena. "Thank—"

He faced empty air.

"Thank the gods you're still in one piece," said Fredrick. "You *are* in one piece, aren't you?"

"As far as I know."

"Good. When you took off and I saw those goblins run after you, I feared the worst."

"So did I."

"Those new clothes? How'd you get new clothes out here?"

Fredrick had finally reached him. He was worn for his efforts: his long-sleeved green tunic showed fresh sweat stains, but his brown pants and boots were holding up well. Corwyn could imagine him pushing himself pretty hard to find him, but he seemed in good-enough shape and spirits.

"You probably wouldn't believe me if I told you."

"Is that right?" His orangish-brown eyes still had a good amount of energy behind them. Enough for a good argument, Corwyn supposed. "Met up with a helpful merchant just 'passing through'?"

"No, I met up with a friend."

"A *friend*?" Fredrick gave the coulee a good, hard survey. "And I guess I must have missed them, then, huh?"

"As a matter of fact—"

"Fine, play your games," he grumbled. "Just know I've been sweating like a pig in an oven looking all over for you and here you—what's that?" He finally noticed the marble tomb. His right hand went instinctively for his mace.

"A tomb."

"So, you're safe *and* sound and have been exploring a tomb, too." Fredrick shook his head. "Typical. But at least it isn't a rock pile." He approached the structure. "Probably where you got your clothes, then, too, I'll bet. You don't seem to mind wearing things from dead people."

"Molly didn't give me clothes from dead people. How many times do I have to tell you that?" He followed the dwarf.

"Looks intact. Anything good inside?"

"Nothing." The reply stopped Fredrick in his tracks, causing him to spin around on his heel like a well-oiled gate.

"Nothing?"

"Nothing but an honored memory."

"So, another worthless ruin," he grumbled, dropping the backpack he'd been carrying to the ground. "What is that now, five?"

"I wasn't really keeping count. This one doesn't have goblins in it, though."

"Funny." Fredrick grinned facetiously. "Seems to be adding up to a wasted summer, if you ask me."

"You're just grumpy because you haven't eaten anything." Corwyn went for the copiously packed bag Lena had provided and pulled out a loaf of rye bread. "Here," he said, tossing it to the dwarf, "this should help."

Fredrick was amazed by the sudden meal. "Where'd you get *this*? We didn't have all this food when we met those goblins."

"A friend."

"A *goblin* friend?" He continued his cautious investigation of the loaf.

"Are you going to eat it or stare at it until it goes stale?"

Fredrick warily bit off a piece. "Not bad," he said after swallowing. "So you mean to tell me I spent the better part of a day looking for you in this heat with no food or water and the thought of you dead somewhere plaguing my thoughts, not to mention the threat of more goblins finding me, and you've been here in the lap of luxury?"

"Well, when you put it like that, it sounds like a *bad* thing."

Corwyn watched Fredrick study him, running his hand down the green-tipped braid flowing from the middle of his bearded chin, contemplating his next question rather carefully. "What happened to the goblins chasing you? I didn't find any corpses along the way."

"They didn't seem to like this place much."

"What's not to like—well, apart from the tomb? You think they would have wanted to take a look inside . . . Course, maybe they already did, and that's why it's empty."

"At least you've found me and have some food."

"You're not going to tell me how you got all this, are you?" Fredrick asked between bites.

"Does it really matter? You know I wouldn't come about it dishonestly."

"I guess not." He plopped down on the grass with a heavy sigh.

"And there's plenty more where that came from." He gave the pregnant bag a gentle pat. "Enough food, water, and coin to get us to Wave's Rest."

"Wave's Rest?" Fredrick's eyebrows rose.

"Yeah. I think it's time to get back to civilization."

"*Now* you're talking sense. Just let me catch my breath and we can be on our way."

"No hurry. You didn't see my hat anywhere, did you?"

Fredrick swallowed another large chunk of the diminishing loaf. "No loss there. You look more respectable without it." He grabbed hold of the waterskin Corwyn tossed his way and took a long draft.

"I've kind of grown attached to it."

"I know. Still, not a big loss."

A soft breeze fluttered through the coulee. With it came a rustling near Corwyn's feet. Investigating, he found his hat. Delighted and amazed that it appeared no worse for wear, he bent to retrieve it.

"There's just no accounting for taste," Fredrick muttered into his beard, watching Corwyn put it on. "Still makes you look like a halfling pirate." He'd finished the bread and was taking another drink of water.

"Glass houses and stones, Fred."

"What you on about now?"

Corwyn took up his lute and began strumming a simple tune. "We'll have plenty of time to discuss it on our way to Wave's Rest."

"So how much money you get anyway?" He eyed the full purse strapped on Corwyn's waist. "Your *friend* as liberal with their coin as their food?"

"It's more than enough."

Fredrick snorted. "Any more and your belt would tumble around your ankles."

"It's really bothering you, isn't it?"

"What?"

"Not knowing how I came by all this."

Fredrick craned his head back to the tomb's stone door. "Nothing inside, you say, huh?"

"If you don't believe me, you can look for yourself," he replied, gesturing for him to do just that.

"I'm too tired to go looking. Do you know how hard it is seeing through this grass, let alone trying to find your trail again?"

"I'm glad you made it here safely." Corwyn continued his strumming. "You must have someone up there who likes you."

"I hope so, but I'm beginning to think I missed the boat. If I'd gotten here earlier, I might have gotten my own bag of goodies and a purse to match."

"I don't know about that."

"Oh, really? And what *would* you know about that?"

"Just get some rest." Corwyn wandered away, continuing with his melody.

Fredrick focused again on the tomb. "I wonder how many more ruins and tombs have been left in the grasslands to be forgotten?"

"I don't know. But I do know *this* one won't be forgotten anytime soon."

"But you said it was empty. So what's there worth remembering?"

"Let me tell you . . ."

He began playing the song he'd just written, the chords and rhythm already becoming ingrained in him the second time around.

THE MORE THINGS CHANGE

1

The lamplighters had just begun lighting the glass-covered lampposts near the docks when Cordell's short figure dashed through the cobblestone streets. Few paid the cloaked halfling any mind. In truth, many didn't think highly of the race in general. This cavalier attitude aided many halflings in their endeavors, which in turn only added to the stereotype of a people already held as larcenous to a man. Even so, he cast a glance over his shoulder now and again, pleased by the lack of interest.

He slowed his gait as he neared the end of the docks, where the coast's sandy beach flowed into the Percillian Sea. Here the clamor of awakening nightlife was muffled by the beige beach and surf. Taking one last look behind him, he made his way onto the sand.

Being shorter than the rest of mortalkind had some advantages, but one big disadvantage was the smaller stride. Add in the soft sand, and his progress further slowed. He'd already begun sweating back in the city; this traipsing about on the beach only made it worse. Over his shoulder, he could see the lamplighters had lit up most of the dock and the areas around it with a warm, cheery glow. It made the beach seem all the darker and lonelier. Casting his gaze toward the sea, he squinted from time to time, peering into the swimming shadows rolling about the waves.

"He better be here," he said to himself through huffs of breath. "If he stands me up, he'll be sorry."

After another quarter hour of walking in a northerly direction, Cordell finally stopped about a mile beyond Caster's Reef. Here the terrain turned more rugged. Sections of broken, jagged rock contended with the water, rising into small serpentine hills slithering their way inland before crumbling back into the beach and the grasslands to the west. Eventually the hills reemerged further north, transitioning into the great Diamant Mountains. The rest of the terrain was empty beach.

Cordell again peered across the waves. "Come on, you fool, don't make me stand out here all night."

"Rest easy." The gravelly voice shook Cordell with fright, causing him a brief moment of confusion while he desperately searched for the speaker. "Over here." The voice directed him coastward. This time he spied another halfling standing on a flatter portion of the rocky area, near the edge of the beach.

"Why'd you do that?" Cordell took a step closer to the similarly darkly cloaked figure. "You want me to die of fright?"

"No." The other halfling snapped his fingers. A small tongue of flame burst into existence between his right index finger and thumb. With it he lit a cigarette he'd retrieved from under his cloak. "If I did that, then I wouldn't get paid." He puffed the cigarette into ignition.

"So, what did you pull me all the way out here for?" Cordell wasn't impressed with the trick. He knew simple magicians who could do the same. "Javier doesn't pay for trivial things. This better be something *really* special."

"Oh, it is." The other expelled a plume of smoke from his stubble-covered lips. "You have Marlon Deplase's word on that."

"I doubt that's worth much coin."

"Here." Marlon tossed a small leather pouch Cordell's way. "This should convince even *Javier* I'm worth the gold." Cordell glanced at the pouch, then back at Marlon. "Just open the blasted thing, will you? If I wanted to do you any harm, I would have done so long before now."

Cordell undid the leather straps and widened the opening with his fingers. Seeing nothing of immediate note he turned it upside down, spilling the contents into his palm. Under the moonlight he saw what looked like a piece of ivory and three small rubies. "You dragged me all the way out here to fence three rubies? What's so special about three rubies and a hunk of ivory that we couldn't have met in the city?"

"Look closer at the ivory." Marlon took the last drag of his cigarette, expelling the creamy white smoke with a sigh before tossing the butt. Cordell turned the ivory in his hand, wondering what Marlon was playing at. It was carved into a figure—a female, judging from the curve of the hips and protruding breasts. And while the piece was worn, he thought he could make out pointed ears.

"So what *is* this?"

"A small piece of many great and rare things I'd be willing to sell Javier, should he be interested," Marlon replied, descending the rocky platform.

Cordell stood taller as Marlon neared. "Tribal knickknacks and rubies barely large enough to be of *mild* interest, even to me? Javier's interested in *gold* and other items of significance. Why are you wasting my time, Marlon? I don't like it when people waste my time."

Marlon grinned widely. It appeared out of place on his rather gruff face. "These *are* trinkets, but what if I were to tell you I've come upon a place filled with all sorts of treasure and objects of historical significance?"

"Bottom line it." Cordell returned the items to the pouch, tied it shut, and tossed it back to Marlon.

The other halfling caught it without taking his eyes off Cordell. "Aquadion relics and riches."

"What?"

"You've heard the stories. There's said to be a race of elves under the waves. A race that hasn't been seen except for the odd sailor's tale or a bard's ballad."

"We've all heard the legends. But old stories aren't tangible. *Gold* is, and that's what Javier wants . . . as do I."

Cordell turned to leave, but Marlon clasped his arm, saying, "I've found your gold and a whole lot more—ancient objects of art and other things of interest, too. Think about it. What would it be like for Javier to corner the market on Aquadion artifacts? Pretty rewarding." Marlon removed his grip.

"It could be. But why are you coming to me? If you have access to such wealth—and I emphasize *if*—then why do you need me or Javier?" He eyed Marlon closely. Few things were as they first appeared in his line of work. Before he'd even think of shaking hands on anything, he always made sure he could see all the angles.

"Come on, Cordell, you know you're the best fence in the city. If I want the reward, I have to make the sacrifice of putting up with you."

"*If* I'm willing to take you on, that is."

"You'll get a hefty cut too," Marlon purred. "I wouldn't dream of stiffing you."

"Hopefully a larger cut than you, though somehow I doubt that."

Marlon shrugged. "It's just business. A halfling has to make a living somehow, but I can't do that if Javier isn't interested in giving me some coin in exchange for my discovery. And it's more than either of you can imagine. I haven't even finished cataloging everything. There's a whole other room and a grotto I haven't even fully searched."

Cordell paused, continuing his exploration of the emerging angles. "And how would Javier know what he got was authentic and not a trick?"

"I'm not *that* much of a wizard," Marlon confessed. "Ask anyone who is, and they'll tell you the spells I do know—the ones I pinch from here and there, that is—are only minor ones. Besides, I'm willing to have it all verified by an expert—even a mage if you'd like—before doing the transaction. I don't want any doubt what I'm offering is genuine."

Cordell nodded. "That could work."

"Then how soon do you think we could get things moving?"

"I would think within a week."

"That should work out fine."

"Next time, though, we meet in the city, at the usual place," he said, turning back toward Caster's Reef. "You don't need theatrics to show me some rubies and a hunk of ivory."

"All right," Marlon agreed from behind. "Let's say the end of next week at about dusk."

"Fine—" Cordell started before discovering Marlon had vanished. "Not much of a wizard, my left foot." Silently he trekked through the sand, working up another sweat and cursing under his breath about why he'd been fool enough to meet out here in the first place.

Late morning found Corwyn Danther making his way down Harbor Avenue in Caster's Reef. The road led to the harbors, providing a natural conduit for the influx of produce and materials from across the Midlands and even the far-off Western and Southern Lands. The smells of spices and salt from the sea perfumed the wind gliding down the street. This same wind made the silk, cloth of gold, and other precious fabrics on display dance in a tantalizing manner, tempting passersby for a closer look.

The avenue was packed with people and carts loaded down for transport either from Caster's Reef or to it. The rest of the people were hawking their goods or buzzing about from shop to shop, vendor booth to vendor booth, like bees in a field of wildflowers. He'd been down this way before, yet every day something would catch his eye. It seemed more booths came and went by the day, keeping a constant sense of newness about the area.

Along the way he noticed the performers on top of wooden crates or in small openings among the vendors, somehow missed by both shop and booth owner alike. These bards sang happy tales, told stories, juggled, put on puppet shows, or engaged in other activities, hoping to catch the eyes, ears, and coin of anyone they could. Children were their biggest patrons, pulling over their parents, who'd drop a coin into the cup or cloth placed prominently nearby.

It had been a week since he arrived from Wave's Rest. With his funds still abundant from Lena's gracious outfitting, he found himself living better than he had in recent memory. He also enjoyed being just a normal person in this thriving and bustling independent city. He'd decided he could do with some rest and enjoy a sabbatical until the end of summer. And by seeing Fredrick safely off that morning, he could now take full advantage of said rest.

The two had parted ways when Fredrick learned of Corwyn's intention to stay on till summer's end. After that he'd make his way to Haven, where

Corwyn would spend fall and winter. And with fall some time off, there wasn't really anything of interest keeping Fredrick in the city. Ultimately, he finally decided Corwyn would be safe enough without him—a small miracle in itself, but probably just practical thinking, if anything. If he wouldn't be wandering off again there wasn't any reason for the dwarf to stay. Corwyn knew Fredrick could also visit with some of his kith and kin in Rockshire. They both could use the rest.

Caster's Reef was on the western corner of Talatheal. Because of this, it had a long, rich, and interesting history. And like many independent cities, it had much to offer those with the financial means. He'd found a place to stay not too far from the heart of the city, which allowed him access to the main ebbs and flows. From there, he'd gone out exploring every day. He'd always had a love of learning new things and soon found himself in congregations of sages and other persons of interest. Talking with sailors and workers on the docks taught him much about the city, as did the conversations he overheard among the local vendors.

About half an hour from noon, he'd made it to the middle of the avenue and another booth where a wide assortment of bric-a-brac caught his eye. The items were scattered on a purple cloth draped over the wooden counter that ran the entire booth's width.

"You need some help?" asked a pleasant female voice. He'd been so engrossed in the objects he didn't even see the booth's occupant until he raised his face in greeting.

"You have quite a selection—"

He stopped when his eyes fell upon a familiar face. "Trina?"

"Corwyn?" The woman was just as amazed to see him.

"You look better than ever." He smiled softly at the brown-haired Telborian. It wasn't an exaggeration. She'd hardly changed since last he'd laid eyes upon her.

"Still a smooth talker, I see."

"What are you doing here? This is a long way from Argos."

"What am *I* doing here? How about you? I thought I'd never see you again. Course, back then I *wanted* to never see you again."

He paused, not sure what to say or do next. Trina apparently was working through a similar challenge. The span of silence sent his mind racing for a solution.

"Is this your booth?" he finally heard himself ask while stepping back for a better look. It wasn't too impressive compared to those he'd seen thus far, but it wasn't the worst either.

"I got involved in some explorations and found I like being more of a sage than a bard. I can make more money, too, selling my services and any trinkets I find along the way."

"I never thought you'd go down *that* path."

"That makes two of us," she said. "But then again, we didn't always see eye to eye on career choices."

"I'm happy to see you've proved me wrong."

"Are you?" The spark in her green eyes got his attention.

"Do you still sing?" he asked.

"A little, but I never really was that much of a singer, you know that."

"I thought you were lovely, actually."

He caught the subtle turn at the corner of her lips before Trina turned to watch the other people passing, putting herself firmly back in the present. "How long have you been in Caster's Reef?"

"I'm just here visiting for the summer, I think."

"You *think*?" She raised an eyebrow.

"I wanted to get some rest," he said, picking up a necklace on a nearby wooden dowel for closer examination. "I've been on the road a lot and needed to take a break for a while."

He could feel Trina's gaze. "You've changed, too. The Corwyn I knew had all these great ideas about wanting to do and see so much before he made his way to Mortis. You couldn't sit still at times."

"I still have plans and places I want to see," he said, returning the necklace to its former location. "Adventures just have a funny way of finding me. And sometimes they can wear me out more than I thought."

"Age will do that." She flashed some teeth. He found himself mirroring the grin on reflex.

"Still sharp witted, I see."

"It comes in handy in my line of work."

"I suppose you have difficult people from time to time." He made a quick study of the space around Trina's booth to make sure he wasn't blocking it from any interested shoppers.

"You could say that." The conversation again fell into a lull, leaving each staring at the other.

"It must get a bit boring when you're out there on your own." Trina deftly broke the silence by peering around and behind Corwyn, no doubt looking for fresh patrons.

"I'm not always alone." His reply snapped Trina's eyes back onto him.

"So, you finally found a poor woman willing to—"

"No. It's not like that. I travel with friends from time to time."

"No one special then?" Once again there was a sparkle in her eyes. She always had a sort of mischievous quality, a faint hint of the scoundrel in training tempting him to join her. And for a while he'd yielded to the temptation . . . "You aren't getting any younger either."

"I think you already mentioned that," he teased. "But I'm young enough and still have years ahead of me. The right one will come along at the right time." The sparkle faded as her attention trailed off again into the bustling marketplace.

"What about you?"

"Someone special, you mean? No." She suddenly became interested in the items on display. "I don't have anyone but me right now, and that's why I'm out here selling every day. Course, who'd want to be married to *me* anyway? A woman who spends her nights with her nose in a book or scroll trying to research her wares or keeping order in the sales ledgers to make sure she's still getting a profit. Not really the stuff of romantic inspiration."

"I think you might be selling yourself short."

"I've heard that before. And from the same source, no less."

"It's still true." Again, the two paused, silently pondering each other. He noticed the fine lines on her face for the first time. They actually augmented her natural beauty, giving it greater depth.

"Still the same optimist." She chuckled.

"I guess some things don't change. How long have you lived here?"

"Long enough to know there's a nice dining hall not too far from here, off Harold and Elliott Street. I think you'd like it."

"I'll have to look into it, then, thanks."

"Why don't you meet me there at sunset tomorrow night?" Her question caught him off guard. "My treat. You should be properly welcomed to the city, which I'm sure you'll want to know more about. And we can get caught up with one another, too. This really isn't the best place for a conversation."

He noticed the people crowding around the booth, searching through Trina's wares. He didn't want to take away any more of her business than he might have already. "What's the name of the hall?"

"The Kraken's Lair. You can't miss it."

"Okay," he said, looking over the booth one last time. "I'm curious to hear how you came to all this, too. That must be a *real* interesting story."

"Hello." Trina greeted another customer with a grin and a nod. "Hey," she called after Corwyn. "I like the hat. It suits you."

He tipped the brim, then continued his trek down the other half of the avenue. But he didn't see much, lost in a daze, already thinking about tomorrow night. Half of him wanted to cancel, letting that part of his life stay in the past, but the other half eagerly wanted news of what she'd been doing since they parted. She didn't look as bad off as she could have, and if she really *was* doing something productive with her life . . . He was so taken with his thoughts he almost knocked over a halfling hurrying down the avenue against the flow of traffic.

"Hey! Watch it, you idiot!" The halfling narrowly avoided getting shoved into a passing open-bed cart.

"Oh." Corwyn came to himself with a start, lowering his head for a look. He couldn't help but take note of the billowing cream silk shirt, black vest, and finely sewn brown pants with matching leather boots. Nor the collection of rings on both hands. Fine attire worn by anyone, halfling or not. "I'm sorry. I didn't see you—"

"Yeah, yeah, yeah," the other grumbled, making his way from Corwyn as fast as his legs could carry him. "That's what all you idiots say. The world isn't full of just you gangly giants, you know."

He watched the halfling depart before resuming his exploration of the avenue.

After his brief collision with the Telborian, Cordell made his way up the crowded avenue until finding Trina's booth and making his way for it rather less politely than others might have. His size limited his view, allowing only his head access above the counter.

"I got everything set up," he informed her.

"Good." She greeted another customer and answered a few questions before returning to Cordell.

"It's still on for tonight, like I told you," he continued.

"Where?"

"The Golden Minotaur." Cordell's face soured when another patron rubbed against him while perusing the items for sale. "Be there an hour after nightfall and look for me. I'll have a table in back for us, and we can get down to business."

"How much is this going to pay?" Trina said plainly.

"Better than the other ones if what he's presenting is as good as he says." Cordell's eyes shifted to the various trinkets beneath his nose. "How's business? It's getting close to the end of the month, you know."

"It could be better. But don't worry, you'll get your cut."

"It better be more than a few coppers." Cordell made sure Trina knew he wasn't making an idle threat. "I can't keep cutting you slack if you can't do what you're supposed to do."

"Don't worry about me. I'm more than good for it, you know that. You wouldn't be here if you didn't think so yourself."

Cordell smiled. "Tough, smart, and beautiful."

"So, you think it's going to be that big?"

"Yeah. If it pans out, you'll be able to live life a little better for quite a while."

"That good, huh?" Trina greeted an elven man studying a necklace on a nearby dowel with some interest.

"*If* it can be trusted," Cordell emphasized.

"You haven't been suckered yet," said Trina.

"How much is this?" asked the elf.

"One hour after nightfall," said Cordell, backing up from the booth while Trina returned to the elf.

2

Night descended upon Caster's Reef like a mist. The new moon added its tint to the lamp-lit cobblestone streets of the city's warehouse district. If Harbor Avenue was the main thoroughfare through which what arrived on the docks made its way into the city, then the warehouse district was the fortress built to protect that traffic flow. Given the place's nature, sailors and merchants often populated the area, mingling with the odd traveler fresh from a boat.

Among the shops and taverns, mead halls, and even a few inns, Trina found what she sought easily enough. The wooden sign over the doorway bore a picture of a golden minotaur, naked save for a loincloth, glaring down in contempt at those below. The name of the tavern was written plainly above the creature in Telboros. Behind the wooden door a pleasant atmosphere greeted her. Smells of stews, fish, and even some stomach-pleasing wafts of beef had her entertaining thoughts of perhaps getting something more for dinner than the simple bread and broth she'd been contemplating.

Inside, the tavern was divided into three rooms. The main room, which she'd entered, housed most of the traffic and the bar. Then there were two rooms behind that, branching off to the left and right. These weren't as well lit, but the glass-topped oil lamps scattered along the main room's wooden support beams helped make things clear enough. In short, the Golden Minotaur wasn't the classiest of establishments, but it wasn't a dive, either. She'd been in worse. Based on previous dealings, she suspected Cordell and company would be in one of the two less illuminated rooms.

"Right on time." Cordell stepped up to her out of nowhere. "I'll take you to the table."

They made their way through the motley crowd of patrons en route to the room branching to the left. As they did, Trina noticed how many halflings were about. So many, in fact, she found it slightly unsettling, since they weren't known to congregate in sizable numbers in many places. She wondered how many of them were connected to Cordell or his fellows. Or maybe they were tied to another organization who had their fingers in other parts of Caster's Reef. If they bore her any ill will, it wasn't reflected in their indifferent glances.

"We already got dinner," Cordell informed her. "You know how the boss likes his seafood."

"Then I'm surprised this place has anything left to sell." She carefully searched the room, looking for the face she'd seen only a few times in her life.

"I'd keep that under your breath." Cordell stepped to the side, inviting her to a table encircled by two halflings and two empty chairs. "After you."

She made her way to the far corner of the room, taking the only empty chair without any food before it. It was also the only chair lacking the thick cushion that lifted the others up to a more comfortable height for the table. Not every establishment in Caster's Reef used them, but given the number of halflings filling the place, she could see why they kept so many on hand.

"Hello, Trina." Javier, an older, plumper halfling, greeted her as she took her seat. On his plate were the bodies of three lobsters he was working through with vigor.

"Javier."

Of all three halflings gathered, Javier was the best dressed. She couldn't imagine him being anything but. Tonight, he'd donned a purple silken shirt under a brown leather vest—both stretched snugly over his large frame. His pants were fine black wool. Amazingly, he hadn't removed any of his copious rings, instead slathering them with butter and lobster juice while he ate.

"This is Trina," Javier told another halfling beside Cordell. "She's the expert we trust will do a fair job."

"Marlon." The other halfling nodded in greeting. Marlon's attempt to size her up was mildly amusing. Of course, she was doing the exact same to him. She'd learned doing this early on helped keep you on the good side of any deal. The stubble-faced and haggard-looking halfling wore the common dark brown tunic and pants, trying perhaps too hard to appear nondescript. His black hair was also long and straight, differing from the other two halflings' short brown locks.

"I'm told you have a potentially big offer." She turned back to Javier.

"The biggest I've come across yet." He spoke while sucking lobster meat from inside a broken leg.

"How big?" Trina's eyes narrowed.

"I've found a burial site—and I believe even a ceremonial site—of Aquadion origin," Marlon coolly replied. "It's *huge* and loaded with all sorts of things and potential profit."

"Aquadion?" She didn't hide the skepticism in her voice.

"Yes, Aquadion," said Marlon. His smile resembled a muted snarl. "And they've brought *you* on to verify my claim before we can move forward." Trina didn't enjoy the subtle dislike Marlon let flutter over the matter. She wasn't the biggest fan of halflings, true enough, but the longer their interaction, the less of a fan she became.

"Think of it." Javier had moved on to cracking the back of another lobster with his pudgy paws. "There should be a whole bunch of religious and other artifacts we could make a *killing* off. Maybe we could even sell the bodies as curiosities."

"Dead bodies?" Apparently, she was the only one at the table uneasy with the notion.

"Why not? Wizards might want them for something, or someone might want to have one of their own. They're a rarity when they're alive— even more so, I wager, dead."

"So what makes you qualified to verify my find?" Marlon's glare burned into Trina's skull. "You don't look so special to me."

"I'm good with identifying fakes and know a bit of the history of the land, too. I was trained as a bard, and part of that is learning a great deal about historical matters."

Marlon turned to Cordell. "You got a bard to prove me? A *bard*? What's wrong with a *sage* or even a *Dradinite*? You have to insult me with a bard?"

"She's good," said Cordell, "and I trust her. *You*, on the other hand, haven't yet been so vetted." Marlon's jaw locked at Cordell's reply.

"You'll be paid well, Trina," Javier said between the large bites of meat he kept digging out of the lobster's midsection. "So you shouldn't be concerned there."

"How well?" She found herself growing less hungry with each wad of lobster Javier crammed into his already-full mouth.

"I told her she'd be paid the usual plus a cut of the take," Cordell informed Javier.

"How much you going to leave for *me*?" Marlon sniped.

"You need someone to take these things and sell them. That *is* why you sought me out in the first place, correct?" Javier wiped the melted butter drizzling out of his lips with a cloth napkin. "Then you have to understand there are going to be expenses."

"Expenses are fine," Marlon huffed. "But now you're cutting into profits."

Javier studied Marlon with a face more solid than stone despite the flabby jowls outlining it. "You came to us, Marlon. You can take our aid or leave it, but you'll be hard pressed to find anyone in the city who can help you more than me."

"So, Trina"—Javier's features softened as he shifted the conversation back her way—"we'd like you to investigate his claim. See if he really has something good to offer."

"How soon would you need me?"

"I think Marlon would like to move on this as soon as possible." Javier took up the last lobster on his plate and broke it open between his fat hands. "That work for you?"

"I could be ready in two days."

"That works for me," Javier managed to say through another mouthful of lobster. "How about you, Marlon?"

"That should be fine, I guess," came Marlon's flat reply.

As she listened, Trina had an idea. It was something that might make things easier, get her a greater return for her services, and perhaps do a few other things besides . . . "I might need extra help getting it all done, if it's as big a haul as you say. And I'm sure you're going to be pressed for a fast turnaround. I wonder if I could bring another with me to help out?"

Marlon scowled. "I'm not going to lose even *more* of my cut—"

"No," Trina interrupted. "No more cuts, just a helper for me to get the verification done faster."

Javier thought while he chewed. "Can they be trusted?"

"I think so."

"*Thinking* so and *knowing* so aren't really the same, my girl," he said before taking a large swig from a nearby copper goblet. "I don't run my business on *thinking* I know things, but on *knowing* I know things." His face matched the steely tone of his words. "Those who've made that mistake now rot behind iron bars . . . or worse."

"Don't worry," she continued, unaffected by the veiled threats. "I trust him with my life."

"You might be doing just that." Javier waved a lobster claw in her direction.

"You can trust him." She realized she was trying to convince herself as well as Javier.

"You're going to take him on sight unseen?" Marlon protested in a low growl. "What kind of operation you running here?"

"Who is he?" asked Cordell.

"Someone who knows a good deal about history and should be pretty good at validating this find."

"*Should* be?" Marlon continued his griping.

"Corwyn Danther," she said, looking Marlon full in the face. He'd been taking a drink from his goblet when she answered. Upon hearing the name he choked, spraying out his watered-down ale.

"I've heard about him," Cordell informed Javier, who contemplated the remains of his meal with a mournful expression.

"Good things?" asked Javier.

"He's supposed to be pretty famous." Marlon's voice was still raw from coughing. "But no matter how good an entertainer, he's still only a bard."

"Never heard of him." Javier took a fresh napkin and cleaned his hands, polishing his rings in the process. "And if I don't know him, then I can't trust him."

She had to act fast; she'd opened a quickly closing window. If anything, she'd feel better with Corwyn around. At least she could trust him. But would he trust her? One thing at a time.

"He wouldn't have to know about all this," she continued. "I could say I came across something and want to get his opinion on it."

Javier stared Trina down, his face looking more piggish now that it wasn't so involved in consuming his dinner. "He won't go blabbing this around, will he?" he asked at last. "He *is* a bard, after all."

"No. He'll keep it to himself if I ask him to. He's a man of his word, if anything." She supposed that much was true. But how much would he have to know to be brought along, and then how much to keep him on? She quickly took herself to task for not thinking this through as clearly as she should have before bringing it up. And why *did* she bring it up, anyway? But what was said was said . . . She needed to start digging her way out of this hole if she wanted to make any progress.

"What else you hear about this Corwyn, Cordell?" Javier inquired before draining the rest of his goblet.

"Only that he's a good performer."

"I've known him long enough to know that he can be trusted," Trina assured him. "If you trust me, you can trust him. Besides, if you have Cordell check him out, he might get suspicious and start digging into this, which isn't what any of us want, right?"

"I don't want anyone more than is needed to see these things," said Marlon, "at least until coins change hands."

"You really think he'll get the job done faster?" Again, Javier's dark eyes bore into her.

"Positive."

"I've come to trust you, Trina, but if this goes down badly, I'll have no qualms about seeing you're held responsible. You understand?"

She gave a small nod.

"Good. Then you can use him to help if you keep him out of the loop."

Marlon didn't say anything, but she could tell he wasn't pleased with how things had transpired. But he couldn't do much about it. He'd be even less pleased to learn how carefully she'd have to plan this all out to bring Corwyn into the picture. In some ways it reminded her of when they were still together . . . Course, back then things were simpler. Though, given their interaction this morning, she was confident she knew how to put everything into place.

3

The next night found Corwyn seated across from Trina in the Kraken's Lair, a fairly decent tavern and food hall not too far from the better part of the city. Nestled in the midst of several modest inns and shops, it was geared more toward travelers than local residents but still remained a welcoming place.

"So have you guessed yet?" Trina watched him as she lifted her copper goblet.

"Guessed what?"

"What this place reminds you of." She took a sip of her wine.

He made a quick survey, trying to see the setting in a new light. "I don't think it looks like anything in particular."

Trina laughed. "You haven't changed all that much, you know that?" She'd chosen to wear a rather nice, but not too outlandish, low-cut red dress. She figured it would hold his attention.

"Really?" He raised an eyebrow.

"Yes." A serving woman approached their table, setting their dinner before them on copper plates with matching utensils. Trina had ordered the catch of the day. Corwyn opted for a bowl of soup.

"Thank you," said Corwyn, flashing a smile. The woman returned it politely before departing.

"Yeah," she continued, "still the same old Corwyn."

"Well, you've changed some," he said, stirring his soup. "The Trina I knew wouldn't be here doing what you're doing now."

"Yeah," she said, taking a deeper interest in her fish, "sometimes we don't always get to choose the paths we take."

"It's still nice to see you again. I know that's probably the last thing you'd expect to hear from me, but it's the truth."

"Time and age smooth away a lot of rough edges, or whatever it was Gath always liked to say." She had to be careful to draw the lines in slowly for everything to work.

"Trina?"

She snapped back to the present, unaware of how lost in her planning she'd become. "Sorry. Just thinking."

Corwyn nodded. "I've been doing a lot of that too since we ran into each other."

"It's kind of hard not to."

"I was surprised you'd even want to talk to me, let alone sit down and have a meal together."

"Same here. I'm happy you took me up on the offer."

"Me too." Thinking the time right, she bent below the table and came back up with a small wooden box. "Which leads me to this." The surprise on Corwyn's face told her she still had her natural instinct for timing.

"You kept it? I thought you tossed it into the lake."

"I lied." She lifted the brass latch keeping the box closed. "I thought if you believed it, I'd get back at you—make you suffer."

"It worked."

The sudden pang surprised her, but she quickly overcame it. She couldn't afford to get distracted. "I'm sorry, Corwyn. It was a foolish thing to do, and I've been thinking a lot about it these past few days."

"I forgave you a while ago, Trina." She couldn't hide her confused and amazed expression. "If I didn't, we wouldn't be here talking right now, would we?"

"No." She couldn't help but follow the logic. "I guess we wouldn't. Over the last few years, I came to forgive you too," she confessed. "You were right about a lot of things. I see that now. Oddly enough, I was sort of hoping I'd find a day when I'd get to give this back to you. I didn't know how or when, and then there you were. And walking right up to me, no less, in front of my very own booth. The gods must have a pretty good sense of humor."

She spun the box around so it faced Corwyn. "Here. It's rightfully yours anyway. And what better time to give it back? We might not cross paths again." She watched him open the box, carefully observing as he took an interest in the collection of rolled parchment sheets tied with a red silk ribbon inside.

"You were right about me too in some things," he said, seeking her face, "but I gave that song to you. It's yours. It was the moment I handed it over."

"You sure?" She wasn't expecting that. Or maybe she was . . . Shaking her head for clarity, she regained her focus.

"I was sure when I gave it to you then and still am now."

She held her tongue, holding firm her trembling lips while fighting back the growing moisture in her eyes. She started to reconsider what she was doing, then forced herself to stop. Focus. She needed to focus.

"So what's this place supposed to remind me of again?" He gave the interior another glance.

"That old place in Argos off of Oak and Muse Avenue," she said, closing the box and putting it back under the table.

"Oh yeah. That place was more run down than this, though."

"I didn't say it was a *perfect* duplicate, and there aren't as many bards here on the street performing for their supper." She shared a wry smirk. "Course, you don't have to worry about that, not if what I hear of your reputation is true."

"I wouldn't believe everything you hear, but I've managed to do pretty well, thanks to the grace of Causilla and constantly working to improve."

"So what have you been up to anyway?" She dug into her fish. "It's been almost a decade. You must have been pretty busy if you kept to all those things you said you wanted to do back in Argos."

"You can say that." Corwyn ate more of his soup. A pleasant discourse followed, each catching up with the other. Eventually, the evening ebbed, leaving the two among only a handful in the establishment with closing time drawing near.

"Dead soldiers?" Trina didn't hide her surprise at Corwyn's latest story.

"Not really dead soldiers but phantoms."

"Still." She finished off the last of her wine. "That had to be something."

"It was." He drained the final contents of his own goblet, this one holding only spiced cider, which he'd been drinking the entire evening. Old habits die hard, she supposed. "But thanks to Causilla, I did some good there."

She fell silent upon tripping into Corwyn's blue-green eyes. The longer she lingered, the more the old feelings stirred, birthing fresh unease.

"You look great," she said at last. "Have I told you that yet? You actually got better looking as you got older."

"I can see someone's had a little too much wine."

"Maybe." And that was probably true. She'd already drained five goblets, if she hadn't lost count along the way. She told herself it had all been to help her relax and enjoy the evening, but now she wasn't so sure, especially given her present fascination.

"But you do look good." Hearing the words before she knew she spoke them, she shook herself from a daze, becoming lucid and businesslike again. Time to pull in the final line and close the deal. "As long as you're here, I wonder if you'd be interested in tagging along with me on something you might enjoy."

"And what's that?"

"I've been hired to help investigate a recent discovery—to make sure it's genuine before more work can be done on it. Since you like seeing old things and seem apt to go on adventures"—she smirked—"this might be perfect for you."

"So you're just verifying it?"

"I'm told it's a possible crypt or tomb for Aquadions."

Corwyn leaned back in his chair. "I don't think I've ever seen anything related to them. But there sure are a lot of legends."

"Especially around here," she added. "Sailors like to keep adding to the collection."

"I don't know if I'd be able to help you too much there. I didn't study much on Aquadions, you might recall."

"But you're good at spotting fakes," she returned, giving the line another tug. "And I know you might come across things that you *do* know more about, and that would be a great help." She deepened her smile. "And it would give us more time together while you're here."

Corwyn thought while Trina held her breath. She realized there had been more truth in that last statement than she cared to admit. What was she doing? If she couldn't keep her head fully in the game—

"It could be fun, I guess."

"Kind of like old times." She carefully masked the fresh swarm of butterflies exploring her stomach. Again, what was she doing?

"Let's hope it's better than old times. I can do without all the arguing. When will you be looking them over?"

"Tomorrow."

"Well, if you think I'd be any help, I'm in. Just tell me where and what time to meet."

4

Late morning found Corwyn and Trina making their way onto the beach around Caster's Reef. With them were the seagulls, diving and soaring above the same waves where fishermen and cargo vessels were busy with the rigors of their trade.

"So how far out are we supposed to go?" Corwyn eyed the long stretch of sand curving north before finally blending into the horizon.

"About a mile." Trina shielded her eyes, studying the same stretch of beach.

"It's amazing to think anything could be hidden on or around this beach." Corwyn kept pace, making sure to keep his hat on whenever a gust flew in from the sea. Both went for simpler attire than the night before: brown pants and, oddly enough, matching white shirts. "You'd think it'd been pretty well explored already over the centuries."

"He's known for his ability to find things that others often overlook, or so I'm told."

"How do you know him?"

"He's someone one of my suppliers put me in contact with," she replied, stopping to retrieve a seashell from the sand.

"So you've traded patrons for suppliers. I suppose it's close to the same thing." Another gust tugged at Corwyn's hat, but he held it true, fixing the leather straps he'd tied under his chin. "You really have become a merchant, haven't you?"

Trina straightened her frame. "It's better in some ways. The coin's steadier than sporadic shows, and the patrons are less demanding."

"Well, it's good to see you finally became so *honest* in your work."

She quickly diverted her attention forward. "We didn't really see eye to eye on that, did we?"

"A little of an understatement." He watched her turn the seashell in her hand.

"Funny how things seem to come full circle in life, isn't it? Makes you wonder if people can start over. Maybe even be given a second chance."

He placed a hand on Trina's shoulder. "You know the Light Gods are merciful and teach us to be the same to others . . . and ourselves."

Trina's misty eyes found his face. "If I was more of a religious person, I suppose I'd have myself thinking Saredhel had something to do with us meeting again."

"Maybe it was Causilla," he offered. "She *is* the goddess of love, after all." The smile following his words squeezed out a few tears.

"You always were the romantic one," she said, fighting back the lump in her throat.

"I just choose to try my best and to see the best in you."

Trina nodded as they resumed their trek, wiping a stray tear from her cheek every so often. "Marlon might not be too happy to see you, did I tell you that?"

"No. Well then, maybe it isn't a good idea for me to come along. I can turn back and—"

"Oh no," she quickly returned. "I need you—to help. It's just—Marlon thinks you're going to take his cut."

"Take his cut?" He shot her a curious glance.

"He's going to get paid by the person purchasing these things if they're found to be genuine."

"So he's a supplier?"

"In a way." She quickened her step. "We'll have plenty of time to talk about it tonight if you like. Right now we have to meet up with our friend. We don't want to keep him waiting too long. He might get a bit grouchy."

"It won't be the first time a halfling's been moody with me." Corwyn matched Trina's pace.

"It's about time you got here," Marlon growled through the half-spent cigarette in his curled lips. Given his demeanor and the remains of about half a dozen spent butts around him, Corwyn assumed he probably had been waiting for a while. "You stop for a *picnic* on your way?" He wore dark attire with an equally drab cloak.

"That was more than a mile," said Trina. She and Corwyn thought it was actually closer to three.

"So?" Marlon huffed out a cloud of smoke. "You got long legs—use them."

"This is Corwyn Danther," Trina said. Corwyn held out his hand. Marlon took a long drag on the last of his cigarette and tossed it into the sandy rock with a disgusted sneer. Seeing this, Corwyn gave up on the handshake.

"Are we *ready* now?"

"Sure." Trina was curt.

"Okay then." Marlon made his way to the lapping blue waves beside them, pulling off his cloak. "We'll have to swim a bit to get to where it's at."

"How far?" Trina planted her hands on her slender hips.

"Nothing to worry about."

"Marlon?" she pressed.

The halfling peered over his shoulder. "It's really not far. Trust me." Trina shook her head, then made her way to the edge of the water. Corwyn followed. "You can hold your breath, right?" Marlon waded into the cool waves.

"I'm not a fish," she said, stopping before she touched the water. "If I die, Javier won't be pleased."

"I'm sure it'll be fine," Corwyn assured her.

"Whose side are you on?"

"Can we keep it moving?" Marlon kept walking into the water, already wading up to his waist. "While there's still daylight?"

"I just wish I'd known we'd be swimming," said Corwyn. "I would have left my hat at the house."

"It'll still be there when you get back," Trina assured him.

"Let's hope so." He placed his hat in what he hoped would be a safe, dry spot, then followed Trina into the water until they were swallowed by the sea. Together the trio swam north and sank beneath the rocky coast into a rough cavern. He couldn't see much of it as they swam—the darkness proved a challenge to finding his own way, let alone trying to follow others. But soon enough they found themselves swimming upward.

A pocket of air formed above them, and all three came to the end of the water and the start of hard rock and darkness. Gulping down mouthfuls of air, Trina and Corwyn began making sense of this clammy murk. It stubbornly refused to reveal any of its secrets, no matter how long they peered into its depths.

"Wasn't too bad now, was it?" Marlon climbed out of the water and onto the cold rock lip sliding into the pool from which all three had emerged.

"I guess that depends on how things look once we can get some light," said Trina as she pulled herself up from the water. Corwyn joined her as their eyes grew accustomed to the dark.

"Leave that to me." Marlon snapped his fingers, and a collection of torches scattered across the nearby cavern wall flared into life. This same wall formed a semicircle, the end of which met the pool. The top of the cavern stood about seven or so feet above them, devoid of any decoration.

"So you're a mage?" Corwyn watched Marlon with fresh interest while squeezing what water he could out of his shirt.

"Not as such." Marlon was rather interested in how Trina's wet garments clung to her figure. "I've picked up some helpful things here and there, but I'm not much of a wizard."

Corwyn noticed a wide golden door opposite where he stood. It appeared to have interesting relief work covering it, but he was hard pressed to make much out of it from a distance.

Trina made for the door, wringing water from her hair along the way. "How did you find this place? This grotto isn't the easiest of places to stumble upon."

Corwyn couldn't help noticing Marlon smirk as Trina passed, his eyes fondling a backside made even more delightfully defined by the recent swim. For a moment he felt a flutter of jealousy. Alarmed and amazed, he pushed it aside and hopefully well out of mind.

"That's not really important," said the halfling. "What's behind that door is, though."

"This is amazing," said Corwyn, drawing near the door. "I've never seen anything like this before." He could see now the blocky pictographic forms of what he could only surmise were elven figures and other flora and fauna. The gold was overlay. He could see places where it had worn thin, and the wood underneath stood out in patches amid the shimmering pieces which remained. As to what the images meant, however, he hadn't a clue. All around the door were varying lengths of pictographic images arrayed in smaller frames, as if the images meant to convey an idea were squished into a sort of box—all following a systematic column layout.

"Oh, just wait," Marlon assured them with a crooked smile. "Push the door aside and you'll see why I've kept it under wraps for so long."

Trina and Corwyn did as bidden. It wasn't heavy and didn't make a sound. As it opened Marlon snapped his fingers and light popped up from the darkness. This time it came from two brass braziers greeting them a few feet from the doorway. The illumination scattered dancing light into a chamber covered with the same raised pictographic blocks all over the walls. The large room must have belonged to a network of caverns that finished at the grotto.

"What are you playing at?" Trina turned back to Marlon. "There's nothing here."

"That's what I thought, too," he said, making his way deeper inside. "But then I walked a little further and found something very *interesting*." He motioned for them to join him at the far end of the chamber.

"What? A wall?"

"Look closer." Marlon pointed to a certain section.

"A door." Corwyn spotted it almost at once.

"A door?" Trina still didn't see it.

"Look at the outline here." He traced the perimeter of a door frame subtly defined among the square boxes framing the pictographs.

"Smart fellow," said Marlon.

"Yes, he is." Trina shared a pleased grin. Corwyn couldn't mistake the familiar twinge at the bottom of his stomach. For a moment he became lost in the past, remembering old feelings, old desires . . .

"Now," said Marlon, giving the stone door a push, "*this* is what I need to have you verify." The door opened silently, spilling out fresh darkness.

He faced them with a serious expression. "You better do right by me. Don't be getting any wrong ideas when you see this haul."

"Why—"

"You can count on us to be fair," Trina cut Corwyn off, motioning for Marlon to continue.

Marlon snapped his fingers again, and the darkness was vanquished by brilliant light. What lay beyond the hidden door made both speechless. "Well, come on. I haven't got all day." The halfling made his way inside.

As he followed Trina, Corwyn couldn't believe his eyes. All around the chamber, light shone from golden statues of life-sized elves. These were clothed in loincloths with the addition of bandeaux for the women. Each held aloft a brass bowl, from which came the room's illumination. The statues were scattered around the room close to the walls, but not touching them, allowing access behind them if needed.

Here again the walls were carved in the strange images found in the previous room. A handful of massive oaken chests—many of them open— were scattered across the area, revealing a rich cargo of precious gems, gold, jewelry, and other items of worth. In a slightly more orderly fashion, large stone boxes carved with the now-familiar pictographic displays rested in the room's center. But there was still more to see.

Other works of art—smaller statues of aquatic life and elven figures carved into solid ivory—stood next to roughly carved humanoid shapes, serving as holders for a collection of various uniquely crafted suits of armor, swords, and spears. The armor especially caught his eye. It consisted mainly of sleeveless leather shirts with what appeared to be some sort of segmented pauldrons crafted from bone. The ivory statues' arms and legs wore matching greaves and bracers.

"I told you," Marlon gloated from behind while weaseling his way through the collection. "You might have your work cut out for you if you're trying to prove me false."

"I don't think anyone said you're a liar." Corwyn let his eyes drift through the room's wonders.

"On the other hand, you can never be too careful." Trina's saccharine grin mocked the halfling. "It's just business. You understand."

Marlon gave a small snort, muttered a few words probably unsuitable for a lady's ears, and made his way for one of the open chests. "As you can see, I found the chests full of all sorts of goodies. The stone boxes, I'm thinking, are sarcophagi, and the armor and weapons held up pretty well, too." He dug into a chest and pulled out a string of black pearls. "Should all be worth some fine coin, I wager."

"Why not sell it yourself?" Corwyn found his way to the nearest golden statue. "I'm sure there are plenty of scholars, scribes, and more who'd pay you enough to retire comfortably for the rest of your life, even after all the taxes and fees."

"He doesn't want to get bogged down with business," said Trina, hurrying to Corwyn's side.

"Yeah," Marlon agreed. "Too many taxes and other things to contend with, like you said. I prefer to keep things simple if I can."

"So, what do you think?" She watched Corwyn examine the golden elven maid. "Can you help verify this stuff?"

"I can tell you if it's real or not, sure," he said, touching the brass bowl. "But I don't know if I can tell you *what* it is exactly. I don't think I've ever heard of anyone finding anything about Aquadions before. Anything reliable, that is."

"I guess I'm just lucky like that." Marlon plopped down on the edge of a nearby chest. "But I do have a life to live, so could you step up the pace?"

"Are those rock crystals in the bowl?" Corwyn stood on his toes, peering as far as he could into the object.

"Yeah." Marlon conjured a tongue of flame and lit a fresh cigarette. "They would have lit up the moment we opened the door, but I put a spell on them to keep them dark as a precaution in case anyone found this place while I was gone."

"Pretty good trick for someone who isn't much of a wizard."

Marlon gave a small shrug and drew in a short drag.

"This all seems pretty old. Too old for mages to have made the crystals light up."

"But a common-enough thing for Shrealists to do, I'd wager." Marlon exhaled a puff of smoke. "They make those sorts of things for mines all the time."

"It's possible," Corwyn agreed.

"Just goes to show how old this all is," Marlon added. "Which makes it even more valuable."

"This is a lot to take in, Marlon." Trina squatted at the statue's lifelike feet. "We could be here for a while."

Marlon's face twisted into a leer. "At least there's a nice view." Corwyn followed the halfling's gaze. Once again the familiar flutter of jealousy returned. And like before he shoved it aside.

"I think I'll take a look at those sarcophagi," he said.

"Knock yourself out." Marlon's full attention fixated on Trina's figure while she continued her examination.

Finding the nearest sarcophagus, Corwyn studied its lid. The whole thing appeared constructed of what he thought could be sandstone. The rest of the object featured a mixture of images, all apparently showing the same person. This figure—a male elf—was involved in a whole host of things. One image showed him holding a spear, another fighting off a rather large octopus, and then there were the rest, telling what must have been his story mingled amid more bizarre images—some so abstract it was nearly impossible to even hope to understand.

"The statues are real enough," said Trina.

"I think we'll find it's all real," Corwyn added. "And I think we'll find it's all Aquadion related. I just have to make sure of one last thing." He gave the lid a light push. It slid quite easily under his effort.

Like summoned hounds, Trina and Marlon hurried to his side, eager for a peek. A skeleton rested inside. Its skirt consisted of shells and small plates of emerald and gold, making for a garment that resembled scale mail more than anything else. On the chest rested a collection of thick necklaces crafted mostly of pearls, small shells, rough bits of brass, gold, silver, and other items.

"Looks dead to me," said Marlon. "Nice bracelets, though." His eyes were hooked on the thick bands of gold in the shape of an eel coiling back to bite its own tail.

"How old do you think he is?" Trina retrieved a bronze dagger from the skeleton's side. "Assuming he *is* a he."

"Oh, it's the same male on the lid, I'm sure, but I don't know how old he is. I told you I didn't take much to Aquadion history."

"*What?*" Marlon shot Trina a hot glare. "You told me this guy knew what he was talking about. Now he says he isn't even *qualified*? What kind of game you playing?"

"No game," she returned, smoothly dropping the dagger back into the sarcophagus. "Javier will get my recommendation on authenticity, if it all checks out. He isn't really concerned about anything else other than to make sure it's real. If he wants, he'll get some scribes to check out the other things if it'll help the price."

"He better give me *top* price. This stuff alone is worth a few bars of gold."

"Wait a moment." Corwyn's eyes went first to Marlon and then to Trina. "You're looking at selling the *bodies* too?"

"Well, yeah," Marlon snorted. "There's a whole host of folks who'd like to get their hands on this sort of thing."

"You can't sell these bones. They were put here in honor and should stay here, not be carted off and sold like they're merchandise." He felt a familiar sinking feeling in his stomach, which only grew worse, no matter how much Trina worked her doe eyes.

"What's going on here, Trina?"

"I was going to tell you soon enough—"

Corwyn shot Marlon a sober stare. "Do I even have to ask if this is on the level?"

"Probably better the less you know, to be honest." Marlon took out another cigarette and lit it by his spell. "If I had *my* way, you'd never have been here in the first place."

"I thought it would be fun," said Trina, gently placing a hand on Corwyn's side. "We'd get to be together again . . ." He didn't speak, merely held his gaze firmly upon her.

His disappointed gaze.

"Hey," Marlon said after a few moments of silence, "you can have your little spat on your own time. Are we done here or what?"

"Yeah, we're done." Corwyn made for the exit.

"Good." Marlon followed him, puffing as he went. "The sooner Javier gets me my cut, the better."

"So who's this Javier?"

"Better if you don't know that either."

"Why do I have the feeling he's another questionable halfling?"

"Corwyn." Trina managed to catch up to the two of them, pulling on his arm to slow him down. "I really was going to tell you."

"When?" He stopped a few steps shy of the door, spinning on his heel to see Trina's penitent face.

"Eventually." She tried a weak smile. "It's just business, Corwyn. Nothing more."

"Then you won't be concerned if I told the authorities, maybe even a couple Gartaric Knights, about your *business*. You could use some help getting this all out of here, I'm sure."

"He's joking, right?" Marlon asked Trina.

"Of course he is," she assured Marlon before checking back with Corwyn. "You're not serious, right, Corwyn?" His stoic face and stiff spine let her know he was *quite* serious. "You haven't changed at all, have you?"

"Neither have you, it seems," he said, continuing for the door. Or he would have, if Marlon hadn't rushed in front of him.

"Marlon?" Trina, like Corwyn, took special note of the dagger in the halfling's hand and the rising hate in his eyes.

"Shut up. It's your fault for bringing him along. I'm not going to have him blabbing now when things are so close to wrapping up."

"He won't talk."

"You can't control him any better than Javier can keep himself from devouring anything put under his snout."

"So what do you plan to do?" Corwyn kept his eye on the dagger. "There *are* two of us, you know."

"*And* we're taller," added Trina.

Marlon's eyes jumped from one to the other. "I know a few spells to help even the odds. I'll just come back with more muscle and we can sort this all out. Javier will still get his goods, and I'll get my cut." He snapped his fingers and the room plunged into darkness. Then came the sound of the closing door.

"Marlon!" Trina shouted.

"Too late," said Corwyn.

"No, it's not. We can open the door if we hurry." Corwyn listened while Trina navigated the darkness. Eventually, she discovered the door but couldn't find any way to open it.

"I told you," he said, coming up beside her. "He probably blocked it with a spell."

Trina kicked his shin. "Idiot! Now we're trapped here."

He staggered back from the attack but quickly recovered. "He'll be back. He wants his cut too much to let this slip."

"So now what? In the meantime, we wait for him to bring some thugs to make us into shark bait? That's *so* much more reassuring. Why do you always have to be so upright?"

"Trina, he was talking about selling dead bodies for profit!"

"And why not? Those bones aren't doing anyone any good just resting in a sarcophagus."

Corwyn sighed. "You never stopped dealing with crooks, did you?"

"After they kicked me out of the college, I didn't have much left I *could* do."

"You had a choice." His eyes continued adjusting to the darkness. He supposed in time he could navigate the chamber . . . for whatever good that would do him.

"So did you," she snapped back. He said nothing. He really didn't want to dig up old ground, but it might be too late for that now. "And I didn't make the right choice, is that it? You get to be all high and righteous, and I'm the lowly thief, right?"

"I never said—"

"You haven't changed one bit." She plopped on the floor, resting her back against the door. "And now we get to sit here for who knows how long and hope they don't kill us when they return."

"I was trying to help."

"How? By threatening to report this all to the authorities?"

"I was trying to help you in Argos," he replied, squatting down before her. "I didn't want you to go down that path. I loved you. I wanted to see you get out of it for good."

"Well, you got me kicked out of the college without a copper to my name. What did you *think* I was going to do?"

"Come to your senses." For a moment each stared into the other's eyes, seeing the same spark that had drawn them together nearly a decade ago.

"Always the optimist." She put a hand to his cheek. "That's one thing I did miss."

"Weren't you the one talking about second chances?" He placed his hand over Trina's. "We could start fresh right now. You could give up—"

"It's not that simple."

"I'd help you. You wouldn't need to steal or deal with any of this business anymore, we'd be able to travel, and—"

His words were swallowed by Trina's lips locking onto his.

"That's for giving me hope," she said, giving his hair a rustle. "You always did spin a good tale."

"Who said it has to be fiction?" His warm smile brought a small pool of tears to the corner of Trina's eyes.

"Will you stop it? I don't want my last moments in life spent sobbing. I'm still damp as it is."

"Then we better look for a way out of here," he said, rising.

"There's that optimism again." Trina joined him.

"We might as well look for something." He headed to the statue they'd been studying before. "We're going to be waiting here anyway, so we might as well be productive." Each made their way around the room, thoroughly inspecting all they could in the darkness. Unfortunately, there wasn't much for them to rediscover—especially without light.

"Pretty ironic we bump into each other only to end up dying together," Trina said after finishing her search, coming to rest before the open sarcophagus.

"We're not dead yet," he said, joining her.

"Look, I'm sorry you had to go through this. I really thought it would be fun."

"Fun to go steal the dead from their graves?"

Trina sighed. "I was going to tell you eventually what was going on, but if I told you the truth before—"

"You thought I wouldn't come down with you, right?"

She lowered her head. "I guess deep down I knew it was too good to be true."

"I did, too. I just didn't want to admit it at the time."

"Damn halflings!" She gave the sarcophagus a kick. When she did, a clicking sound rose from where her foot hit a small section of icons around the structure's base. This immediately drew Corwyn closer for an inspection.

"What is it?" She tried peering over his shoulder.

"It sounded like a lock. I wonder . . . give me a hand with this." He began pushing against the sarcophagus. Together they managed enough force to move the stone box perpendicular to its base, revealing a stone staircase.

"What's that?" Trina peered into the stairwell descending into even greater darkness with more than a little trepidation.

"Possibly our way out of here," he replied while trying to get a better grasp of what the ancient stairs afforded. But in the dark he could only discern a few steps.

"You're not going down there, are you?"

"You want to wait for your friend to come back?" As he began to descend, a blast of light rose from below, nearly blinding them.

"Light's better than darkness," said Corwyn, blinking the flashing spots from his vision. The illumination apparently covered most of the stairwell. When he felt confident enough, he continued his descent. Trina followed.

The stairs were old but had aged well, like the rest of the artifacts. The light itself came from a collection of stone-crafted oysters with open shells revealing a glowing crystal inside. By this light, both could see the stairs were carved into a natural opening in the cavern which had been widened and artfully altered.

The further they went, the cooler and damper it became. Eventually, the stairs ended in what looked like a large cavern which had seen better days. Parts of it housed fallen rock but otherwise appeared sturdy enough for them to pass through. It was still lit here and there by the same carved oysters, but these were lesser in number, crushed by broken segments of the cavern wall where they once rested.

"So there's another cavern under the one we were just in?"

"Looks that way," said Corwyn. "Though I think there's something more here than meets the eye."

"What do you mean?"

"Look around. This place has seen looting."

Trina scanned the area. "It's been damaged from the rockfall, but—"

"A lot of the signs point to things being dragged—lots of *heavy* things—which all seem to lead there." He indicated a dark section of the cavern.

"And I suppose you want to check it out."

"I don't see any other way out around here, do you? If someone dragged stuff out of here, then there must be a way out."

"You first then." She motioned for his lead.

"I don't know how deep we are, but there might be a way to another pool leading to the sea. If we can get out of here before your friend returns, we'll both be better off."

"You planning on leaving town when you get back?" She followed him into the darkness, slowing her pace until her eyes fully adjusted.

"After I make my report to the authorities."

"Figures."

"Now *that* could be a problem." Corwyn's sudden stop brought Trina within an inch of running into him. In the middle of another, smaller, cavern rested a great mound of gold, silver, and other rare and wondrous objects. The entire cavern was lit by a small collection of statues like the ones they'd encountered above. This pooling illumination also revealed other things hidden alongside the treasure—bones piled to one side of the cavern like in a refuse pit or animal lair.

"Why do I not have a good feeling about this?"

"Maybe because of that," said Corwyn, pointing out a large skull peeking out of the shadows across from them. Though larger than any animal either had seen, it held some familiar traits he knew both of them recalled from their schooling.

"Midgard, isn't it?"

"I'd say so, but I'd have to get closer to be sure."

"Let's just stay where we're at for the moment. I tend to favor my life continuing for as long as possible."

"It's either wait for your friend or have a look around."

"And since when has Corwyn Danther been so brave?"

"Since he's been searching for a way out of a situation he was fool enough to fall into." He made his way forward.

"You still fell—came along. Don't go blaming *me* entirely for all this. You could have chosen not to come," she reminded him as he moved deeper into the cavern. "You had a *choice*."

"I know, and I made a poor one."

"You saying you shouldn't have believed me, then, is that it?" he heard her ask as he faded into the shadows near the linnorm's skull.

"Let's just focus on getting out of here for now."

The cavern fell silent while Corwyn searched the darkness.

"Corwyn?" Trina's voice called after him. "*Corwyn?*"

"I think I found something."

"Where?"

He heard her begin the tentative steps closer to the skull. Soon enough he caught sight of her from where he stood near a battered section of rock. It had once held a doorway similar to the golden one they first entered in the room above. The hole looked big enough for something as large as a Midgard to fit through. Among the debris were more bones, scattered weapons, trinkets, and other assorted items neither invested much time in identifying.

"It looks like it goes to another pool and could be a way out of here," he said.

"What do you think happened?"

"Probably a fight of some type."

"With whom, though?"

"Maybe that Midgard," said Corwyn, stepping over the bones.

"Did I tell you how much I *hate* halflings?" Trina squeamishly followed.

"If we can hold our breaths long enough, we might be able to find our way out of this."

"How are we going to see in the water?" She studied what resembled a large pool, larger than the one they'd come through the first time. "It's pretty dark."

"Those glowing stones on the stairs should help. If we each hold on to one, we should be able to see well enough ahead to make sense of where we're going."

"Maybe. But if we don't know the way or get trapped . . ."

"We have to try something."

Trina sighed. "Okay. Let's go." She marched for the steps. Once each found a globe to their liking, they worked to pry it free.

"If we don't get out of this," said Trina, "I just wanted to say I'm sorry."

"You already said you were sorry."

"I know, it's just that—I really *am* sorry." She stopped, making sure he could see she was serious.

"Sorry it didn't work out as you thought or that I got pulled into this mess with you?"

"Both."

"Well, in either case, I don't think your friends are going to be too pleased with you after this." He could feel his stone coming loose. "You might have to find a new line of work—a new place to live."

"Let's focus on getting out of here first, okay?"

"All right." A sharp snap accompanied the globe breaking free from the wall. "I think we can agree on that point." After a few more tugs and twists, Trina's stone gave its own crack and pop as she yanked it free.

"Now to test it out."

5

Both made their way onto the beach a safe distance from where they'd first entered with Marlon. Heaving for breath, they dropped onto the wet sand. The ancient glowing globes rested beside them like freshly laid turtle eggs, shimmering with their own inner light.

"Not so bad . . ." Corwyn gasped.

"Speak for yourself." Trina collapsed onto her side.

"Got a nice . . . sunset though . . ." He motioned to the reddish hue darkening across the horizon. "Red sky at night . . ."

"Sailors' delight," Trina chimed in.

They remained where they were, catching their breath and wringing out their hair and shirts before letting the breeze finish drying them. The glowing stones had served them well, guiding them all the way out. And it hadn't been too arduous a journey. In fact, the cavern had been fairly open and rather easy to navigate. With the added light, they quickly found the exit and then the surface.

"I don't suppose you'd take me up on my offer?" he asked, watching Trina stand.

"Of me traveling with you?" She smiled. "You really are a hopeless romantic, aren't you?"

"And I don't believe you're a lost cause," he added, dusting sand off his legs as he rose. "You still can start over and make good on an honest life."

"With you?"

"I'm more concerned with helping you right now."

"I see. Get your life straightened out first, and then we'll talk."

"It would be easier. I'd be there to help you. I have some contacts that could help get you up and running in the right direction—"

"Let it go, Corwyn. We were both foolish to think anything could be rekindled. We're too different. Always were. Always will be."

"But people can change."

"Well," said Trina, peering deep into the ever-reddening sky, "*I* don't think we've changed over the years, and we probably won't anytime soon."

"So what are you going to do?"

"Something will pan out. Javier likes me and Cordell trusts me. Marlon might flap his gums, but in the end, any rough spots can be smoothed over. I should be able to get back into their good graces easily enough and keep making coin as well. I'll have to pin all the bad things on you, of course."

"Of course."

She gave her glowing stone a soft tap with her foot. "These should help, too. Unless you're set on keeping them from me."

"No, not the stones"—Corwyn rolled his Trina's way—"just you profiting from the dead . . . among a few other things."

"We still might be able to make money off that place too—even if you tell the guard and the Gartaric Knights."

"How—"

"Best if you don't know." She scooped up the stones. "I suppose we better start walking. It's going to be dark enough when we get to the city, and who knows what might be lurking about, thanks to Marlon's lead. What about you, though? Still going to leave right away?"

"Since I've made some not-too-happy friends, it's probably for the best. For both of us."

"I'm sorry you're being chased off."

"My choice from the beginning." He started walking. "Besides, I can make a few stops along the way back to Haven. I haven't been to too many places along the coast, and now I'll have some time to enjoy it."

"Well, you shouldn't be worried about ever coming back to Caster's Reef. Marlon's resentment will only stir things up for so long. Before you know it, everything will be smooth sailing again. So don't feel like you have to hide yourself away forever. It might be nice seeing you from time to time."

"We'll see."

"At least you can buy me dinner."

"What for?"

"You owe me for last night."

"I didn't know you were keeping score."

"Yeah." She smirked. "You haven't changed one bit."

The next day found Corwyn contemplating the lapping waves, watching Caster's Reef sink into the horizon of the Percillian Sea. A breeze tried to take his hat, but a quick hand held it in place. It was a small miracle he still had it. On their way back he and Trina had come across the spot where they'd waded in with Marlon. Apparently, he hadn't had any use for Corwyn's hat. So much for Fredrick's notion of it being coveted by fashion-conscious halflings. Needless to say, Corwyn couldn't have been happier to retrieve it, even if Trina gave him a little ribbing when he did. But that was a fading memory, like so much of these last few days.

The ship on which he'd booked passage happily received him—and his coin—putting him in a fine location for his voyage. By the next morning he'd be in a new town, opening up new options for consideration. And yet, while anticipating the future, he couldn't escape revisiting the past few hours.

Without much to pack, leaving the city hadn't been hard. It didn't take him long to locate someone to take over his abode. After he'd told some government officials what had been discovered and what was going on with the hidden Aquadion tomb, he'd been introduced to a helpful Telborian merchant who happily took the residence off Corwyn's hands. He had also introduced him to the captain of a boat sailing early the next day.

It happened so fast he still wasn't sure if it was more daydream than reality. In time it would all sink in, and the matter, like so much of his past relationship with Trina, would fade into distant memory. For a brief time he'd entertained raking up old embers, hoping for a spark that could blaze into something new. But it was wiser leaving the past in the past—for everyone involved. It'd take some time for those raked embers to cool, but for now he simply watched the past fade behind him while the future opened wide its embrace.

It was evening by the time Trina returned home. Her day had been an eventful one. Marlon had spewed what venom he could, but in the end, much as she'd told Corwyn, she'd been able to smooth Javier's ruffled feathers. It helped that Javier was so widely connected on so many levels in Caster's Reef. His fat fingers reached into almost every aspect of the city. The only place he didn't have any contacts was with the Gartaric Knights. Despite this, he was able to recover much of the loss from the sizable fine that had been imposed. And then there would be taxes and other fees to pay, but when he finished the game of cycling the coin through various hands, he'd still make out rather well.

Trina didn't even get into any hot water with the authorities. It seemed Corwyn might have been milder in his report about her actions than she first feared. A hopeless romantic to the end. In a few days she'd be back to her old life, and it would be like Corwyn had never interrupted it.

She'd managed to turn some nice coin on those glowing stones, too. She didn't tell Marlon or Javier about them and made the deals herself without Cordell. If she'd learned anything from these last few days, it was to make more connections of her own. You never knew when they might come in handy. And who said Javier or Cordell needed to keep all the profit? In fact, it might be wise branching out further still, perhaps making her own ventures and forming her own associations, cutting Javier's fingers out from any future gain.

Entering her bedroom, she sought her familiar box—the same one she'd shown Corwyn at dinner. She kept it safely hidden under her bed. Sitting on the bed's edge, she placed the box on her lap. There she opened it and took careful stock of its contents. No matter how often she looked inside, it always held the same impact. It was hard keeping herself under control when she'd shared it with Corwyn. And yet he remained steadfast in his desire for her to keep it. She thought she saw a spark in his eyes when he told her, too. Maybe that had been foolish dreaming, the wine perhaps taking her feelings too far. Still, it was nice having toyed with the thought of something being possible again . . . even if just for a moment.

She wondered if Corwyn felt the same way. She supposed it didn't matter now. He'd left, and Trina was wise enough to know he wasn't coming back, no matter what new fantasies she entertained. It would sink in soon enough, she knew, and she'd move back into the routine she'd known before. And, of course, she'd still have her box, to which she now gave her full attention.

Once more she carefully unrolled the parchment pages, reading the notes and lyrics written with a careful, loving hand. Once more she heard the song they composed in her head—a loving melody from a different time. A time when things seemed simpler, her life brighter, and the world a better place. Once more she savored the music in her heart until reaching the song's end. Once more she rested the final sheet upon the others as the silence returned. And once more she cried.

APPENDICES

APPENDIX A
Corwyn Danther's Timeline

The following is a chronological list of the various events that have taken place in the life of Corwyn Danther, both prior to and as revealed in the stories collected in this book. While not inclusive of all the events of his life, they do touch on the more monumental or pivotal moments.

734 PV   Born in Haven, Talatheal.

746 PV   Corwyn travels to Maiden Rock for the first time.

747 PV   He arrives in Argos, Belda-thal, and begins his bardic training.

757 PV   He completes his training in Argos and returns to Haven. He later travels the Midlands, mainly Talatheal.

759 PV   "Rainier's Legacy"

760 PV   "Maiden Rock"
"Where Dreams Go to Die"
"Charity for Halflings"
"Sellswords and Snake Oil"
"The Forgotten"
"The More Things Change"

APPENDIX B
The Crown of the World

At the top of Tralodren, beyond the Northlands, lies the Crown of the World. Many myths and tales have been told about this place, and little in the way of exploration or solid factual insight has done anything to confirm or deny them.

Many hold that Tralodren is a world rich in water. Following the Great Shaking, which helped define recorded time, the great landmass that had once been the only continent on the planet shattered into the continents and islands currently populating the Northern Hemisphere. Speculation has been put forth that there are lands formed by still more fragments to the south, beyond the Boiling Sea. But information as to their number, size, and population remains unknown.

Tales do tell of the monstrous races who got a greater hold over the Northern Hemisphere from a bloody and vast southern migration. Because of this, some sages, scholars, and priests have suggested there would have to be a sizable chunk of land beyond the bubbling waves: not as many landmasses as are known in the Northern Hemisphere but perhaps a sizable handful capable of supporting such a horde.

The other side of Tralodren, the reverse of the known world, as it were, is open to wild speculation and debate. None know what is there for certain. Prevailing beliefs, generated by those who have sailed the waters in times past, have said it is an empty, vast, massive ocean. As such, they call it the Great Ocean. Naturally, such a grand background provides a rich seedbed for stories of what might lie still hidden among the waves. These tales range from a virgin continent rich with all the good things lost and exploited during the times of the dranors to a land filled with dragons and other horrors, waiting to waken and attack those on the other side of the world. A few more esoteric theories speak of portals to other planets and planes and realms. But until someone succeeds in the circumnavigation of Tralodren, we will never know.

With the Crown of the World, however, there have been records of travels and trips to its outer rim. While none have ventured too far beyond this territory, it has been consistently reported that it's a quite cold and very inhospitable place. Some have said it is so cold that large chunks of ice float about the waves like islands, and that the water has even been known to nearly freeze the closer one gets to the center of the crown. What lies at the exact center of this region is still unknown, as none have sailed into it for fear of losing control of their vessel and falling into the empty waters on the other side of the world. How this could be is rather unclear, but it is a common fear that has kept the handful of those who've sailed there from proceeding any further.

—*An excerpt from "A Basic Primer of the Land" by Elliott Nedlah, a sage in the employ of the king of Romain*

APPENDIX C
The Muses of Tralodren

The following is a child's rhyme that tells a story of the muses, insofar as their current locations are concerned. These are specific to the Northern Hemisphere, since none know much of anything about what's beyond the Boiling Sea.

THE RHYME OF THE MUSES

Thirty maidens to inspire and delight,
By goddess' command, get up and take flight.
Three to the South to plant seeds in the sand,
Five to the Midlands—inspirers of man.
Four more to the North, mixing beauty with ice,
Six to the West, championing virtue over vice.
Six more venture beyond the Boiling Sea.
And six with the goddess forever shall be.

Three maids traveled south, spreading their charms,
And were greeted on the shores with open arms.
Kira, Jasmine, Amira—all flames in the mind,
Greater beauty in life none shall e'er find.

Five sisters also came to Midlandic shores:
Alanna and Ella—sights to behold.
Mortal minds to enlighten, inspire, and mold.
Hannah, Keely, and Lena the other three—
Delight of men and mortals be.

In the lands of the North four more made their home:
Erika, Mia, Andra, and Leela constantly to roam
Over snow and field, sharing what light they may,
In hopes of bringing forth a brighter day.

And to those in the West six others were sent,
Sharing their gifts wherever they went.
Alison, Ashley, and Sana sang out o'er the land,
Calista, Adina, and Bala gained favor with man.

Six muses would stand beside Causilla's throne,
These always calling Delecta their home.
So Causilla has blessed the world with her gift
While the spirits of all has she sought to uplift.

It is widely known that Causilla, goddess of beauty, love, and the arts, fashioned thirty beings at the creation of Tralodren to further spread the beauty of creation and her nature to all who would receive them. Six of these she took for herself—to inspire her own realm and the greater cosmos; the other twenty-four made their home on Tralodren.

What makes muses unique is that, unlike other divinities and gods who have to hide their true nature and power through a guise of flesh, the muse is present in their full nature on Tralodren. This means they have a great deal of power and ability at their disposal, more so than any other divinity. Despite this, each muse has sought to use her talents to the betterment of her charges and not for her own selfish gain.

Muses appear as the loveliest of human maidens but have been known to take on the guise of other races when and where needed. Their true form reflects their purest nature, which is breathtaking to behold and beyond words to describe. Their main purpose, though, is helping spread the nature of their creator in and through their given charges wherever they can. To this end, they will work with people from all walks of life to accomplish what they feel is in the best interest of their goddess' mission.

THE TERRESTRIAL MUSES

In the beginning of creation, the muses ranged over the entire supercontinent that once dominated Tralodren. After the Great Shaking, the current landmasses appeared. The muses cast lots to see where they should go and whom they should adopt as their charges.

Thus, the twenty-four terrestrial-bound muses were divided as follows:

The Midlands
The five muses who found their way to the Midlands were Alanna, Ella, Hannah, Keely, and Lena.

Alanna: Assigned to the northernmost landmass of Arid Land.
Ella: Assigned to Colloni.
Hannah: Assigned to Draladon.
Keely: Assigned to the southernmost landmass of Arid Land.
Lena: Assigned to Talatheal.

The Northlands
The four muses who found their way to the Northlands were Andra, Erika, Leela, and Mia.

Andra: Assigned to Frigia.
Erika: Assigned to Troll Island.
Leela: Assigned to Valkoria.
Mia: Assigned to Baltan.

The Southern Lands
The three muses who found their way to the Southern Lands were Amira, Jasmine, and Kira.

Amira: Assigned to Menessa.
Jasmine: Assigned to Belda-thal.
Kira: Assigned to Antora.

The Western Lands
The six muses who found their way to the Western Lands were Alison, Ashley, Adina, Bala, Calista, and Sana.

> **Alison and Ashley:** Assigned to Breanna, Caradina, Irondale, and Black Isle.
> **Adina and Bala:** Assigned to the Pearl Islands.
> **Calista:** Assigned to Rexatoius.
> **Sana:** Assigned to Napow.

The Southern Hemisphere
The six muses who found their way into the Southern Hemisphere were Jalena, Kasia, Nadila, Vanya, Velra, and Xondara.

> **Jalena:** Assigned to the Crimson Isles.
> **Kasia:** Assigned to the Thalian Islands.
> **Nadila:** Assigned to the Gartaric Islands.
> **Vanya:** Assigned to Sargona.
> **Velra:** Assigned to Thalia.
> **Xondara:** Assigned to Sethra.

The Celestial Muses
The six muses chosen as Causilla's personal handmaidens are as follows: Azni, Carine, Deshi, Havana, Kamia, and Maali.

APPENDIX D
The Bards of Tralodren

The following is an excerpt from an essay written by Petra Crates, a somewhat famed Patrician bard of the last century who lived in the Western Lands, namely Rexatoius. In it, Petra provides insight into both what bards do and what they are believed to do in Tralodren. Though a little dated, this work is still useful in gleaning basic information about bards and the bardic traditions on Tralodren in general.

What is a bard? Well, I guess you can say we are a curious sort who love to travel. We have a hard time being in one place for too long, and not being able to do something creative would drive many of us wild with boredom. We are a people who are creative, yes, but are more in love with the act of creation than the item that's produced by it. Is it any wonder we are thought of as we are?

Far from layabouts and wandering vagrants, we are very dedicated workers of our craft . . . though each bard's craft is far from being as certain and uniform as one might think it should be when compared to mortalkind's other endeavors. "Surely," one could say, "the blacksmith makes tools for the same purpose and in the same manner, the baker always makes his loaf of bread like so, the cooper always plies his craft to similar tasks, so why is the bard so different?"

My dear friend, it would be foolish to try to label the works of my fellow brothers and sisters as so certain in the progression of their craft that you would expect such uniformity. Are all songs alike? Are all stories told the same way each night around the fire, even by those who don't share in the Bardic Order? Why, then, put us in the same category?

Bards work with organic things—songs and tales, dance and music and art, and so many other wonders and blessings Causilla has showered upon us. We have been given the light of jubilant energy with which to craft such pleasing and inspiring works, not only for our benefit, but also for all those around us who might later delight in our creation. This is what it is to be a bard. But then, how does one become a bard? Now that, my friend, is an interesting tale.

One is not necessarily born into it, as some might have you think. Those are the flashier of my fellows who are trying to both elevate their station and probably make extra coin off your donations in the process. A bard, truth be told, is a man like any other (though we have a great many women in the order as well) who feels that this is the life he wishes to lead.

Just as I'm sure there are some who want to be blacksmiths and bakers—and oddly enough, yes, politicians—there are also those who wish to become bards. And these, as with the former examples, will follow this desire as best they know how. Many will never rise to the level of skill better-known bards have come to be known for over the past few generations. Instead, these will be modest men of simple means—more musician and street performer than accredited herald of the goddess—and unlikely to get a great audience in even the largest of cities. Rather, these fellows are often the ones who work for the true bards—those who have had a great deal of training.

And how does one get training? Good question. As I have said, the average fellow might be a great artist, singer, taleteller, etc., but he might not be able to find a way to get proper training and so will never ascend to that higher level of recognition of accomplishment all bards crave and need to further their careers. So it is this training that is the dividing point among a great many. It is also a dividing point because of the costs of education, offered in only select areas. As with mages, the bard has to learn his art. And like a mage's magical academy, the bard has a college which he attends.

There are two types of bardic colleges. A general school, which provides basic musical principles and understanding, voice and instrument training, and even instruction in performance and dance. The other is a more specialized school that, while it teaches the same things as the general school, also instructs the student in the ways and understanding of Causilla and the spiritual nature behind the profession. Naturally, these schools are found in close association with Causillinites, so it should come as no surprise many temples also house a section for bardic instruction; priests actually serve as teachers to these young bards on most occasions.

So does one need to go to college to get training? No, not really, but it is much easier to advance in your career if you do so. There are tutors and older bards who have now retired and take on students to keep bread on the table, and so one could find a path to instruction that way. However, in doing so, one loses out on the great contacts and connections the colleges afford. I'm far from one to say which is better, as I've had friends who've gone to college or self-funded their way to their dreams by the various tutors, and both turned out fairly well. They're not famous, mind you, but they don't have to sing for their suppers every night, either.

Once you have your training, then what do you do? Well, after you leave the college and get good enough on your own that people actually want to listen to you perform, you have many options. Many bards find being more universal in their approach helps at first but hinders them later on, because they aren't known for anything specific, being a jack-of-all-trades but not really a master of anything in particular. If you want to do birthday celebrations and weddings and other events, then you could do very well, but you won't get your name out there beyond that.

Instead, many bards soon look to find a niche where they do well. This is probably something they had training in during college or are inclined to with the gifting given them by Causilla. In either case, many find out what their niche is and look to develop it and exploit it to the best of their ability. What are some of these niches? Writing various stories and plays, dancing, a myriad of musical stylings, including playing a certain musical instrument, and simple storytelling. There are a whole host more and just as many bards to fill them, but it's how many bards get a start at standing out among the crowd.

To this end, many have done well and found a decent life, but still others add the final element of touring to their talents and do even better. This isn't to say the other bards don't travel from town to town, but they don't do it as an overall strategy for both bettering their performance and increasing their renown. And while taking on larger tours of whole regions or nations can be grueling, it gets your face and name out there and a fresh audience before you with each new stop. Better still, if you're *really* good, you can generate excitement for your upcoming event before you even get there. All this is to the advantage of the bard who knows how to do it right and play to his strengths. A little showmanship goes a long way too and helps garner name recognition and a fat coin purse.

So what does that mean? That all bards are people who chase after coin all over this world like a hound after a rabbit? I'll let you be the judge of that; I can only speak for myself. And for myself, I can think of no greater service to offer mortalkind than the sound of music, a tale to pass on and inspire and teach, a song to lift the spirit, a joke to waken a smile on a crestfallen face, or even a simple reminder of what is great in life for those who might have forgotten. Yes, this is Causilla's blessing of the bard.

Chad Corrie has enjoyed creating things for as far back as he can remember, but it wasn't until he was twelve that he started writing. Since then he's written comics, graphic novels, prose fiction of varying lengths, and an assortment of other odds and ends. His work has been published in other languages and produced in print, digital, and audio formats.

ChadCorrie.com | @creatorchad

Scan the QR code below to sign up for Chad's email newsletter!

Enjoy podcasts? Chad also produces the following:

Cauldron of Worlds
Corrie Cast

Further information about the world of Tralodren can be found at Tralodren.com as well as on social media (@tralodren). Chad also produces two monthly podcasts delving into the setting, stories, and what's happening in general with current and forthcoming works as well as sharing additional insight and information:

Tralodren: Behind the Scenes
Tralodren: Legends and Lore

All these podcasts can be found on ChadCorrie.com and wherever else podcasts are available for listening and/or subscription.

Tralodren.com